I0588951

A Gathering of Dragons

{ Deanna Cooner, PhD }

Stones in Clay
PUBLISHING

A Gathering of Dragons
Copyright © 2018-19 by Deanna Cooner, All rights reserved

Unless otherwise indicated all Scripture quotations are from the Holy Bible, New American Standard Version, 1995 by Lockman Foundation; A Corporation Not for profit, La Habra, Ca. All rights reserved.

No part of this publication may be reproduced, stored in a retrieval system or transmitted in any way to any means, electronic, mechanical, photocopy, recording or otherwise without the prior permission of the author except as provided by USA copyright law.

This is a work of fiction and any similarities to any person living or dead is purely coincidental, other than those historical persons used for the story. Any details used about them are public domain.
The opinions expressed by the author are not necessarily those of Stones In Clay Publishing.
Some extracts that appear to be Scripture quotations are an amalgam or paraphrase written by the author.

Stones in Clay Publishing
P.O. Box 1302
Newcastle, Ok 73065

Living stones, being built up as a spiritual house for a holy priesthood, to offer up spiritual sacrifices acceptable to God through Jesus Christ. 1 Peter 2:5,
But we have this treasure in jars of clay, to show that the surpassing power belongs to God and not to us.2 Corinthians 4:7

Cover Design and Graphics by Mindi Stucks
Book Design by Gary Cooner
Edited by Amy Mykytiuk
Published in United States of America
ISBN: 978-0-9989522-2-2
Young Adult Fiction / Religious / Christian / General
2019.6.26

Stones in Clay
PUBLISHING

Even a coward is brave with hope

OTHER NOVELS BY DEANNA COONER

The Dragon and The Mask

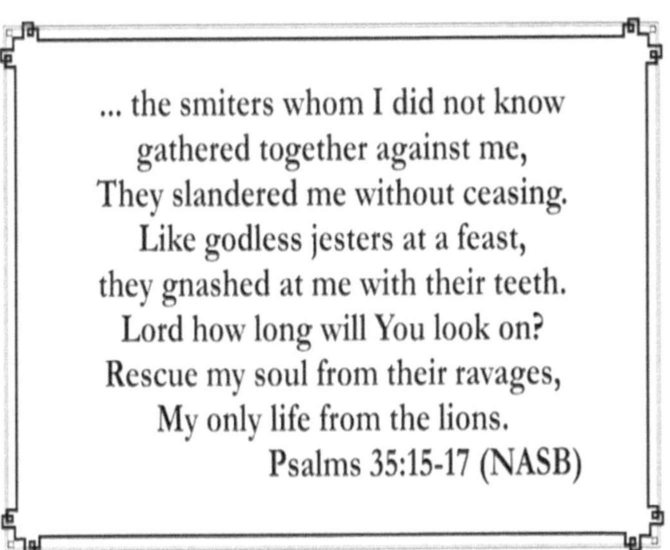
... the smiters whom I did not know
gathered together against me,
They slandered me without ceasing.
Like godless jesters at a feast,
they gnashed at me with their teeth.
Lord how long will You look on?
Rescue my soul from their ravages,
My only life from the lions.
Psalms 35:15-17 (NASB)

Contents

1

Fearful Recognition

An appalling and horrible thing has
happened in the land.

-----Jeremiah 5:30 (NASB)

Burlington Heights University, 1971

AT THE SOUND of rustling paper coming from the hall, Barbara Troye froze in mid-stroke while putting on mascara. *Who is there?* She pulled the drawer of her vanity open and picked up the 22 caliber revolver her dad gave her when she left home. *Please Lord, don't make me shoot anyone . . . or get shot.* She stepped into the hallway hidden in shadow. She took a deep breath in an attempt to calm her rapid beating heart and steady her breathing. *Maybe it's just a rat.*

The shadow of the intruder moved toward her. Her free hand flew to her mouth and her breathing stopped.

Beads of sweat tickled her spine. Her addled mind searched for an escape. She felt body heat and a drift of air when a shadow passed. Standing still she didn't perceive the second shadow until it towered over her. She flattened herself against the wall. The entity pressed closer, standing from floor to ceiling.

The man moved toward her desk. The dragon followed. Her lungs were about to burst holding in her breath, she exhaled knowing it would reveal her position. It appeared neither of them heard her gasp for air. The man walked around the living and kitchen area as though he lived there. He made no effort at stealth. The dragon followed close behind the man, tracing each of his steps. Barbara wondered if the man knew a large dragon followed him. She shuddered at the sight.

A cold crept up over her body like a glove covering a hand. She held her gun close but she could feel her whole arm shivering. Surprised to see a dragon again, she groaned inside at the unexpected sight.

She watched the man rifle through the papers on her desk. The make shift desk of a poor college student made of a plywood board with screw-in legs couldn't stand under the rough search. A moment after the intruder pushed everything to the floor with a swoop of his muscled arm, the desk toppled to the floor. Paper, pencils, pictures, and a melee of various brick-a-brack sprawled broken around the room.

Barbara raised her left hand in front of her face. Again, she held her breath. Neither figure looked at her. She eased back into a dark corner. The second form stood next to the first, but they didn't acknowledge each other. The dragon raised his serpent-like head over the intruder.

A strange noise reached her ears. *A growl?* Barbara yelped. The man turned from her, toward the window. A strange, orange glow emitted from the dragon and surrounded the man like a cloud.

Barbara gasped. This time the intruder heard. With quivering hands, she slipped her finger over the trigger. Her legs felt like they were made of wax. How could---

At that moment the man looked directly into her eyes. One side of his mouth turned up in a smirk. Barbara gripped her gun and braced herself to shoot. He walked toward her, snickering.

Barbara wanted to run for the front door but the dragon blocked her path. She had nowhere to go except deeper into the hallway.

"Hello there; it's been a while," he growled.

"Who . . . who are you?"

"You don't recognize me?"

Barbara shook her head. He did look familiar. Still she didn't recognize him.

"I'm not surprised," he said. When she reached the end of the hallway, he kept coming.

Barbara fired.

He kept coming. The dragon no longer followed the man, but settled on his haunches in the dining room. He flicked his forked tongue over the man's head.

She fired again; he jerked a little. She hit him, still he kept coming. The dragon lowered his head over the man.

"Take whatever you want!" Barbara screamed.

"I found what I wanted," he said as he placed a sheet of paper in his shirt pocket.

"Then leave," Barbara demanded.

"Oh . . . you don't frighten easily."

"Why should I be afraid of a clown in orange?"

He hesitated. His facial expression changed. "Orange?" He looked down at himself and brushed his chest.

"You think I'm a clown?" he mocked. With the statement he raised his arm and pointed directly at Barbara's head.

Something knocked her to the floor. Her hands trembled and she heard gunfire as she fell.

Orange man groaned. She both felt and heard him fall beside her. Staring into his blood-stained face he exhaled. His breath stank of sulfur.

With great effort she pushed herself up only to fall into something wet and sticky. Blood.

She heard a voice say, "The planting of seed is singular, but the harvest comes in multiples."

A wispy orange cloud floated in front of her just before blackness engulfed her.

2

The Unknown Threatens

> My soul, My soul! I am in anguish!
> Oh, my heart! My heart is pounding in
> me; I cannot be silent, Because you have
> heard O my soul, the sound of the
> trumpet the alarm of war.
>
> ---Jeremiah 4:18 (NASB)

WHERE AM I? Barbara heard no answer. Neither could she see anything. Blackness enveloped her all except for an orange wispy cloud moving from side to side. Am I dead?

The voice coming from the darkness aroused her curiosity at first and then sent chills of terror down her spine. She lurched to sit up but felt herself pulled down . . . hard. She opened her mouth and screamed, no sound came out. With no alternatives left she fell still and silent. She took deep breaths to slow her racing heart.

"That's better." The illusive voice cooed over her.

"Who . . . what?"

"You know me, we met . . . oh. . . let's see... about three years ago."

"I can't see you."

"Yeah, I hate the darkness but sorry I have no lightbulbs." The voice laughed out loud as though his words were funny.

"Where did we meet?" Barbara strained to calm her voice.

"On the couch in your family's living room."

"What? I don't understand." Barbara whimpered through course tears streaming down her cheeks. She tried to wipe them away but couldn't move her hands.

The voice laughed. "You remember the night you awoke and saw that strobe light in your parent's den?"

"Uh uh," Barbara moaned.

"I introduced myself to you by showing you how I could make your world sparkle. You sat down in front of me and I touched you."

Barbara felt her resolve returning and she felt strong enough to argue with this faceless voice, "The horrible mask on the wall touched me, nothing else."

"I am the spirit behind the mask."

Barbara turned her head toward the voice and with all her resolve cried out. "Go away."

"It's not that easy to get rid of me. I've been waiting years to have this conversation with you, no way will I leave now."

"What do you want?" Barbara groaned.

"Everything, your life." The voice growled the words.

"No!" Barbara screamed and started crying and fighting the bonds around her arms. A fearful laughter filled her ears. She blinked hoping to find a shred of light. The weight of the darkness pressed upon her like concrete. With short breaths and gasps she struggled against the force holding her down. "I will never give my life to a dragon," She choked out the words.

"I'm not a dragon." The voice answered. Barbara sensed something overpowering in this voice,

"Then what are you?"

"I'm your god,"

"No, I only serve one God."

"So you tell yourself, but you will soon learn who your true god is."

The voice stopped speaking. Her shackles loosened and a bit of light entered her vision. She took a deep breath and called upon all her strength. She tried again to raise her arms without success. At the same moment she gazed into a strange room. There were people standing around her. Her parents and her roommate, Sharon Simmons. They were talking among themselves as though she wasn't there. She tried to listen to them. They were mumbling, she couldn't understand. She watched as her daddy left the room.

The weariness in her body overcame her desire to speak. She closed her eyes and drifted into a restless sleep.

3

Fear And Worry!

> Behold, the noise of the bruit is come, and a great commotion out of the north country, to make the cities of Judah desolate, and a den of dragons.
>
> ---Jeremiah 10:22 (KJV)

SHARON SIMMONS, BARBARA'S friend and roommate needed to clean up the apartment before Barbara's parents, Buster and Merilee Troye arrived. She may not be able to get the place in good shape for visitors but at least she would put things in order.

The college apartment rented by Sharon and Barbara, the summer before their sophomore year of college, felt secure and safe. At least until an intruder broke in and created this mess.

The relationship she and Barbara shared went beyond friendship. They knew each other's backgrounds, hopes and dreams. They shared a sisterhood not born of blood but of calamity. They shared grief. Now they shared concern and fear. Sharon shuddered. The break-in didn't have any rhyme or reason. The girls didn't possess anything valuable. A thief entered their apartment and took nothing except their sense of security. This thought created fear because it brought a question of possible motive to the forefront of Sharon's mind. A motive she didn't want to consider.

Barbara still lay unconscious. That meant the only source of information about the event lay in this mess. She didn't want to clean; she wanted to inspect. The police took pictures of the muddy shoe print. An excellent idea. She pulled out her camera and took pictures of everything.

She picked up the stack of envelopes the intruder threw to the floor. The task took time and effort because of the amount of paper. When she finished she studied the number of unexposed frames left on her roll of film; only one. A scan of the scene revealed her need for a wide angle. She stood on a chair and looked through the camera lens. She gasped when she saw a strange imprint in the shag carpet. How did I miss that? She moved the camera directly over the strange looking indent. She shook her head in disbelief. It resembled a clawed foot.

Sharon shivered and snapped the picture. She placed a rug over the blood stains in the hall carpet. There lay a piece of paper, she picked it up and stuffed it in her purse and headed for the door. There she stopped, and looked at the intact door lock. I wonder how the intruder got in?

Sharon didn't realize how comforting it would be to have the Troye's present. She decided to ask Barbara's mother, Merilee, about the strange message on the paper she had found.

When Merilee read the message her hand flew over her mouth. She looked at Buster and extended the note to him. He looked at it and groaned.

"Again?"

Sharon didn't understand.

"Where did you get this?" Buster raised his voice as if he were angry at Sharon.

Sharon answered in a meek voice, "I found it on the floor near the spot where Barbara lay."

"I'm sorry, I didn't mean to yell at you."

"If you don't mind, can you tell me what it is?" Sharon questioned.

Buster nodded.

Merilee picked up the conversation. "We had a sculpture in our home that we called the mask because it looked like one. It kept---" She stopped.

"It kept changing?" Buster intoned. Sharon cocked her head to one side and looked at Buster for an explanation.

"I know, it's weird. The store owner gave this list of previous owners to Merilee when we returned the mask." "Previous owners?" Sharon raised her eyebrows.

"Yes, the thing has been around since the 1800's." Merilee elaborated.

Buster sat down beside Merilee and put his arm around her. "You see, it's an idol that can't be destroyed, but it destroys all who own it.

Look at the last name on the list." Buster instructed Sharon.

"It's your name." She turned to Merilee.

"Yes, I still have it, so no one else will feel the pain of the vile thing. I can't destroy it, but I can keep it from others and prevent future suffering."

"Do you think this list has something to do with the intruder?" Sharon pondered.

Buster and Merilee shook their heads, "It has everything to do with it." Buster confirmed.

"Read the last line."

"The planting of seed in singular but the harvest comes in multiples." Sharon read. "I don't understand."

"Don't feel alone, we don't either. We only know it's the signature of that awful dragon."

"What?" Sharon stood up and yelled in a loud voice. "Are you saying there was a dragon in our apartment?"

Buster stood and put his hand on Sharon's shoulder to calm her. "It's okay, I doubt you have a dragon here."

"Then what's this?" Sharon walked over to the imprint and pointed to it. Buster stood over it and pressed his lips together. Merilee watched the color drain from Buster's face. He turned to Merilee and said, "It's not over."

4

The Piercing Light Of Justice

> Wash your heart from evil, O Jerusalem, that you may be saved, How long will your wicked thoughts lodge within you?"
>
> ---Jeremiah 4:14

SHARON WORKED AS a nursing assistant at the university hospital in addition to her studies to become a registered nurse. It helped pay the rent and buy the groceries. Barbara had been preparing for a job interview at the same hospital when the invader appeared.

To preserve the imprint Sharon found in the carpet, Buster sprayed it with oil then pressed a brown paper sack over it. He used Barbara's face powder to spread it over the oily print. It wasn't great, but it gave proof of its existence. He shampooed the carpet after he obtained the proof. No one else would see it, unless he allowed it.

"Can we go to the hospital now?" Merilee asked. "I need to be with my daughter, not hunting a monster."

"Yeah, it's almost time for my shift." Sharon agreed and drove the Troye's to the hospital where Barbara lay unconscious.

With a little extra time before her shift started, Sharon took the opportunity to look at Barbara's chart. There wasn't much in there that she didn't already know, except for one nondescript page, a mental health evaluation. As she closed the chart and put it up, she shook her head and moaned.

Sharon met Barbara during her high school years. The daily courtroom drama faced by Sharon's family during her father's trial turned her heart to stone. Every day a gathering of press camera flashes went off in her face. The pictures appeared in the newspapers the next morning for the world to see. Sharon took to walking with her head down and her hands covering her face.

The tears didn't hold back when the judge announced a final sentence of fifteen years. She sat there for a while dreading the scene outside the courtroom, and worse, going home with a distraught mother and absent father. Sharon leaned over to her brother and whispered, "I know how the gladiators must have felt. This crowd is like barking hounds out for blood."

Her younger brother held tight to her arm as he leaned into his older sister. A tender young boy in a grown man's body fighting the fear and loss of his father with a grimaced face.

Once life resumed without dad and his paycheck, Sharon watched her friends pull away, leaving her alone. She no longer received invitations. The looks of pity from her friends hurt her the most. Being the oldest child in the family made her the keeper of her younger brothers' emotional health while her mother locked herself away with a bottle of wine.

Then she met Barbara Troye, another lost girl searching for her place in the world. Barbara lost her friends due to death by massive bomb. It seemed a natural step for the two, lonely, shocked, teen aged girls to cling to each other when they met at church camp the following summer. Their wounded hearts met at the prayer garden on opposite sides of the same tree. As one listened to the prayers of the other, they felt an immediate kinship. Now a year later they were both beginning a new course of life.

They rented an apartment from college housing. Sharon enrolled in the nursing program; Barbara floundered in her direction. She eventually joined Sharon in the nursing program, at least it would give her an occupation. They were putting their tragedies behind them; until a stranger invaded their living space

Why would someone break into their apartment and take nothing? He only trashed a desk with nothing of value. Sharon shuddered at the memory of the second set of footprints she saw in the camera lens. She didn't speak of them to anyone except the Troye's. Every day she dusted a thin layer of orange dust from the furniture. The strange color made if feel like trouble rained on them.

For the next few days Sharon served as hostess to Barbara's parents. With a few days left before enrollment, Sharon gathered Barbara's enrollment forms, as well as her own. On the way home from campus, she stopped by the hospital room to check on Barbara.

"Hello, Mrs. Troye. How's she doing?" Sharon asked Merilee when she entered the room.

"The doctor says there isn't any physical reason for her to be in a coma," Merilee told her. She sat beside Barbara, kneading the sheet and stroking Barbara's forehead. "He said that's good sign." Merilee's voice quivered as she spoke.

"You don't sound convinced."

"She won't wake up." Merilee wiped a tear from her face. "It's hard to believe that's a good sign."

"Maybe it's allowing her body to rest and heal."

Merilee nodded and let her mouth curve into a slight smile. "I hope you're right. I can't think of anything except that my child is hurt."

Sharon looked at Mr. Troye, sitting quietly on the other side of his daughter's bed, his brow turned down in a frown. "How are you doing?" she asked him.

"I keep asking why the dragon came to Barbara?

Merilee choked back her sorrow.

Sharon felt a shudder come up her spine. The reaction of these two strong people scared her. "What if?"

Buster stood and faced Sharon. She backed away. He and Merilee were both watching Sharon for the completion of her thought. She sat down on the edge of the bed and buried her face in her hands.

"What if someone connected to my father did this?" She blurted out her deepest fear. "I have a hard time figuring out why he would choose our apartment. We are only one of hundreds, and we are all mostly poor college students."

"I've thought of that too?" Buster lamented.

"Only thing different I can't understand is the list of names," Sharon answered.

"Why did Barbara have that list?" Buster queried.

Merilee buried her cheek in the palm of her hand and shook her head.

"What's the significance?" Sharon prodded.

Merilee looked up at Sharon, "I'm not sure, but that mask changed Barbara." Merilee answered. She rose from the chair and walked over to the window. She stared down at the parking lot and crossed her arms in front of her. "Will we never be free of that monster?"

Merilee reminded Buster of the change in their daughter the night the mask pricked her. "It seemed like a different personality poured into her soul; a haughty, selfish person."

Sharon frowned. Merilee noticed and attempted to comfort her. "How is your family doing without your father?" Sharon didn't answer but grimaced and nodded.

Merilee understood Sharon. She lost a daughter to the evil of an idol, which she herself brought into their home. Merilee reached over and took Sharon's hand.

Buster shook his head as he stared at Barbara, "What's going on with you, sis?" he said in a whisper.

Merilee sighed, "Buster is this happening because of that dragon?"

Buster nodded and rubbed the back of his neck. "Could be."

"What can we do?" Merilee moaned as she walked up to the bed.

"Sometimes there's nothing you can do . . . except pray."

Merilee saw the mist forming in Buster's eyes. He walked over to the door. He turned and took one last look at his daughter's form before he walked into the hallway. Merilee started to go after him but stopped when she saw him turn to the right toward the chapel. He needed to be alone to prepare as a warrior fighting an old enemy making a personal attack against his daughter. Merilee watched him walk down the hallway and saw the slump of his shoulders. The battles with the dragon weighed on both his soul and body.

"Life is a series of battles," Merilee explained. Sharon didn't understand, but she nodded.

That same moment, Barbara blinked and slowly opened her eyes. She groaned with a harsh voice.

"She's awake!" declared Merilee with tears streaming down her face.

The nurse came in when Merilee squealed out. "I heard shouting and . . ."

"She's awake," Sharon exclaimed.

"You've been hit in the head. You need to take it easy." The nurse instructed Barbara as she tried to sit up.

"Please help…sit." Barbara pleaded with the nurse. The nurse helped her up slowly to the edge of the bed. Sharon and Merilee on each side of her.

It took a few minutes for Barbara to feel steady. The doctor entered the room. "Are you her family?"

They nodded. He proceeded to look at her wound and give Barbara instructions to follow his finger, etc. At the end of his exam he looked at the anxious faces of those in the room.

"I can't see any damage, but time will tell. The doctor continued, "Because of the possible psychological activity surrounding her wounds, and the criminal activity which caused them, I have asked the judge to admit her to an experimental group Dr. Abby Greenstein is putting together."

"What do you mean criminal activity?" Buster inquired.

"There are many unanswered questions regarding the intrusion and shooting in your daughter's apartment. I think she has information she is unwilling or unable to share. The group may help her explore and define what she saw and did that night."

"So why is there a judge involved?"

"Because of those unanswered questions, there is possible criminal charges that can be brought against your daughter. This way the court will have more information and your daughter will have a chance to explore her part in the event."

"This sounds serious." Merilee moaned.

"It is; I highly recommend you admit her to the class. For her own sake."

"I would like for her to attend one of the experimental groups called the "Victims of Violence and Their Psychological Response." The family nodded but didn't say anything.

The doctor continued, "I'm not sure what's going on with her, but our conversation leads me to think there is some psychological impact too."

"Thank you doctor," Merilee answered.

"That swatch they shaved off your head is going to mess up your hairdo," Sharon joked as she rubbed the stubble on Barbara's head. "I hope it didn't block out your memory because we're all full of curiosity and questions." Barbara nodded but kept silent. However, her thoughts were loud and persistent, *should I tell them what I saw? Who he was? What he said? Should I tell them about the orange cloud in the room?*

Finally, Merilee spoke up, "So, are you going to tell us what happened?"

Barbara just shook her head. "Strange things." She turned to Sharon, "How does the apartment look?"

"Like we haven't moved in completely," Sharon answered with a smile.

Barbara adjusted her position on the bed to better suit her balance. "I don't know about the mess in the apartment, but I know one thing." Barbara spit the words out slowly and with great difficulty.

"What's that?" Sharon asked while Merilee listened.

"I'm in a mess."

5

The World Changed

> "It shall come in that day," declares
> the LORD "that the heart of the king and
> the heart of the princes will fail; and the
> priests will be appalled and the prophets
> will be astounded."
>
> ---Jeremiah 4:9 (NASB)

MICHAEL DONOVAN AND his two buddies, Russ and Sid, picked up their duffel bags and loaded the "Freedom Bird" otherwise known as a C-451 cargo plane. The soldiers headed back to their "world"— their term for America, their home.

The three managed a weak smile at the sight of the plane. These men spent their hours and days in survival mode while wading in Delta waters and living with the continuous smell of death. During that time, they lost the skill of laughter. They left their home world as teenagers to enter into a realm of the unknown, a place called Vietnam.

Once they left solid ground, Michael, Russ and Sid shivered so bad their teeth chattered like maracas. The seats lining the unheated cargo plane didn't provide any creature comforts. Michael eyed the pile of duffel bags at the back. He reached for the bag closest to him.

"I bet we can find some extra clothes in there."

"Yeah," Russ agreed and pulled one of the bags open. He rummaged through it and found a long-sleeved shirt. He threw it to Michael and grabbed another bag.

"Thanks," Michael answered as he pulled on the extra clothing for warmth.

The two of them passed clothing to the other men. As the shirts made it down the line, the men wrapped themselves in a bit more warmth. Soon the shivering and groaning quieted. Only the dull hum of the plane's motor engine could be heard.

"At least we won't break our teeth chattering now," Russ exclaimed as he settled with three extra-long sleeve shirts. Then he added a thought to no one in particular, "When I get home, I'm going to kiss the ground."

"According to the articles in *Stars and Stripes*, you may not want to," Sid admonished him.

They all grunted. "It don't matter none," Russ responded with a grin. "Whatever it's become, it's still home with my sweetheart waiting for me."

"My wife will greet me with my son I've never seen," Sid said. A little mist clouded his vision. "What about you, Michael, you still got a girl or wife?"

"I'll see," Michael replied. He hadn't received any communication from his wife in the last nine months. He didn't know what awaited him.

Soon Michael relaxed a little. He and the others fell into a state of sheer exhaustion. This band of soldiers waited silently to arrive in Hawaii where they would make connecting flights to San Francisco and then each to their individual homes.

Michael's final destination would be Ft. Worth, Texas. He sighed, *I have no home*. His father had sold the family farm during his Vietnam tour and moved to a small town in South Texas. He drifted back to memories of his family before Vietnam.

Memories from another life passed through his mind. He recalled his grandmother's old family farm filled with aunts, uncles and cousins gathered for Sunday afternoon lunch and baseball games. The warm homey memory caused the corner of his mouth to lift in a smile.

Alas, he loved the memory but reality fast approached. He would soon see his folk's new home and his new bride he left there. A shudder came over hi. He felt lost. His life before Vietnam no longer existed.

The connecting flight to San Francisco provided a commercial jetliner with soft seats and a warm atmosphere; both in temperature and in service. The stewardesses smiled and talked to them, in unbroken American English.

"You sound so good," Sid said as he sat down.

The stewardess smiled but didn't respond to his familiar statement. A few minutes into the flight to San Francisco, Sid screamed out and batted at the air with his closed fists.

Michael came out of his melancholy sleep instantaneously. He rushed to Sid sitting a couple rows behind him. When he neared Sid he saw the image of an angel hovering over him, in the form of a stewardess, whose name tag read, Donna.

She cooed in a soft voice to arouse him. It took a while before Sid came back to the safety of the plane from the horror of his mind. She handed Sid a cup of cold water.

"The war is over for your body, but it will take your mind a long time to leave it."

Michael watched the kindness and patience of the stewardess. "How long have you been doing this?" he asked.

"You mean, escorting you guys home and getting you there in one piece?" Donna asked. "About a year." She paused for a moment and then said in a soft tone, "It ain't easy."

"Sounds like you've had some battles of your own."

"I have, my first day on the job," she said. "Another returning soldier went to sleep like this fellow. When the nightmare started his heart couldn't endure. He had a heart attack and died."

"On the way home?" Michael exclaimed.

"Yes, on the way home."

"Have you had some special training?" Michael inquired.

"We get retired early from this job, so I've been taking classes on my time off, to prepare for that eventuality."

"What are you studying?"

"Psychological nursing."

"Sounds right for this job," Michael smiled at Donna.

"On this job, all that schooling just gets thrown out the window."

"What do'ya mean?"

"The demons . . . there are awful demons in that land, and you guys bring them home with you,"

Michael exchanged glances with Russ and listened as Donna moaned about the destruction to the mind caused by a war with no rules of combat.

"Especially from a war like this one." She concluded.

"Everybody and everything could be the enemy. They moved their villages overnight and their loyalties quicker," Russ jumped into the conversation.

Michael nodded; he suspected Russ referred to the event they shared. Donna saw the knowing look between them.

"Tell me about it, it may help to talk."

"It started with the sweet vision of a pudgy little toddler," Michael began.

"Cute as a button, just a baby." Sid joined the conversation with a whisper. The words came slow and arduously.

"We entered a village and saw a group of women and children standing near one of their hooches, that's the name for their houses. One little girl moved away from her spot toward us. Russ noticed a wire coming out from the little girl's dress; it led to a detonator."

Sid shook his head as he moaned the words with great grief, "In the mother's hands."

"Just as we stopped, the mother hit the button causing that little girl to be cut in half." Russ raged red faced as he continued, "Why sacrifice her own baby?"

Michael picked up the details, "Her flesh sprayed all over us. That sweet little girl. Why would anyone destroy their own child? Monsters," Michael said with quivering voice. He bowed his head and covered his face with his palms.

"We had given her our candy bars. She had just taken a bite of chocolate when---." Sid couldn't finish his sentence.

Donna took a deep breath and wiped the mist from her own eyes. "I never get use to the horrors you guys experienced." She disappeared into the galley and returned with complimentary drinks for the guys.

Michael continued the discussion. "Nature proved to be a formidable enemy as well."

"Did you know there are over a hundred different snakes in that country, and every one of them except two are poisonous?" Sid interjected.

"I remember Carl and the one-step snake." Russ shook his head as he mumbled the words to the floor.

"Why one-step?" Donna asked.

"Because if you got bit you could only walk a few steps before you dropped dead. That's what happened to Carl. He yelped; we saw the snake slither away, and Carl fell to the ground—dead." Russ shuddered with the memory.

"But the foot rot plagued us all. We watched the skin on our feet turn white and fall off after stomping through the brackish water of rice paddies or in the thick mud of the Mekong Delta." Michael shuffled his feet. "Still hurts."

The numerous other soldiers on that plane groaned in agreement and the soft sound of shuffling feet could be heard. Another young man who had been silent up to this point muttered in a voice barely audible enough to hear, "I don't ever want to speak of it again."

The others nodded, and a cloak of silence fell over the war-weary soldiers.

Donna made one more admonition, "Just remember if you don't expunge those memories, they'll follow you wherever you go and whatever you do. Keep close to each other. You don't have to talk."

The guys nodded in agreement. Russ spoke up to voice their thoughts. "You just have to know. Those who have never been there will never understand, but we will always know." A collective moan of agreement came up from the group.

Michael leaned his head back and quietly said, "God, if you're there, please help me readjust, and help my family still love me in spite of the things I've seen and done."

The plane dropped ever closer to the ground, and every soldier on the plane looked out the nearest porthole. The door opened, the steps dropped. Where scared young boys once had boarded a plane many months ago, today war-weary men deplaned.

"Remember, men, hold your head high. What you have done is honorable, and let no one tell you otherwise," Donna encouraged them, knowing they were about to step out into another war altogether.

Michael thought it a strange comment. He didn't have time to think about it because a noise coming from the fence on the tarmac grabbed his attention.

A large group of young people about the same ages of the men deplaning were screaming and yelling. They held signs and pumped their hands in the air. The men waved at the crowd and smiled. "Maybe it's not as bad as we've been led to believe." Russ pondered.

Once the soldiers had both feet firmly planted on the ground, Russ dropped to his hands and knees to kiss American soil. Just as his lips touched the tarmac, he felt a powerful kick on his behind that sent him skidding across the asphalt, opening the skin on his nose, lips and chin. With pain coursing through his face he rose and saw Michael and Sid barreling into a red-faced young man. At that time three of the kicker's friends came baring fists and anger at Michael and Sid. Airport security stepped in and stopped the assault while pushing the men toward their connecting flights.

"At least they look worse than we do." Michael said as he picked up his duffel bag holding his head high and straight. For the first time he read the signs held by the screaming crowd, "baby-killers." One particular sign displayed the image of actress Jane Fonda pretending to shoot a Vietcong gun at American soldiers. The sign read, *'Jane's right. You are all liars.*

6

Life Goes On

Thus says the Lord, "Stand by the ways and see and ask for the ancient paths, where the good way is, and walk in it; and you will find rest for your souls."

---Jeremiah 6:16 (NASB)

EXCITEMENT SPARKLED THROUGH the air like lighting. The freshman students gathered in the lobby of the student union. Boys watched the girls and the girls watched the boys; watching them. The ritual of the college mating game had officially begun.

Barbara could care less. She didn't have much regard for the male gender and didn't care what they did. She didn't plan on dating or getting married. Her ability and intelligence served as her life goals, not becoming someone's wife and mother. Her heart's desire focused on developing her skills into a professorship. She wanted respect in her field, which meant she needed the education. Her chosen field of study in theology proved to be her biggest obstacle.

One of the upper-classmen called the group to attention. At that moment she turned her head toward the tall student with the chiseled features and movie-star good looks. Barbara felt only disgust. She had known his type. With arrogant demeanors, they had little respect for women as people. She wanted nothing to do with them.

As the man gave instructions about up-coming events, she listened. The girls in the audience looked mesmerized by his words. She noticed a student or teacher behind him dressed in the gaudiest orange suit she had ever seen. He turned and looked at her and making eye contact.

"Ugh." She said out loud.

"Shh," Sharon scolded, "we need the information."

"Sorry," Barbara whimpered.

The students played games to encourage mingling.

"What, or rather, who are you staring at?" Sharon nudged Barbara.

She pointed to the man who introduced himself from Montana.

"Whoa!" I thought you were going to ignore the male sector." Sharon pointed out.

"I was, but he's different."

"He's okay, but nothing to hang a gaze upon," Sharon protested.

Another game started. The upper classman stood in front of the group giving instructions. After the fellowship time she saw him standing at the refreshment table. She couldn't help herself, she took a glimpse at his name tag---Daniel Holloway.

While fulfilling the requirements of registration to see a curriculum counselor, Barbara stood in the middle of a line that stretched the length of the cafeteria. She wasn't sure she would be able to endure the long wait. Her hospital release three weeks ago left her in a weak state. The vending machine across the room caught her attention. A snack would give her some strength. She also noticed Daniel Holloway sitting across the room staring at her. For that brief moment she felt comfort in his gaze. She offered him a coy smile but before he could respond she heard her name called. She entered the office of Mr. Phillip McCord.

He motioned to a chair. Without saying anything he studied the file in front of him. With a heavy sigh he finally looked up at her. She sucked in a deep breath when she saw him. She felt as though she gazed into the face of her old high school superintendent, Dr. McCoy. She groaned realizing the name of the counselor sounded similar to her high school superintendents' name.

"Barbara Troye," came a hoarse voice from the man setting behind the desk with his fingers intertwined and index fingers steepled. The face may resemble Dr. McCoy, but not the voice. Nothing made any sense. Barbara pulled her sweater a little tighter around her.

Mr. McCord, the counselor at the university, peered into her eyes. "It says here you want to teach theological studies." He stated as he jabbed at the file.

"That's right." Barbara responded.

"Why?" He prodded with dead eyes staring directly into hers.

"Why, what?" She responded with an edge to her voice.

"Why theology, you can study for an elementary education to teach children." He reprimanded.

"I'm not good with children. I want to teach theology at college level, and for that I need a degree." Barbara retorted.

"Whatever you teach, as a woman, you'll not get a theology degree from this university, probably not from any other reputable school."

Barbara opened her mouth to protest, but Mr. McCord continued, "It's nothing personal. There's limited space in our theology program. First choice is given to the young men who will someday be our pastors and evangelists."

Barbara took a deep breath so as not to alienate the man who held her future in his hands. "I understand, but those young men will need training, and I can provide that as a college professor."

Mr. McCord laughed out loud. "A woman teaching men. You may as well grow another head."

Barbara shrugged her shoulders and crossed her arms in front of her with a clenched jaw. Her stomach churned and her resolve melted. He mocked her desires.

Barbara rose from the chair and stood beside it. She put her hands on the back of it and ducked her head. She struggled to build up her courage. When she raised her head a cold fear gripped her. Mr. McCord morphed into Dr. McCoy both in his appearance and the sound of his voice.

"You and your family gave me trouble for years. Now it's my turn to torment you." Spoke the voice of Dr. McCoy. He mocked her with a chuckle and a crooked smile.

With the strange pronouncement, she watched Dr. McCoy change back to Mr. McCord. He leaned back in his chair with his hands behind his head. He sighed with a crooked smile, "Young lady, you'll make some lucky pastor a happy man. Nonetheless, I can't admit you to the theology program."

The voice reverted back to Mr. McCord's voice and face. Barbara wondered if Mr. McCord had been aware of Dr. McCoy's appearance and statement.

Mr. McCord insinuated the meeting had come to its end by closing her chart and folding his hands in front of him. Barbara saw the futility of arguing especially with a creature who kept changing his appearance and sound. She felt defeated by his judgment pronounced upon her.

"You'll notice I put you in music classes; your chart said you are an accomplished pianist. Churches love a pastor's wife who can play the piano or organ." He grinned and made the last stab at Barbara's confidence, "If you major in music you can graduate with a hot pink tassel."

Barbara held her tongue in check with a tight grimace. She felt the steam of anger building into a full -blown blaze. She searched for some biting searing words to put this devil in his place. She threw the schedule he handed her into the trash with a forceful thrust.

"You better pick it up, or you don't go to school at all." McCord said.

Before she walked out the door, she wanted to make one last defense. She turned to speak, instead her whole body froze with fear. Before her sat the most repulsive creature she had ever seen. His huge teeth were green from decay and orange slime crept down the corners of his mouth. Barbara let out a little squeal at the horrible apparition. It had to be her imagination. She grabbed the school schedule from the trash and ran out of the room. With a sucking gasp she shut the door, looked at the secretary and crumpled into the nearest chair becoming a small body of tears and fear.

She took the schedule and pushed it into her notebook. As she did, she noticed the signature of the "counselor." There in large letters read the name, Phillip Donnigan McCord. Beads of sweat formed on her upper lip.

"Are you okay?" the secretary asked.

"Yes, I mean I think so. I just saw his signature."

The secretary looked at her puzzled. She tried to explain simply and logically, "Phillip Donnigan founded my hometown in the late 1880's. I thought it a strange coincidence."

"The secretary nodded, "Yes, it is. What is your hometown?" she asked Barbara.

Barbara could feel the perspiration of anxiety dripping down her spine. She politely said, "Church Creek Falls." She hoped the secretary hadn't heard of it.

"The town wiped out by a bomb?" She asked with a high pitch voice of surprise. Barbara nodded wanting to get on her way. "That's strange. Mr. McCord's resume listed that town as his last position." Barbara stared at the woman behind the desk with her mouth open. Finally, she managed to say, "What?" The secretary nodded with a big smile.

Barbara shuddered and mumbled, "the dragon . . . it wasn't an illusion."

7

Choices

You shall also say to this people, Thus says the LORD; Behold, I set before you the way of life, and the way of death.

---Jeremiah 21:8 (NASB)

BARBARA'S EIGHT O'CLOCK English literature class started her day with enjoyment. Then came the dreaded music classes, one right after the other. In all, she endured four hours of music. Afterwards she felt exhausted and ready to quit. She read music, that didn't make her a musician. And sitting in class amongst some of the most talented people on campus, augmented her inadequacy. Her whole body felt stretched beyond its limits from the tension of attempting to do something she couldn't. She knew she would not last a semester.

Walking past the theology building between every class made her heart ache with longing. The pain increased when the students, all boys, emerged from the building discussing the exciting new details they learned in the lectures they attended.

Sharon came up behind Barbara. "Hey, woman, wanna go check out the bowling alley and get in a game or two."

"Only if I can throw a fifty-pound ball at Mr. McCord's head."

Sharon laughed, "You'd have to get in a long line for that one."

"What do'ya mean?"

"Every student he counseled came out of his office scared and mad."

"I didn't know that, but I'm not surprised." Barbara scoffed.

"It'll get better," Sharon insisted. Barbara tilted her head and stared at Sharon.

"Don't make empty promises to a scorned woman with a big problem."

"You mean the problem of playing the piano?"

"No, my problem is practicing the piano. I hate it."

"What are you going to do when jury time gets here?"

"Jury?"

"Yeah, didn't they tell you about that?"

"No!"

"You have to play three pieces for three instructors, and they judge your proficiency, that will be your final grade."

"This just gets worse."

"Look at it this way, it's too late in the semester to get any money back, so just use the time for your own pleasure, then drop the music classes before finals."

"Good idea." She said to Sharon with a renewed spirit." And yes, I would like to go bowling."

"You sound in a better mood," Sharon noted.

"You gave me at least one way out of this maze of a troubled life."

"Dropping music?"

"Yeah, now I don't have to be the perfect pastor's wife," Barbara chided remembering Mr. McCord 's direction for her life.

"I have no idea what you are rambling about," Sharon responded.

Barbara had a scheduled hour of practice time, starting now. She climbed up the massive steps into the music building, with a dose of self-confidence. Holding her head up and with a broad smile on her face she congratulated herself for overcoming the depression of lost opportunity. She whispered to herself, "I don't need God, I can take care of myself."

Sitting on a bench a few feet away, a military man with the name, Davis, sewed on the right pocket flap, heard her comment.

Life must go on and that meant practice time every day. The old and smelly music building still stood as a bastion of exceptional talent. Barbara felt out of place. Her shoulders slumped. The last room on the long hall served as her practice room. She could hear the professional musicians. For that reason, she never practiced. If these people heard her playing they would die laughing. She entered the room, closed and locked the door. She looked at the old studio piano sitting in the middle of an empty room, pulled up the one chair in the room and sat down. She rubbed her temples. Leaning back, her gaze landed on the water-spotted ceiling before she bowed her head to pray.

"Dear Lord," She stopped, opened her eyes and looked around. "What do I pray for?" She tried again, "Dear Jesus, I really want to know more about you, but You let them put me here---Music? Really Lord. You didn't give me musical talent, so why? I don't understand what you are doing. I came here to learn more about the Scripture. I hate this. The only reason I learned music is because my mother sat on the bench and made me practice. God why are you asking me to do something you didn't give me the ability to do? Are you there?"

She sighed and said, "God, do you care?"

Ever since her hometown blew up and she lost friends, believing in a good God proved difficult and at this moment it proved impossible. God just didn't make sense any more.

She leaned back and said, "I can't do it anymore." Having made the admission of failure as a called disciple of Christ, she felt relief. She no longer had to strive to be a good Christian. Instead she could be a mediocre heathen. But strangely, she still wanted to take those theology classes. Maybe to discover why God claimed to be good, when his true character proved to be vindictive and absent or to prove to God with His own words that she didn't need Him.

She spoke out loud in response to her thought, "If you don't care, why should I?" She pulled a book out of her backpack and started reading about 'the problem with no name,' from *The Feminine Mystique*. Each word caused her heart to harden a little bit more against God. A coat of spiritual ice formed around Barbara's heart. Nearby an orange glow settled on her hair and shoulders.

8

A Woman's Place?

> My soul, I am in anguish! Oh my
> heart I cannot be silent, Because you
> have heard, O my soul, . . . the alarm of
> war. Disaster on disaster is proclaimed.
>
> ---Jeremiah 4:19-20a(NASB)

MORE THAN A year had passed since the strange man invaded Barbara's life by intruding in her private space at home. At least it made her tough and independent. A trait causing some of her family and friends to mock her.

Since the break-in, her parents visited on a regular basis. They would be going home tomorrow. Barbara felt grateful her daddy had seen the kitchen light and came to join her. He may be an old-fashioned religious nut, but he loved her. That one fact she knew and because of that she truly trusted him.

Barbara's father prepared a midnight snack.

"What are you doing up at this hour?" he probed.

"I had a nightmare."

"About the intruder?" Buster surmised.

"No, I dreamed about the Sunday I surrendered to go into full-time Christian service. Do you remember?"

"I remember. There's no greater life than serving the Lord," Buster reflected.

"Do you remember what else happened that day?"

"We had dinner with the Barnhill's and celebrated."

"What were we celebrating?"

"Your decision."

"And- - -"

"And Johnny's."

"Which one do you think people remembered? How many opportunities did Johnny get after that day? How many did I get?"

"Opportunities to do what?"

"Teach. He even preached several Sundays. He received honors for every little thing he did, he graduated high school, he went to college, etc. etc. The church made him the youth pastor and gave him a huge scholarship. You know why?"

Buster nodded.

Barbara threw her cookie onto the dining table, rose and paced the room, raising her voice, "Because---because, he surrendered to be a preacher. What did I get daddy? Tell me, what did I get?"

"Nothing." Buster whispered. He saw the pain in his daughter's face, "Sugar, it doesn't make your decision any less meaningful."

"I know, but why? Johnny lived up to his reputation as the meanest boy in school."

Buster moved toward Barbara and held her in his arms. "I know baby."

"He used the group for his own amusement. He made crude jokes and poked fun at everyone. Do you know what he said to Darrell?"

"The little boy with the lisp?" Buster clarified.

"Yea, he mocked him and called him a baby in front of the whole youth group, then preacher Dan brought him up front on that same Sunday morning and gave him scholarship money because God called him to be a preacher."

"I remember." Buster recalled the Sunday morning service when the dragon revealed himself at the feet of the preacher. He also remembered the words the dragon whispered in his mind, 'it goes on and there is nothing you can do about it.' Buster became aware of Barbara still talking.

"If he's an example of God's man, I don't want anything to do with that God. Do you know where Johnny is today?' Barbara blurted out.

Buster nodded, "In jail."

"For what?" Barbara screamed. She knew the answer but she wanted to know if her daddy knew.

"Rape!" Buster divulged.

"That's right and you know what daddy? He almost raped me."

Buster stood up red-faced, "What? When?"

"That Sunday at the Barnhill's house when everybody congratulated him. Susan invited me to the barn to play some records. I followed her there, but we walked in an empty barn, except for Johnny. I heard the barn door close and lock."

Buster looked at Barbara with his mouth open, "Sis, I didn't know."

"He touched me and tried to kiss me. He even ripped the sleeve on my dress. I remember shaking and screaming loud, but nobody heard." Barbara started crying and Buster couldn't make out her next words.

"Daddy, the dragon, the dragon on our farm stood behind him telling him what to do." She sobbed.

"Did he. . . did?"

"No."

"How did you get away?"

"You called my name. Johnny jumped up and left out the back way. That's when I ran to you."

"I remember," Buster groaned with the memory.

"When you called, the dragon stopped smiling. It stopped telling him what to do next and it disappeared with Johnny."

"I'm so sorry baby."

"It's like if we don't beg boys to have sex with us then we girls aren't worth anything."

"Did Johnny do that to you?" Buster asked.

"He acted like I should be happy. You know what he said to me?"

"No." Buster answered.

"He said I would make him a great preacher's wife."

Buster shook his head. After a few minutes he changed the subject and asked a question more relevant to the current situation.

"Sis, the dragon in the apartment . . . did it look the same as the one on the farm?"

"I don't know, the one in the apartment emitted an orange cloud. The one on the farm didn't?"

"What about the one behind Johnny?" Buster whispered the question, clearing his throat.

Barbara hesitated and thought. She shook her head, "Yes, the orange cloud surrounded it."

"Sis, you've gotta resist this orange thing."

"That's what I'm doing, that's why I go to the meetings." Barbara answered.

Buster asked, "What meetings?"

"It's called NOW, which stands for National Organization for Women," Barbara stated.

"I never heard of them."

"It's a fairly new group."

"They promote women's rights."

Buster chuckled, "So women have different rights than men?" he repeated with an air of sarcasm.

"Yeah, it's women who have the children and raise them but get no recognition and become second class to men. Just like I was to Johnny," Barbara sat back and crossed her legs and folded her arms in front of her.

Buster knew his daughter's behavior; she hid more than she shared with him.

"Sis, what's going on?"

"Nothing." She ducked her head as she said it.

Buster recognized the code for 'nothing I want to share with you right now.' The conversation ended. He changed the subject.

"Have you made any friends at these meetings or do you attend alone?"

"I go alone, that way, I can leave when I want, but, I have met one girl. Can't say we are friends but we always sit together. We don't get as involved as some others."

"What's her name?"

Barbara laughed as she answered, "Teresa. Do you know any more than you did? What difference does her name make?"

"A name is how we identify ourselves. How will I know you're talking about a friend if I don't know her name?" Buster winked at Barbara. "Do you know what your name means?"

"Not really? What?"

"Barbarian." Buster explained with a broad smile.

"Thanks a lot for that information, now what do you want me to do with it?"

Buster leaned forward in his chair and pulled her hands away from her body. He held both of them tight in his own hands. "It also means stranger, a traveler from a foreign land. My sweet daughter, you are in a foreign land, and you are fighting like a barbarian, but when you are ready to come home, your mother and I will be there to greet you."

Barbara stroked her father's sun-burnt rough hands, "I know, Daddy. I just don't want to live on the farm."

"That's not what I'm talking about. I mean your soul, not your body."

"What?" Barbara responded.

Buster reached over and kissed her on the cheek, "I love you peanut, and I pray for you."

"I appreciate it, but don't waste your time, God doesn't care about me."

"You may be right." Buster remarked as he rose and took his glass to the kitchen sink. Barbara's mouth fell open and she followed her daddy with her eyes.

"That's a surprise answer. What are you saying?"

"I'm saying; "The eyes of the Lord are toward the righteous, His face is against evildoers. In Ezekiel it says, "Woe to rebellious children who have a plan, but not Mine."

"Daddy?" Barbara moaned.

"Cursed is the person who makes flesh his strength and trusts in mankind," Jeremiah 17:5."

"Okay, enough with the Bible verses, I get what you're saying; I'm rebellious. You're right. I don't believe any of the stuff from the Bible, it's all designed to give people money and power over others or to instill guilt. I'm not falling in that trap. I'll take care of myself."

Buster leaned over the sink for a few minutes, taking a deep breath. Then turning towards his daughter, he said, "At those meetings, listen to the ideas of the opposition, those who have been around a while and remember why the fences were put up in the first place."

"We're not on the farm. We don't need fences because there are no cattle."

Buster smiled, "Are you sure the bull hasn't been set free?"

"Still not gettin' your meaning."

"Just be sure you know where all the livestock is before the fence is torn down."

Barbara rose from the couch and walked into the kitchen. She didn't want to have a conversation with her daddy about women's lib. She especially didn't want to have the conversation in riddles. Her struggle between the concept of an independent woman versus a wife and mother lay beyond her father's understanding.

After her parents left, Barbara noticed her book, *The Feminine Mystique* open on the coffee table. Her mother must have read it. Barbara couldn't wait to hear her opinion.

9

Brotherhood With A Sister

> And I thought, 'After she has done
> all these things she will return to Me'; but
> she did not return and her treacherous
> sister Judah saw it.

--- Jeremiah 3:7 (NASB)

University Medical Center, Burlington Heights, 1972

"WHY DO YOU THINK I should make application? I'm not a veteran." Barbara studied the blank form. "I don't even want to be here."

"I know, it's not just for vets; it's an experimental class for anyone suffering from violent trauma---"

"And you think I qualify?"

"Yes, I do." Dr. Greenstein answered. "This is part of your treatment."

"But my wounds are healed. Besides, it's been over a year since the incident," Barbara argued.

"Only the physical wounds are healed, your physician thinks you still carry some anxiety."

Barbara crossed her arms in front of her. "Are you saying I have mental problems?"

"Your family doctor and I think the class can provide you some clarity," Dr. Greenstein stated in a comforting voice.

"When does all this take place?"

"The meetings are held once a week on the psychology floor."

Barbara filled out the form and with a frustrated sigh and handed it to Dr. Greenstein.

"Now what?"

"Now you show up Monday." Dr. Greenstein replied.

"What is this group called?" Barbara asked.

"I call it a class for victims of violence."

When the elevator door opened, Barbara looked around. In the hallway sat a table with a coffee pot, sodas, and treats. A group of young men surrounded it. A door leading into a large room stood directly in front of the elevator. Barbara walked in. She found a row of empty chairs and sat down on the end. Another man came and sat on her left side. He handed her a soda and cookie.

"Thank you, that's thoughtful," she said as she took the refreshments. Grateful to have something in her anxious hands.

A man in a wheelchair pulled up beside her. He smiled and introduced himself as Paps.

"Rough duty." Russ, the man who brought her refreshments said. Paps only nodded with no expression.

Barbara ignored the remark. Finding herself the only female in this group caused her heart to speed up and her hands grow clammy. Anxiety crept around her like a dirty blanket. She wanted to go home. Her head pounded. She rose from her chair and stood in a corner of the room, away from the men.

A man in a white coat came over to her. She assumed he must be the leader of the group. He introduced himself, Carl Young, R.N.

"I guess that's an appropriate name for the leader of a mental group." Barbara smirked. "If I'm in the right place, Carl Jung."

He smiled, "my name is one of my biggest assets in this setting, however, few people get it."

"I gather this is the meeting for the victims of violence?"

"Yes, you're in the right place." He assured her. He turned toward Paps and introduced himself. He continued the pattern of speaking to each person as an individual.

The two men who had been sitting on either side of Barbara were now conversing with each other. Everyone ignored her. Her heart rate slowed, and her spirit quieted.

While she took deep breaths, another man walked up to her on shaky legs. Can I sit with you?"

She smiled at him, "Of course."

He pulled up a chair beside her. "My name is Sid, and I just fell off the bird from Vietnam."

"Bird?"

"Plane." He took a sip of coffee as Barbara tried to make sense of his words.

At the same time a disembodied voice called out, "Barbara?"

"Michael!" She squealed, as she recognized her cousin's voice. She jumped up and ran to him smothering him with a big hug.

"When did you get back?"

"Last week."

"How are you doing?" Barbara asked clinging to his arm.

"I'm here and that's a good thing. Why are you here?"

"I thought it was a mistake but I've been told this is a group for victims of violence." Barbara answered.

"What? Why?" Michael probed.

"Seems violence breeds camaraderie or something like that."

Michael gasped, "What violence?"

"An intruder broke into my apartment and he shot me."

"Since you're here he must have been a lousy shot."

Barbara smiled. "Yeah, thank goodness."

"Who and why?"

The leader of the group, Mr. Young, started the meeting before Barbara could answer. Michael pushed Sid onto the next chair and sat by Barbara. Grateful for his presence, she looked forward to spending time with her favorite cousin after a three-year absence while he served a tour of duty in Vietnam. At least now, these meetings may be tolerable.

"Welcome to the first meeting of the 'Psychology Class for Victims of Violent Acts.' Each of you were hand-chosen or directed by your physicians to attend this on-going class."

"I thought this would be a one-time thing, I didn't know I made a lifetime commitment."

Michael smiled at her remark while he sifted through the sheaf of papers they were each being given.

"Does this mean we have homework?" she complained softly but the class heard.

"Spoken like a true college student," Michael sneered.

Barbara changed the subject with a troubled voice, "It's so good to have you home."

Michael studied her face, but before he could address her, the leader stood up and spoke. He directed his comments to the changes the group would experience.

"By being here today, most of you will discover the symptoms that are manifest now will be reduced as you return to civilian life. Your trauma is a problem you have today, it isn't a problem of your future, although your future decisions and worldview will be colored by your experiences, they need not impact your future negatively."

Barbara noticed Michael's shaking hands. She looked at her own. Then she looked at the rest of the group and studied their physical appearance. All of them had at least one part of their anatomy shaking uncontrollably or missing.

The leader continued. "None of you are the same today that you were before your service or your trauma." Mr. Young said. At least she had to agree with him in that assessment. Orange could never be her favorite color. She smiled at the silly thought.

"You have changed emotionally, the way you think and the things you think about are different." At that statement Barbara ducked her head and started twining her fingers together. Michael reached over and put his hand over hers. She relaxed.

"Spiritually, you've changed. Your beliefs, spirituality, faith in people, even your faith in your god has transformed."

When the meeting ended Russ asked Michael, "You wanta go get somethin to eat?"

"Russ, this is my cousin; you mind if she comes with us?" Russ gave Barbara a once over. He smiled and answered, "Sure, it will be nice to have some female company as cute as you." He winked at Barbara and heat rose to her fair cheeks.

Barbara bit her lip and didn't respond because if she did it would be a diatribe on the evil thinking of men. Why couldn't he appreciate her as a person?

"I'm not cute." Barbara blurted out. *I sound like an idiot.*

Russ' facial expression softened. "I'm sorry, I didn't mean---"

Michael took her head, "Careful boys, she's a bit-"

"Abnormal?" Barbara finished the statement.

"Yes, that's the word; we're all abnormal. That's why we're here."

Russ jumped in after the scolding from Barbara, "I'll call my fiancée and see if she can come too." Sid stepped up and heard the conversation. "Mind if my wife and I join?"

Barbara's prepared speech deflated. The company turned out to be delightful and Barbara enjoyed being with the group. The women were beautiful and both of them had exciting jobs. Russ' fiancée attended college to be an architect. Barbara noticed Sid's wife smiled when she spoke of her baby.

"I'm surprised you invited me, I thought you would bring Elizabeth," Barbara commented to Michael when they left the cafe.

"Like the man said, we've changed," Michael explained as he closed Barbara's car door. "Be careful and I'll see you next week." He clicked his tongue and pointed his index finger at Barbara. As he turned away, she noticed the bottle of whiskey sticking out of his pocket.

10

N.O.W

There shall not be found among you anyone who makes his son or his daughter pass through the fire, or one who practices witchcraft, or a soothsayer, or one who interprets omens, or a sorcerer, or one who conjures spells, or a medium, or a spiritist, or one who calls up the dead.

---Deuteronomy 18:10-11 (NASB)

BARBARA MOTIONED TO Teresa to come sit with her and Sharon. With an oversized crowd, seats were hard to find so Barbara saved one for Teresa. Soon the audience quieted down and all eyes focused on the girl at the podium.

After the short speech by the woman calling herself Moonbeam, she introduced the main speaker. The woman presented a more pleasant appearance than any of the other speakers. As she stood and walked to the podium she had control of the room. Her business-like suit gave her an air of confidence and authority. She wore light make-up, clean hair, parted in the middle and combed nicely to each side. She possessed a natural combination of the innocent cheer-leader and the business matriarch. The big bug-eyed glasses she wore made Barbara smile. Moonbeam introduced Gloria Steinem to an excited crowd. Barbara knew Ms. Steinem, as she liked to be called, served as one of the founders of the second wave of feminism. Barbara didn't understand all the terminology, but she knew this journalist from "The New Yorker" magazine, held some notoriety with this audience. She found herself smiling and feeling an inner excitement generated by the crowd lusting to hear their founder and cheerleader.

Moonbeam continued to speak, causing some agitation among the crowd. Barbara saw the familiar orange cloud settle beside Steinem. Surprised by its presence she watched it change into the shape of a man dressed in an orange suit. When he raised his cane the room erupted in applause and wolf whistles. When he let it down the noise subsided. He stayed by the side of the speaker. The churning of anxiety increased in Barbara's stomach. She looked at her friends.

"Do you see the man on stage?" she ventured to ask Teresa.

"There are no men here, this is a meeting for women only tonight." Teresa growled.

Barbara turned toward Sharon, sitting quietly, shuffling her feet looking at the program. She wouldn't see anything on stage. Barbara decided to turn her attention to the speaker and become better acquainted with the purpose of the meeting; ratification of the Equal Rights Amendment or more commonly known as the ERA.

The speaker wailed about the injustice of her childhood. The filled room watched and listened with rapt attention. This meeting possessed a different message. Barbara could feel its power. The orange man controlled the response of this audience. He mouthed the words that came from the lips of the speaker.

"Sex is the only way women can gain power," Ms. Steinham said.

"Guess we better get a boyfriend," Barbara heard a girl sitting a few chairs down from her. Heads of people around them turned and shushed them. Barbara focused on the woman and the words she could hear orange man speaking to her.

"A coven of 13 members of WITCH (The Women's International Terrorist Conspiracy from Hell, celebrating witches and gypsies as the first women resistance fighters) demonstrates against that bastion of white male supremacy: Wall Street. The next day, the market falls five points."

"More witches and some black-veiled brides invade the Bridal Fair at Madison Square Garden. They carry signs ("Confront the Whore-makers," "Here Comes the Bribe"), sing, shout, release white mice in the audience of would-be brides, and generally scare the living daylights out of exhibitors who are trying to market the conventional delights of bridal gowns, kitchen appliances, package-deal honeymoon trips and heart-shaped swimming pools."

Ms. Gloria Steinham shouted to the crowd as they cheered her on.

What? Witches? Rats? Barbara's hand went over her open mouth. Barbara experienced both intrigue and disgust, as well as confusion. Ms. Steinham promoted the destruction of objects women use to lighten their household chores, in order to gain power over men. That doesn't make sense. *If I have no washer, who is going to do my laundry. I think that advice is more work not more power. And, what does it mean when she says power comes from sexual manipulation of men?* The strange idea stunned Barbara. She wanted to be a strong independent woman. She didn't want to manipulate men, she wanted an equal opportunity. This plan sounded ludicrous, violent and wrong. Still this talk about witch terrorists intrigued Barbara. It may be strange but it did peak her curiosity.

When the meeting dismissed, Barbara turned to Teresa, "Wanna go get a burger?"

"Yes, I'm starving," Teresa answered.

Barbara looked at Sharon. She shrugged her shoulders and replied, "I'll go. Listening to that nonsense made me hungry."

The three girls settled into a booth, and discussed the speech they had heard.

"What'd ya think?" Teresa started.

"Not sure if that woman is delusional or brilliant," Barbara reasoned.

"Why do'ya think she could be delusional?" Sharon quipped with a wrinkled brow.

"Her comments made men sound like the creation of hell." Barbara answered.

"That's how I felt when I saw my dad hauled off to prison. It made life hard." Sharon reciprocated."

"I didn't get that message," Teresa announced.

"What message did you get?" Barbara asked her.

Teresa winked and smirked as she answered with the guttural sound of a movie star, "Men only want us for sex."

Sharon didn't laugh, she sighed and dropped her head into the menu. "It's not funny. I really missed my dad."

"Sorry," Teresa apologized.

"Teresa, whadya think about the witch remark?" Barbara turned the conversation topic to one less personal.

"Not much, but I've been thinking about the power remark."

"You mean without using sex?" Barbara smirked and Sharon laughed.

"It's all twisted together. In order to have any influence or power in the arena of ideas, women have to put out sex or marry into power. Sex and marriage take all independence from women."

Barbara didn't say anything, she ate her meal in silence, but her mind whirred. Barbara wondered, *is marriage the problem?*

Once Sharon regained her composure she exploded with her defense, "Marriage is God's idea and it's a pretty good one."

"Phht." Teresa mocked. "I bet you got that answer at church. The answers from there make it simple don't they?"

"God uses the simple to confuse the wise," Sharon responded.

"Power is not simple when you get it," Teresa said.

"Do you have power?" Barbara mocked.

"Yes, and I will show you how to get it when you're ready to put Mr. McCord in his place." Teresa said.

Barbara smiled and muttered, "That would be nice."

"What would you do to him if you had the power?" Teresa demanded.

"I would have him grow a tale that wouldn't let him sit down comfortably." Barbara chuckled.

Teresa studied Barbara, "Your kidding? That's what you would do?"

"I don't know; it's an impossible scene so why not have fun with it." Barbara responded.

"Think about it as real. Now what would you do?" Teresa restated.

Barbara put her burger down and put her hands palm down on the table in front of her. Her gaze lifting up. "I would... I would take something precious away from him."

"Now you're talking." Teresa advocated. "So what's precious to him?"

"I don't know, his looks?" Barbara declared.

"That's already gone." Sharon grunted. "You better think of something else."

The girls giggled for a few minutes, then Barbara leaned back and raised her hands behind the back of her neck. A slight smile crept upon her face, "His reputation."

"Good one." Teresa slapped her on the shoulder.

"Girls this is all very interesting and speculative, but I've got to go and Barb, you is my ride," Sharon interrupted the celebration of ideas.

Teresa suggested, "You take Barbara's car, and I'll bring her home, I need to talk to her alone anyway."

Barbara handed Sharon the keys.

Sharon stopped and turned toward Barbara and Teresa, "Before I go, I want to say one more thing; marriage is a picture of God. Remember, He made man in His image."

"Yeah, man, but woman he made a sex object." Teresa retorted.

"No, He didn't, women are equal to men, but different," Sharon added.

Teresa started to speak, but stopped when Sharon rose from the table. "This is an interesting conversation but I've really got to go now. Glad to have met you Teresa and I wish you the best."

Barbara watched Sharon leave. She took her final bite of burger and chewed slowly. Teresa ranted.

"What are you trying to say?" Barbara demanded. After a while? "I have a secret, but so do you, if you tell me your secret, I'll tell you mine," Teresa urged.

"I do have a secret but I have no desire to tell it and you are busting at the seams to tell me yours."

Teresa frowned and nodded. Then she looked around the room as if searching for privacy. She leaned in toward Barbara and whispered, "I think I'm pregnant."

11

Family Strength

The prophet who has a dream may
relate his dream, but let him who has My
word speak My word in truth. What does
straw have in common with grain?"
declares the LORD.

---Jeremiah 23:28 (NASB)

THE ASSEMBLY LASTED an hour, but it felt like three.
Barbara stretched and yawned as the student body filed out
of the auditorium. These required assemblies could be the
highlight of the week or a good naptime. Today had been
the latter. She gathered up her belongings and stood up.

"Got any plans this afternoon?" Sharon asked.

"Yeah, I've gotta go to my crazy meeting.'"

"How's that working out?"

"I'm the only girl and non-vet. Those guys had some scary experiences. The psych man is pretty savvy though."

Barbara didn't usually talk at the meetings, but tonight, the leader focused on her.

"Barbara, you haven't spoken," Nurse Young said.

"I don't have anything to say."

"Okay, whenever you're ready."

After the meeting dismissed, one of the guys came up to Michael. Barbara overheard their conversation. "You got a place to stay tonight?"

"Not yet, you offering?"

"My box isn't big enough for both of us." The two men laughed a knowing but painful laugh.

Barbara moved over to Michael, "Are you homeless?"

"In a way, yes, Elizabeth kicked me out, said she's afraid of me,"

"What? Why would she be afraid of you?"

"It's the nightmares, I can't control them and I act out when I'm having them. Frankly, they scare the liver out of me too."

Barbara leaned in a little tighter. "Tough, huh?"

"Yea, I have the same recurring nightmare," Michael said.

Barbara nodded, "I know that feeling. You're coming home with me," Barbara reasoned; leaving no room for Michael to resist.

After dinner, Barbara brought Michael and Sharon a cup of coffee and a piece of pie.

"Wow, this looks great," Michael said as he took the treats.

"It should, its Aunt Maggie's recipe."

Michael took a big bite, closed his eyes and leaned his head back. Swallowed and said, "Yea, tastes like my childhood, and mother's cooking. How'd you know?"

"You mentioned it in one of the meetings, and I knew I had the recipe. Nobody could make a cherry pie better than Aunt Maggie. At our family meetings, us girls drew the job of cutting the cakes and pies, so it was easy for me to hide a piece of her pie."

Michael laughed a genuine belly laugh. "I remember those Sunday afternoons at Granny's house with all us kids playing ball."

"Well, you played ball, I chased balls," Barbara remembered.

Sharon volunteered to clean up the kitchen after she brought some clean sheets to make up the couch for Michael. "Maybe tomorrow we can get you a real bed."

Michael questioned Barbara, "what does she mean?"

"The complex has two apartments they rent only to vets. The rent is based on your earnings, so you can get the apartment without a job and start paying rent when you have one."

"Do I have to be a student?"

"No, but they encourage you to take some classes to help transition back into life."

"Wow, it's nice to know there are people who still care." Michael lamented.

Sharon bade the two of them good night and Barbara rose to go to her bedroom.

"Barb, can you talk a minute?" Michael asked.

"Sure."

"Why won't you talk at group?"

"Mr. Young thinks I'm delusional," Barbara answered with the mysterious reply.

"He needs to know what's going on your head. You need to talk." Michael admonished her.

"Your kin to me, you have to love me whether I'm crazy or not, right?"

Michael laughed. "Yeah."

"People like Mr. Young could have me committed; they don't love me; they see me as a freak." Barbara moaned and put her head on her balled fist.

"He can commit you even if you don't talk." Michael reminded her.

Barbara stared at him with pursed lips. "I can't talk about it."

Michael glared at her. She squirmed and tried to look away from his piercing gaze.

"Why not?" he followed her eyes.

"It's crazy, and I'm not ready to be labeled as a lunatic yet."

Michael softened his gaze and took her hand. "You will not recover until you talk about it."

"How do you know?"

"Remember we are victims of violence, that's why we are here. All of us have secrets and buried horrors."

She squeezed his hand and turned her head away from his gaze., before she blurted out her secret,

"I saw a dragon."

"Is that all." Michael grinned.

"You don't seem alarmed."

"I served in Nam, remember, that's the land of dragons."

"There's dragons in Vietnam?" Barbara squeaked the question.

"I've seen dragons both literally and spiritually."

"What are you saying?" Barbara questioned Michael.

"Dragons are sacred in the East. There are reports of their existence in ancient writings. The spiritual reverence of that area is found in the dragons…real dragons." Michael waved his arms in the air as if pointing to the dragons.

"I … I'm flabbergasted." Barbara sputtered.

"Technically, Vietnam is communist, so the religion is atheism, that's the star, but humans are spiritual creatures and they will worship something, even themselves. Like it says in the Bible, we trade the truth for a lie and worship the creature instead of the creator, that's the spiritual side of Vietnam."

"How did you stand it as a Christian?" Barbara repeated.

Michael sighed and leaned his head back. A big smile exuded from his mouth. He took Barbara by the hand and led her to the couch, now made into Michael's bed.

"You remember the night before I shipped out and Aunt Merilee made dinner for all of us?"

"Yea, I felt so worried. Everybody cried and hugged you; I wondered if I would ever see you again."

"But what did Uncle Buster do?" Michael asked Barbara as he put his arm around her shoulders.

"He prayed. He had you get on your knees in the middle of the floor, then he poured oil on your head. Then we all touched you and prayed and prayed and prayed – it seemed like hours."

Michael chuckled. "Funny, it felt like seconds to me. I believe with my whole heart that prayer meeting and many others like it are the only reason I returned. There were so many times I should have been dead, but I wasn't even injured."

"What are you saying?"

"I'm saying I lived in the middle of the devil's territory and the prayers of my family protected me there. I watched the native people try to meet the impossible and horrific demands of their evil gods, at the same time my Lord carried me through hellfire." Michael took her hands in his and kissed them. "Little one, we're all at war with evil."

Barbara leaned on Michael's shoulder and wept. "If God is watching over you, why are you drinking?" He sighed, patted her on the hand and said, "Good night little one."

Barbara smiled when he used his pet name for her. It gave her a wonderful sense of security. She forgot about the whiskey.

12

Montana Man And Horses

> But this is what I commanded them,
> saying, 'Obey My voice, and I will be your
> God, and you will be My people; and you
> will walk in all the way which I command
> you, that it may be well with you.'
>
> --- Jeremiah 7:23 (NASB)

THE NEXT MORNING Barbara noticed the sheets folded on the couch. The smell of fresh coffee permeated the room along with bacon, toast and eggs. Barbara picked up a piece of bacon and took a bite. She noticed a note on the table.

I have a busy day planned. I'll be looking for a place to live and a job. Thanks for putting me up last night. Keep praying.

The last two words stood out in neon to Barbara, "Keep Praying." *I gave up praying when God quit listening.* Michael's prayers would have to come from someone else.

She didn't have any. She noticed the open Bible laying on the coffee table. *That's a waste of time too.*

Sharon came into the kitchen, "Thanks for getting the coffee. She took a sip of the hot brew and noticed the food on top of the stove. "And breakfast too? You're a good roommate."

"You can thank Michael, I just got up."

The girls took their food and coffee to the dining table. "Where's our house guest?" Sharon asked. Barbara tossed the note to her. After she read it, she turned to Barbara.

"What 'cha doin' today?"

"I don't know, any suggestions." Barbara replied.

"None. But I know one thing, I like having breakfast. We should do this more often." Sharon recommended. Barbara nodded and took a big bite of toast.

"Let's go to a movie." Sharon suggested.

The girls both jumped when the phone rang. Sharon answered it. She flashed Barbara a big smile when she heard the voice on the other end. She handed the phone to Barbara.

"Who is it?"

"Daniel Holloway," Sharon chortled.

Barbara took the phone and listened. She smiled and then put her hand over the receiver, "he asked me to spend the day with him. What should I do?"

"You are such a dunce; you can make the easiest thing hard. Say yes," Sharon answered and rolled her eyes.

Daniel told her to dress in jeans and comfortable shoes. Barbara couldn't imagine what they would be doing, but it wouldn't be the usual dinner and a movie. When he arrived Barbara answered the door, he took her breath away. He stood there in cowboy boots, jeans and plaid cowboy shirt with a ten-gallon cowboy hat which fit his five foot nine frame very well.

"Where'd you park your horse, cowboy?" Barbara said.

"In that trailer, and I have two."

She leaned out the doorway and saw the horse trailer with two horse heads bobbing up and down. She ran back into her room and exchanged her flimsy tennis shoes for her substantial and broken in cowgirl boots. It had been months since she had ridden a horse. She couldn't stop smiling.

When she came back down, Daniel looked confused. "I wondered if I scared you off."

"Heck no, I had to get on the proper shoes; how'd you know?"

"I do my homework, girl. I called your dad and asked what you enjoyed doing."

"Have you ever ridden a horse?"

He hesitated, "Don't worry, I can hold my own." He smiled at Barbara and winked.

"Okay, let's go."

The day turned out to be picture perfect. Daniel grew up on a ranch in Montana. His riding expertise soon became evident to Barbara.

"Where did you find the horses?" Barbara asked when they stopped for a picnic lunch under one of the few trees around.

"I actually brought them with me from home. I stable them at a nearby ranch, but keep them available for my own use. You can imagine my delight when your dad told me you loved horses."

"At one time, I decided I would be a barrel racer in the rodeo. You should have seen me and my horse. It didn't take long for me to realize my horse and I were better at chasing rabbits than barrels."

Daniel laughed. "How many did you catch?"

"None! We didn't want them, but we did catch a barbed wire fence. It cut up my horse's leg pretty bad. After that she didn't do much running. In fact, I didn't bother with saddle or bridle. If I wanted to go somewhere else, I pulled her mane or gave her a direction with my knee. She trusted me and I trusted her."

Daniel laid back and stared up at the puffy white clouds in the sky, "Sounds like you had a good horse," he said. "Trust is an important thing in relationships whether it be humans, animals, or God.

Barbara didn't like the direction of the conversation.

"What's really on your mind?" she asked him.

"I'm wondering how I can bring this conversation to a kiss," Daniel said without looking at her.

"You know I heard what you said in assembly."

"What?"

"That I would be your wife."

Daniel blushed slightly. "Yep, I knew it the minute I saw you."

"Isn't that a bit presumptuous?"

"I guess, but the Lord told me."

"What? Why would He care?"

"He does," Daniel said as he sat up and contemplated Barbara's face. Leaning in he stole that kiss.

"Smooth," Barbara said as she ducked her head. "Does this mean we are engaged now?"

"Yes, and no. We're engaged, but not formally."

"All I see is male arrogance and ego trippin."

"Yeah, the Holy Spirit told me you would be a challenge."

"What else did He tell you? How many children we're going to have and what they will be?" Barbara said in a huff.

"As a matter of fact, we will have three of our own and two others, not sure adopted or inherited, but we will have five and they will all be wonderful people, no matter what they do," Daniel said with a big smile and tweak to Barbara's nose. "Silly."

Barbara laid back on the blanket and looked up into the sky,

"Keep dreaming, rich boy."

"What makes you think I'm rich?"

"Horses aren't cheap."

"I raised them from foals. I stable them at my uncle's ranch, for free. He even furnishes the feed. He and my dad have worked hard and neither of them are rich." Daniel defended himself. Then he stopped. "Besides it doesn't matter. You'll marry me no matter what I have or don't have."

Barbara felt her spirit splitting in two with both fondness and disgust for this man. He intrigued her. Yet his good-nature wrapped itself in a bit of male arrogance. They remained quiet for a few minutes, each lost in their own thoughts.

"What else did my daddy tell you?" Barbara asked.

"He said you were in trouble, and you need someone to stay close by."

"I guess you volunteered?"

"Not exactly, but yes, I'm to be your prayer warrior through your battle."

"What is it with prayer today?"

Daniel didn't understand the comment, but he felt it best to leave it alone. He didn't respond.

"It's getting late, I better get the horses back, do you mind if we take them first?"

When he brought her home, he shook her hand.

"I had a nice time, I hope we have an opportunity to do this again."

He gave her a little peck on the cheek, and waved goodbye. Barbara responded with a wave noticing the dimple in his cheek when he gave her a big smile and a wink. Barbara shook her head as she entered her apartment.

"How'd the date go?" Sharon asked with a giggle.

"Nice, until the end, it felt as though he couldn't get rid of me fast enough."

"Maybe it's that funky orange glow over your head."

"What are you talking about?" Barbara demanded.

"Ever since you got out of the hospital, it's been there. It's weird." Sharon said before turning away to go to the kitchen.

Barbara sat down on the couch and released a heavy sigh.

"Wanna talk about it?" Sharon asked as she joined Barbara on the couch, handing her a cup of cocoa.

Barbara nodded her head.

"Do you know what it is?" Sharon started the conversation.

She shook her head and managed to utter a garbled, "No."

"It's okay. Orange is not your best color, but we can work with it. Just don't wear any pink for a while."

Barbara snorted at the comment in the middle of a sip of cocoa. After she gained control she said, "Sharon, I think the orange glow may be alive.

13

Rally

What will you do? Although you dress in scarlet, you decorate yourself with ornaments of gold, you enlarge your eyes with paint, in vain you make yourself beautiful, your lovers despise you, they seek your life.

--- Jeremiah 4:30 (NASB)

THE FIRST SPEAKER should not have been on stage. She looked awkward and out of place, plus she couldn't complete a thought. Being the author of a book entitled, *The Feminine Mystique* provided Betty Friedan's only notable characteristic.

"If men would act more. . . humm. . .hu ah. . . like . . .hum . . . women, than we could get jobs and a... and a... you know have freedom... like men."

"What is she trying to say?" Sharon asked Barbara as she leaned over toward her. But the woman continued in her disjointed thoughts and her inability to speak rationally, "The children they uh . . . they uh. ... belong to the men too. So women should be able to work."

Barbara couldn't help but laugh at the poor woman. She obviously wasn't a speaker.

"I wonder whose keeping her kids?" Barbara whispered to Teresa.

"She may not have kids." The woman on the other side of Barbara commented.

"Yeah, she does, look at the author notes on your book." Barbara pointed to the sentence relating her family relationships as the mother of three children and married.

Sharon squirmed in her seat. Barbara fidgeted, and Teresa scolded them both. "They'll kick us out if you two don't settle down."

"I hope so." Sharon answered and Barbara giggled. Sharon pointed at something on the side. There were big signs to their left that read, "We're Here, We're Queer, Get Use to It."

"What does that mean?" Sharon whispered.

Barbara gave her a big grin and answered, "I guess that's our welcoming sign." Sharon elbowed her in the side. "You do have a queer sense of humor and a high regard of yourself."

Gloria Steinem, the final speaker, rallied the emotionally charged women into a frenzy. She caused the undercurrent of anger in this group to start boiling over.

Barbara punched Teresa, "Let's go, quick; we've heard her before and I don't like the way the people react to her."

The girls headed toward the doors. Before they could exit, the crowd flowed like hot lava out onto the streets. They chanted slogans, "Don't cook dinner, starve a rat." The next small group of women shouted, "End Human Sacrifice, Don't Get Married." But the strangest sign Barbara noticed read, "Women Have the Right to Choose, So Do We, Gay Liberation Movement." While being focused on the signs and the shouts Barbara stumbled and fell. She called to Teresa and Sharon but the crowd swept them out of sight. Barbara shouted over the noise of the crowd, but they didn't hear. She tried to get up, but the crowd kept moving in march step, stumbling and stepping on her.

Barbara screamed, but no one could hear her. She couldn't even hear herself. *I'm about to die in a stampede!* She pulled into her body in a knot with arms over her head. As the multitude of women passed, their knees jammed her back and sides. The shoving and tossing bruised her skin and muscle, causing agonizing pain. Pulling her feet under her in order to stand, another woman would push her back down before she could gain enough momentum to move with the crowd. Fighting panic, she curled in a ball shape. Those who tripped over the stumbling block of a curled up body cursed as they attempted to remain erect themselves.

With no way to rise from the floor, Barbara waited it out and endured the pain. In the midst of the resignation of impending injury or death, an arm wrapped around her. She looked in the face of a large woman hugging her.

"Move left when you stand." The woman pulled Barbara up and shielded her with her own body. Once they were clear of the crowd, Barbara turned to thank her but she had disappeared.

She didn't know how they made it out of the mob. She leaned against a wall to catch her breath and let her muscles relax. A uniformed policeman offered her a paper cup of water. "You okay miss?"

She shrugged her shoulder pulling herself away from his grip. "I guess I am. Thank you." She spat the words of gratitude like a curse. She took another large drink. Her rescuer watched the crowd with intensity. Out of curiosity she asked him, "Why are you here?"

"Extra work; we're hired to be here. So extra pay, that's why we're here." He scowled at her and then ran off toward a brawl between several women.

As the crowd flowed past them, a few of the women stopped, looked at the policeman, snarled and spit on him. Others used vile curse words ending with pig.

"My question, is why do you women think you need security. There's nothing meaner than thousands of angry women," the policeman stated without raising his voice or snarling.

Each of the five men put on riot gear before they headed out into the middle of the fray. The policemen brought more wounded women to the first aide area. Still the women tossed rocks and any object they could find at the uniformed men. Their lips curled up as nasty monologues spewed from them. Most of them were slinging their bras over their heads and shouting.

The policemen were busy containing the bedlam occurring on city property. The one policeman standing next to Barbara heard one of the women say, "You don't get it. You're a stupid man." The woman spit on him and moved on.

He wiped the spit from his face. When he did he saw Barbara staring at him. As if he needed to defend himself, he gave her a mini-lecture. "You gals don't get it. Women are the best of God's creation, and you can't accept your own value or beauty." Then the man disappeared into the crowd, using his nightstick to ward off the attacks of a mob of angry women.

"Call an ambulance," the policeman shouted as he bent over a young woman, attempting to breathe life into her limp body. The room came alive and Barbara backed up against the wall, shaking.

"There's more in this girl besides hate." The policeman said.

"You mean drugs?" asked another policeman.

"Yea. I'm not sure she's going to make it."

About that time an ambulance attendant stepped up and looked at her limp body with blue hands, "I agree." The siren sound wailed, people moved about screaming and shouting. Barbara put her hands to her mouth and begin to whimper. Her stomach roiled, and she felt herself getting weak in the knees. Memories of the bomb in Church Creek Falls flooded her mind.

"Miss are you okay, you look kinda pale." Said a young man standing next to Barbara. Probably one of the ambulance attendants.

"Sorry, this brings back memories," Barbara explained to him.

"I understand; it reminds me of the Vietnam protests."

"Why?" Barbara didn't get the connection.

"Same tactics, same complaints. Even most of the same people. The gays and women libbers take advantage of the war protests."

Barbara didn't respond. She still felt weak and didn't want to get into an argument. She had been a participant in one of those protests and knew he spoke the truth.

"This is the age of Aquarius you know," the young man said as if he were offering an explanation.

"I have no idea what that means." Barbara chuckled.

"I looked it up in the library." The young man fell silent. After a while Barbara could stand the silence no longer, "Okay, smartie pants, tell me. What does it mean?"

"You'll probably laugh but it means Christianity will be replaced by a world ruled by elite people with special knowledge, to rule with absolute power over all people."

"You saying all these protests are for that purpose?" Barbara mocked.

He stood up straight and wiped the sweat from his brow. He looked at Barbara and said, "Isn't that why you're here?"

He left Barbara in a quandary of confusion. Why did she come here? What did she hope to accomplish? Why did she feel so much anger toward men?

Before she could formulate any answers to her questions she saw the orange cloud swirling around in front of her. It formed a shape, but not the usual man she saw, instead an older woman stared directly at Barbara. Her stoic wrinkled face fit her large frame. Her clothing displayed the same blue and orange colors of orange man. She came close to Barbara and spoke in soft monotones, "Knowledge will make Christ offensive, and then all people will serve the one true master." Barbara saw the familiar yellow eyes of a dragon. She shuddered.

How weird to promote the demise of religion. . . and Christians. She scanned the crowd for the old woman. Instead she saw an orange cloud hovering over the unruly crowd. She stared at it until she heard Sharon yell from a few feet away. Teresa waved at them as she made her way across the room.

When Teresa joined them, Sharon exclaimed, "You don't look good." Noticing blood streaming down Teresa's face.

"I think I got hit in the head with a rock."

Sharon reached up and pulled a chunk of glass from her head, "Maybe a glass bottle?"

Once the girls were safely on their way home, Teresa told the story of her adventure, "I saw Barbara fall, but the crowd carried me. Once we exited the building the crowd thinned on the plaza. I noticed several barrels of fire. Those women were taking off their underwear and throwing it in the fire." Teresa chuckled at the memory.

"What was so funny about it?" Barbara asked.

"The irony. These are women protesting the dominance of men over women and they are pulling off their underwear in public."

"Still not getting the funny," Sharon prompted.

"Isn't that giving men what they want, to get women out of their underwear." Teresa laughed out loud.

Sharon and Barbara joined her in the laughter at the scene.

"What did you do, just watch?" Barbara prodded Teresa.

"Naw, I saw a bra on the ground and picked it up and started to throw it in the fire, but then I saw the tag on it."

"And?" Sharon asked.

"It said Neiman-Marcus and it was my size." Teresa pulled a beautiful bra out of her purse. "I just couldn't do it."

The girls inspected the bra. "Man you truly got a bargain here." Sharon said upon examination.

"I wonder who bought this for her?" Barbara pondered.

"Don't go and get all moody on us now," Teresa lectured her.

Barbara smiled. "So does this mean we're not feminists?"

"We're wise feminists. Why protest with expensive underwear?" Teresa laughed.

"How should we protest the inequality of men and women?" Barbara asked her.

In a solemn tone Sharon answered. "By refusing to take our underwear off."

14

A Texas Bar B Que

> I have listened and heard, they have spoken what is not right: No man repented of his wickedness, Saying, 'What have I done?' Everyone turned to his course, like a horse charging into the battle.
>
> ---Jeremiah 8:6 (NASB)

BARBARA WOKE UP, sweating and shaking. The dreaded nightmare struck again.

"Another nightmare?" Sharon asked when she heard Barbara in the bathroom at two in the morning.

"Yea. Sorry I woke you."

"You think there's more going on here than a dream?" Sharon asked.

"Yeah, but if I tell you what I think you'll have me committed."

"I already have."

"Wha?"

"The meetings you're going to." Sharon turned and looked at Barbara with a slight smile and winked. "Come on, since we're up, let's have some hot tea. Do you think we could do something besides political protests tomorrow; I mean today?" Sharon said as she handed Barbara the tea.

"Like what?"

"A Texas barbeque, and invite all our friends."

"All two of them?" Barbara smiled at Sharon.

"We have more friends than that. What about the people in your group meeting? You always talk about them like friends." Sharon suggested.

"Yeah, that's a good idea," Barbara reasoned.

The girls chattered about possibilities. "We need to make definite plans instead of throwing out every idea that crosses our brains," Sharon concluded. "Like the basics. When? Where?"

"And how?" Barbara muttered.

"This party is a great idea," Daniel complemented Barbara as he arrived. "I think we all need some recreation after studying for finals."

She smiled at him, "I really wasn't thinking of finals. It happened because I had a nightmare and couldn't go back to sleep."

"Wanna talk about it?" Daniel asked.

"Not sure; it's about a wicked man coming after my friends."

"Are you in danger?" Daniel asked her.

"No silly, you are; I said he comes after my friends." Barbara elbowed him and laughed.

Daniel joined in her laughter. "Guess I better start looking for a wicked man. By the way, what does a wicked man look like?"

Barbara gazed at the stars when she answered Daniel without hesitation, "Orange."

After a moment she came out of her reverie and turned toward Daniel. "The problem is not the dream, it's the people." Barbara continued.

"Tell me more?"

"The guy threatened my friend in high school for real. Now I'm dreaming about it."

"The mind is a funny thing." Daniel replied. He started to explain a paper he had just read about this very thing.

Barbara didn't give him time. She picked up the thought and asked, "Daniel, do you think there's something wrong with me?"

He stared at her, "What makes you ask that question? All of us have nightmares."

"Does everyone have orange men hanging around them?"

"Why do you think you have an orange man hanging around you?" He ventured with a grin, "Does this mean I have competition?"

"No, silly. Imaginary men." Barbara chuckled.

"I'm not imaginary," Daniel took her hand in his and raised it to his lips and kissed it. Barbara felt heat rising to her cheeks. This man certainly did raise her blood pressure.

Daniel lowered his voice and with great caution asked, "Is there a chance we are. . . you know. . .us?"

Barbara leaned in to him. "I hope so. I really need you. Even though I hate to admit it."

"Not the answer I hoped for, but I'll take it as long as I'm in competition with an orange man." Daniel kissed her hand again, then asked, "Tell me about him."

Barbara laughed at the absurdity. "You know about my hometown?"

"You mean the bomb that wiped it off the map? Yea, everyone knows about that."

"Before the bomb went off, we saw a... a... oh, I can't say it?"

"An orange man?" Daniel prodded with a smile.

"In a way yes. But it wasn't a man."

"So what was it?"

"A dragon, a real live dragon living in our field."

Daniel was silent for a few moments. He didn't show any response or facial expression.

"Are you gonna run away from me now?" Barbara asked him in a whisper.

"Let's say you have my attention. Do you think orange man is that dragon?"

"No, I know he isn't. He's different." Barbara said and ducked her head.

"Different how?"

"Dragons are ugly and mean and evil . . . you know. . . a devil."

Daniel didn't laugh. "Tell me about this. . . this dragon."

"I don't want to talk about him," Barbara whimpered.

Daniel didn't push, after a few minutes Barbara began to talk. "My mother bought a sculpture to hang on our wall. It was a terrible piece."

"Why?"

"We couldn't get it down, and it started growing. One time I sat on the couch in front of it, and a piece of it had grown into a tentacle that stabbed me."

"Did it hurt you?"

"A small charge of electricity went through me, but it didn't hurt, instead it made me feel . . . eerie. It wasn't long afterward that I started seeing the orange cloud."

"Did you tell anyone?"

"You kidding? I'm not ready for the psychiatric ward yet." Barbara almost shouted at him. "But daddy said the dragon came to our community to deceive and the mask was his idol."

"So... when did you see the cloud for the first time?" Daniel prodded again.

"I think I saw it several times but ignored it. The night of the intruder, I knew---"

"Knew what?" Daniel asked.

"Nothing, it's not important." Barbara said before she walked back into the group of her guests.

He followed her. "You can't leave it like that." Daniel put his arms around her, both to comfort and to keep her from leaving.

She rested her head on his chest. She could hear his rapid heartbeat.

"I'm afraid that if I tell you then you'll---

"I'll what?" Daniel demanded but held her close.

"You'll leave me, thinking I'm a freak or something."

"I'll stay with you until the end of time if you'll love me as much as I love you."

Barbara didn't lift her head but continued to listen to his heart beat in rhythm with her own.

"Why do you love me?" She asked without looking at him.

"That's a good question, and the only answer I have is that God made me love you." He twirled his fingers through her strawberry blond locks of hair. "My friends all tell me I should quit pursuing you."

Barbara raised her head, "They do, why?"

"Barbara, really, you won't even hardly acknowledge I exist unless you are in one of your funky moods. I get nothing from you." Daniel moaned. "Besides, you're more interested in your women's rights than you are a relationship."

She peered into the distance. Daniel's right. She didn't want a husband. She wanted a career. She desperately wanted it. She wanted to be in charge and do things the way they should be done. . . her way.

"Barbara?" Daniel said, then walked away when she didn't answer.

In her reverie she forgot about him.

"Where are you going?"

"Giving you space to be alone with your thoughts. I think I'm intruding."

"Daniel, wait, I didn't mean---"

"I know, you never do. When you want to be with me you can come get me."

"I want you here because I want to tell you." Barbara begged him.

"Okay."

She stood as close as she dared, hoping he would reach for her. He didn't.

"Okay, I think orange man is a demon sent by the dragon," she blurted out in one breath. Daniel put his arm around her waist and pulled her toward him. They clung to each other in the comforting embrace for several minutes without conversation. Daniel stared up at the stars. Leaning closer to Daniel she let her head rest on his shoulder while she cried. "I'm confused and scared."

Daniel whispered in her ear as he held her. "I'll never leave you."

Michael and Sharon walked up beside Barbara and Daniel, "Great party, Little One."

Paps wheeled up to join them. A strange woman walked beside his wheelchair. She gave the impression of being petite and fragile. Dressed in a simple white blouse and black skirt, her dark hair framed a heart-shaped face. When she looked up at Barbara, it took her breath. Her eyes were smoldering as if they had been on fire. As Paps and the woman came closer, Barbara noticed her eyes were a dark brown surrounded by a well-defined make-up job. The burned look had to have been an optical illusion. The woman smiled and extended her hand to Barbara.

"I understand you're our host." She observed.

Paps offered the introduction, "Barbara, I want you to meet my friend, Patti, she works at the library."

Barbara shook her hand. "I'm glad you came; I'm one of the hostesses, and this is my roommate Sharon, the other hostess."

"I hope you're having a good time," Sharon responded.

"Paps is a good host," She demurred with tilted head. She stared at Paps. She reached down to the arm of his wheelchair and patted him.

"Paps, it's good to see you smiling too," Barbara said.

"Yea, I don't know why, but this young lady makes me remember what it's like to have fun. Something I've forgotten." Paps looked at Michael, "Ain't that right, son?"

Michael nodded. Paps kept talking, which was a strange phenomenon since he seldom talked. Barbara noticed he kept looking at Patti and touching her hand.

"Paps, Patti doesn't have anything to drink, did you offer her a soda?" Barbara asked him. He looked surprised and exclaimed, "Oh my, can't believe I didn't notice. I'll be right back."

Barbara smiled as he wheeled toward the refreshment table. She commented, "He has a good heart. He really likes to help others."

In response to Barbara's comment, Patti whispered low, "Not always."

Barbara missed the comment but Sharon heard it and pondered its meaning. "Why not always?" She asked Patti.

"Not important, just thinking out loud," Patti said.

The moment she said the words, orange man appeared to Barbara and a loud noise permeated the party. All the guests stopped and looked toward the direction of the noise. They heard the shouts of war protestors. *Oh no!*

Barbara ran to the courtyard on the other side and saw them approaching carrying their signs, pumping their fists in the air and shouting nonsense about Jane Fonda's inept knowledge.

Orange man spoke to her with the growling voice of a dog. "Trouble, trouble everywhere, and thou does think it sweet."

Your work is never sweet.

The sound of the protestors stopped as suddenly as it started.

Daniel called, "Barbara, Barbara." He called to her. She looked at him, "I'm right here, don't yell."

"Did you see them?"

Barbara nodded and walked toward the center of the courtyard and sat down at one of the picnic tables. Daniel followed her.

"Did you see them? Were they real?" She asked Daniel.

"The sounds were real, and you saw them. Now they're gone. Do you think they were real?"

"No, I think the . . . the . . . orange clown made me see them and everyone else hear it."

"But why?" Daniel grunted. Barbara slipped her hand inside his arm. Daniel accepted it with a squeeze of his arm against it.

"He's a jerk and wants to steal our fun times." Barbara scowled. She pasted a smile on her face and attempted to return her guests to a party mood.

"We can't let this spoil our evening," Barbara pleaded with the group.

They stared at her with weak smiles.

"I'm sorry, little one, but the damage has been done." Michael contended. "It's a reminder of what life is really like; we don't feel much in a party mood anymore."

"I know, but we can't let the orange m---"

"Can't let what?" Patti's head jerked toward Barbara when she commented. Barbara saw a nervousness in Patti along with her raised voice.

"Nothing," Barbara plopped down next to Daniel.

The orange man blew her a kiss. Barbara's heart raced, her hands turned clammy, and her breathing became labored. She turned away from him. He again appeared in front of her face. Looking past him she saw Patti walking toward the gate into a shadow that seemed to swallow her.

15

The Testing Of The Mind

> The children gather wood, and the fathers kindle the fire, and the women knead dough to make cakes for the queen of heaven; and they pour out drink offerings to other gods in order to spite Me. "Do they spite Me?" declares the Lord. "Is it not themselves they spite, to their own shame.
>
> ---Jeremiah 7:18-19(NASB)

WITH A HOT CUP of coffee in her hand, Barbara sat down on the couch while waiting for Teresa to arrive. The cut on Teresa's head appeared to be infected. Barbara agreed to go to the clinic with her.

She picked up the morning paper from the coffee table. Sharon walked into the room and saw her reading. "What's so interesting?" she asked as she sat.

"Look! This, this story, it's my nightmare," Barbara continued.

"Coincidence?" Sharon queried.

On the way to the clinic. Barbara told Teresa about the oddity of the newspaper story. Then she laughed out loud.

"That's not funny." Teresa responded.

"No, you're right, but I remembered how I'm the crazy one but we're going to get your head examined."

Teresa chuckled at Barbara's analysis. "Both ends," she added.

"Huh?"

"I'm . . . you know. . . ---." She put her hand on her abdomen.

"So you're getting both ends examined?" Barbara said with a smirk.

"Go ahead and laugh, some day it will be the other way around."

"No doubt I need my head examined," Barbara responded in a quiet voice. "At least I don't need to get hit in the head to know I'm crazy,"

"Life isn't simple," Teresa mused. The conversation died as the girls reached the clinic. Once inside, they both picked up old magazines and started thumbing through them as if it were a required ritual to see the doctor. The nurse called Teresa back.

"You don't have to go with me," Teresa said to Barbara.

"Good, I didn't plan to."

Barbara slumped in the waiting room chair and sleep tried to claim her. She closed her eyes but before she drifted off, she heard something. It sounded like a distant voice being carried by the wind. She raised up but didn't see anyone else in the waiting room. She heard the radio static. Even though it wasn't clear she still caught a name, Roy Molder. She tuned into the words;

"Molder was captured as he tried to escape from the VanLang farm where he attacked Mrs. VanLang with a broken coke bottle. Mrs. VanLang suffered minor cuts. No one else was attacked. The motive is unknown.

Barbara shook her head and muttered to herself, "He's just mean." *Could her dream be reality.* "Can a dream cause this? How? Did I cause this with my nightmares?" Barbara said out loud in a hushed tone since she was talking to herself.

Soon Teresa came out of the doctor's inner sanctum and joined her in the waiting room. Barbara's gaze dropped to the empty row of chairs across the room from her. Except one wasn't empty, a man dressed in orange occupied the chair. Barbara shuddered. He stared straight into her eyes.

"Are you okay? You look like you've seen a ghost," Teresa said.

"Or a demon," Barbara muttered.

Barbara didn't want to discuss the orange man, so she changed the subject, "What did the doc say?"

"He confirmed I'm pregnant."

Barbara looked up at Teresa, "How'd that happen?"

Teresa stared at her, "I hope you're not serious."

"No, I mean, you don't have a boyfriend---oh, I forgot about skuz bucket. Is he the father?"

"Yes, and his name is George."

"He looks like a skuz bucket."

"He acts like one too." They sunk into a mutual silence.

After a few moments, Teresa punctured the silence with a strange announcement. "The doctor said I didn't have to have the baby."

Barbara stared at Teresa, "Who? The doc? What does he mean?"

"He said the law now lets him remove the product of conception. That's what he called the baby. A court case called Roe v Wade made it legal."

"That's awful," Barbara grimaced.

"No, not really. I still have a lot of things I want to do and I really don't want George in my life forever. I'm seriously considering it. What do you think?"

"Doesn't matter what I think, it's your baby; your decision."

"You're right. It's my decision." Teresa said with new resolve.

"What about your parents? Shouldn't you discuss it with them?"

Teresa moaned. "I guess I'll have to. I need $400 to pay for it."

"Yikes, that's a lot of money." Barbara winched.

She couldn't help thinking of Molder and his attack against a mother and her children. The doctor sounded a lot like Molder except he charged the mother to kill her child.

"I don't understand how you could kill your baby."

"Sometimes things are out of our control. "Teresa said in a soft voice.

Barbara took a deep breath and haggled, "I am always in control of my body."

Teresa looked at her. "This is coming from the woman enrolled in a psyche group and says she sees a man dressed in orange?" Teresa didn't laugh but Barbara saw the corner of her mouth lift in a half-smirk.

"That doesn't mean I'm not in control of my body.

"What?" Teresa hollered.

"I am the master of my own fate." Barbara stated with confidence.

"If you truly want to be the master of your own fate, you should come to a secret meeting with me." Teresa segued into a new topic. Aurora has been invited to a party in my honor this weekend. Do you wanna come?"

"Who is Aurora and what kind of party is that?"

"I'm Aurora."

"What kind of party?'

"A party in the grove of trees high on the hill."

"Sounds spooky." Barbara teased.

"Some think so. If you don't want to come, I understand." Teresa replied with a note of sadness.

"I wonder why would I think it's spooky?" Barbara grumbled

"Because I'm a witch. It's a secret witches' coven meeting. If you come, I'll show you how to get that power to hurt Mr. McCord like we talked about."

Barbara stared at Teresa.

"Don't worry, I'm not going to turn you into a toad."

"Okay, that makes me more comfortable, I guess I'll go. Maybe you can turn me into a unicorn instead." Barbara giggled.

"Be ready at 10:30." Teresa announced.

"Why so late?"

"Because midnight is the witching hour. Bawhahahaha."

"Stop it." Barbara smirked. "And what do you mean you're Aurora?"

"That's the name I use at our coven meetings. You better find one for yourself pretty quick, make it something to do with nature," Teresa said.

"What's Aurora have to do with nature?"

"Aurora Borealis, the Northern Lights," Teresa said with a smile. "Besides I think it's pretty."

"Okay. Call me Maize."

"What does that mean?"

"Maize is a grain my daddy grows. It has a full red head and is pretty, like me." Barbara tossed her light red hair back with her hand.

"Witchcraft is about nature and if you believe that the gods and the goddesses are in everything then you will see some real magic. We select our alternate names to honor our spirit guides. The woods surround us with images of our goddesses."

"So why is it secret?" Barbara questioned Teresa.

"No one must know about it, and you must never tell anyone."

Barbara felt her heart beat speed up. She fidgeted in her seat with a big smile across her face. Teresa watched her as she drove them to the coven meeting.

"I can't tell if your excited or scared." Teresa remarked.

"What will we do tonight?" Barbara changed the subject.

"Tonight is all about me. We will be seeking an answer about my pregnancy."

"You already know your pregnant, what more do you need?" Barbara queried.

"Whether to keep it or have that surgery."

"I still can't believe it's legal to kill your baby before it's born," Barbara stammered, not knowing what else to say.

"There were docs doing it before, so now, they can do it and advertise."

Barbara shuddered, "I can't believe you want to kill an innocent baby."

"What's wrong with you?" Teresa asked Barbara.

"I killed a baby once." Barbara answered while looking out the window.

"Really, did you have an illegal abortion?"

"No, I ran over her with my car. It was truly the worst moment of my life. I just don't understand how you could want to kill your baby."

"It's not a baby yet, so I'm not really killing it, and you didn't either, you had an accident." Teresa justified.

Barbara didn't hear much of what Teresa said. She was pondering.

"What are you thinking about so deeply? Teresa asked her.

"About how stupid I am about the things that go on."

"You're not stupid you just haven't been enlightened." Teresa instructed. "Tonight will be your first step into the adventure of true life with the power of the goddess."

Barbara smiled at the word, *power*.

When they arrived Teresa parked on a grass lot with other cars. There wasn't much else around them.

"We have to park far away so the car engines won't interfere with the energy flow," Teresa explained. "Balance is key, you know."

"Oh." She didn't know but she didn't want to show her ignorance. She had no idea where they were or what they were going to do. Although she wished she had taken time to put on better walking shoes. By the time they reached the clearing, her feet hurt from the hills and rough ground.

"What is this gathering?" Barbara asked as she absorbed the strange sights.

"We are a Draconian coven," Teresa stated. Barbara skipped a breath.

"A what? You mean like. . . a . . . dragon?" She gasped.

"Yes, that's exactly what a Draconian coven is. We put our emphasis upon dragons and dragon lore."

"And what does that mean?" Barbara could feel her heart racing and her pulse pounding in her temple. "Do you see dragons?"

"Sometimes, we are delighted when we do." Teresa said with a sing-song voice.

"Teresa, do you---"

Teresa interrupted her. "We are actually a rare group of witches. The draconian is much more popular in Asian countries like Vietnam. You know dragons are real; not just cartoon characters."

"You don't have to convince me," Barbara said in a soft whisper to herself, but Teresa heard her.

"See, I knew you would make a good witch. I saw it in you at the meetings."

Barbara didn't respond to Teresa. Instead, she had a question pounding in her head she needed to ask, "do you. . . do you?"

"Do I what? Spit it out." Teresa urged.

"Do you have a dragon here?" Barbara stammered.

"No silly, we invoke the dragons during the magical incantations. They are ruled by the sun god and the moon goddess."

"What do these dragons do?"

"Whatever we ask of them." Teresa noticed Barbara shaking. "It's okay. We do no harm, our incantations and rituals are for good."

"Teresa, you're summoning a dragon! Do you understand what a dragon does? How can you say it's for good?"

"Of course, that's what witchcraft is about---"

"What? Dancing with dragons?" Barbara yelled in hysterics. Teresa put her arm around her and spoke softly. "Maybe you should just observe tonight. You'll see. Pagans have been around since before Christianity. In fact, there are several Christians here."

Barbara looked at her and then down at the ground. *No there isn't.* Before Barbara had time to ponder her own objections a woman greeted them with a bow. She wore a black velvet corseted dress with rayon jacquard embroidered trumpet sleeves. The v-neckline trimmed in a gold braid connected to her waist with a gold chain belt hanging loosely around her hips. At the hemline of the dress were three asymmetric tiers of material lined in blood red, ending in a slight train. Barbara had never seen such a garment. It enthralled her with its beauty and repulsed her by it darkness.

"Close your mouth and I will introduce you to our high priestess," Teresa snickered.

Barbara looked into the dark, almost black, eyes of a beautiful woman. Yet, Barbara felt a blanket of cold slide over her shoulders.

"Hello, Barbara."

Barbara couldn't speak, she just stammered, "hel... he. . . lo"

"This is our high priestess Madame Lilith."

"The night monster?" Barbara drawled.

"Oh, we have one with knowledge. Yes, you're right. Welcome," the Madame said with restrained, but obvious delight. "It's good to meet you," Madame Lilith acknowledged.

Barbara felt stupid in the presence of this woman. Madame Lilith turned toward Teresa and remarked within Barbara's hearing." I love the way these Christians crumble when they see real power." She took Teresa by the hand and headed toward the large rock in the center of the clearing.

"Teresa, what about your friend? You letting her watch?" Madame Lilith questioned.

Teresa nodded, "Yes, your highness." Teresa bowed to her.

Barbara could feel her heart pounding so hard, it felt as if it would burst from her chest. She knew she didn't belong here.

"I can't Teresa, I can't stay---" Barbara stammered and stumbled trying to escape.

"I need you here." Teresa pleaded.

"You don't understand; this is. . ."

"No, you don't understand," Madame Lilith scolded and touched Barbara's shoulder. Barbara felt an electric charge go through her. Similar to the pain she felt when the sculpture pricked her. She stood unable to move or speak. Madame Lilith removed her hand and cupped Barbara's chin in her palm. "Barbara, this isn't a garden party."

In spite of her quivering Barbara spoke, "Madame Lilith, how. . .?" Before she could finish her question the eyes of the high priestess turned vivid yellow with a vertical black iris and orange smoke came from her nostrils and mouth. Barbara felt her body go limp. She offered no further resistance, but watched Madame Lilith walk away swaying her hips in rhythm to the pounding drums. The flutes joined in a discordant cadence that made Barbara feel weak and helpless. She grabbed Teresa's hand as they walked toward the center of the grove, "Please, get me out of here," she begged Teresa.

Teresa gave Barbara a stern look of authority, "You can't."

"Please Teresa, you don't know what's happening."

"Yes, I do. Tonight we summon the dragons for an answer to my dilemma."

Barbara let go of Teresa's hand and stood planted in place. She could physically go no closer to the center of the grove. Nor could she turn away. She could see the altar without any obstruction.

Teresa and Madame Lilith approached the big rock at the center of the clearing. Barbara saw several objects on the flat surface. Among them were two knives, one with a black-handle and the other with a white handle. A bell sat in the middle with a broomstick, some candles, a wine goblet and a small iron Dutch oven. A variety of flowers, and plants were scattered over the rock. On one end of the altar sat a loaf of bread and two eggs. The high priestess approached the rock and held a wooden stick in her hand. She waved it in a circle, took the broom and made a sweeping motion ringing the bell. Everyone turned toward the rock.

Barbara wanted to shrink into the background. She rocked back and forth holding her arms tight around herself. Fear gripped her in a vise causing her stomach to roil with the memory of the dragon. Today is different. She is standing alone among dragon worshipers; summoning the dragon instead of her Christian family fighting it. She watched the sky with wide eyes and pounding heart. The words spoken by Madame Lilith didn't make sense. Barbara didn't want to know what the words were or what they meant. She wanted to leave this place where the darkness sucked in more darkness; a place where cold and isolation enveloped her body and mind.

Roar! The noise overpowered all other sounds. She blinked. There above the trees she saw him; Nisroch.

He called Teresa's name. Barbara stared at the same ugly reptilian monster which had bit her mother's friend, Mrs. Waithe. Teresa walked to the rock and lay down on it.

The other women and girls were bowing their heads with eyes closed.

Oh no, they're worshiping this monster. Barbara screamed in her head.

Nisroch dropped his huge head in front of Barbara and stared at her with one eye. He flicked his tongue and knocked her down. The familiar drool dropped on her feet. She pulled back and screamed. He laughed.

"No! No! Barbara screamed out. The other girls rose from their bowing positions at the sound of her scream.

"Please, no!" Tears fell down her face in a mixture of fear and anger. The dragon laughed at her. "See how they love me." Nisroch said to Barbara's mind.

Barbara watched as the circle of girls took their braided flower headbands and threw them onto Nisroch. She turned to the girl nearest her. "What are you doing?"

"Giving our offering to the dragon." The girl answered as she stared at Nisroch with a silly grin.

"Do you see a dragon?"

"No, but I feel him. His love is so deep and satisfying; I know he's there.

"See how they love me?"

"They don't know, please don't hurt them."

"Tsk Tsk, silly Barbara, it's what I do. I cause chaos and I hurt people. I love it. Watch this." he turned to the young girl to whom Barbara had been speaking. She walked up to him as if she could see him.

"I'm guiding her. She knows me and trusts me," The dragon explained to Barbara's mind. Barbara wanted to run away, but her feet wouldn't budge.

Nisroch winked at Barbara and then opened his mouth slightly and emitted a whoosh of fire, setting the young girl's body on fire. She screamed and fell in front of him writhing in pain.

"And yet, she still loves me. Strange creatures, you humans," Nisroch said.

"I abhor you." Barbara spat as she tried to reach the girl and put some dirt on her.

"Don't bother, she'll die no matter what you do and then. . ." he laughed." I'll play with her like this forever."

Barbara raised her eyes to the heaven's and called, "Please God, help her!"

Nisroch laughed, "You're in my church now. He doesn't come here. Besides why would he answer you?"

"He's everywhere and you can only do what He allows. God help her."

"Nice answer, I bet you learned that in Sunday School. All you church people call on God when your helpless. Then you ignore Him when He blesses you." Nisroch laughed out loud. "He's stupid to try to rescue you people."

"I'm here and He lives in me." Barbara heard her plea coming from her own mouth. Her childhood teaching failed her understanding as she stared at a demonic beast. *What does that mean?*

Nisroch opened his mouth and set a group of trees aflame. He laughed out loud as Barbara's eyes followed the flames leaping toward the sky, it appeared the night sucked them up, they produced no heat and little light. Barbara stood mesmerized with the phenomenal sight.

"See how easy it is to distract you. Even your Christian Bible says your heart is wicked and deceitful and there is no cure. You all belong to me."

Barbara heard his mocking in her head, and she silently prayed. "God, if you are real, help this girl." She waited for the girl to be revived, instead, she continued to burn. Barbara fell to her knees and began to plead with God.

Then she heard His voice, "Why have you turned against Me?"

"God, You are more powerful than this evil creature." She continued to plead for mercy.

"You don't come to Me anymore.; You won't listen to Me. You want to do it your way, so I will let you."

"But what about her?" Barbara pointed to the screaming and burning young girl. Then a strange feeling came over her. "God?" What?" She felt her palms being lifted up. She watched as an iron tipped writing pen cut into her hands. It kept cutting deeper and deeper as she screamed in pain. The blood mingled with the ink coming from the iron stylus until the blood disappeared and only black ink remained.

Then she heard God's voice again, "Repeated willful sin stains the soul so deep there is no hope for redemption."

Then a pressure built inside her. It pounded like a hammer with each beat of her heart. She gasped for air and felt her body being crushed from the inside out. She cried out to God for relief. Again she heard His voice in the word of His Scripture, "My heart swells with pain as my people love to wander and seek other gods. Even if Moses and Samuel were here pleading their cause, My heart could not be with them for they have destined themselves to death and captivity."

"Oh, my God, it hurts, it hurts so bad. I can't bear it." An intense pain entered her chest as if a vice squeezed her heart. She could feel her life flowing out of her. Suddenly, the pain stopped. She bowed her head and wiped the tears away, "I understand," She felt the Lord's spirit depart. The vacuum left by His departure caused her to suck in air deep and longing. "Don't go, please."

"Now you pray!" Nisroch mocked her. "I told you He doesn't come to my church when my people come to praise me."

She felt the warm tears flowing down her cheeks and falling on her hands as she remained still on her knees clasping her sore chest.

"He showed you His heart, didn't He?" Nisroch smirked.

Barbara didn't answer Nisroch. However, his statement revealed the pain in the heart of God. She felt herself shaking. She looked back at Nisroch, she felt void of fear.

She shouted at him, "What are you going to do now?"

"Destroy you!" he thundered.

Nisroch raised his head toward the sky and roared with the sound like a pride of lions. Barbara covered her ears. She noticed the other girls were raising their hands and shouting words of love to the roar of dragons. Barbara shouted at them to stop, but they couldn't hear her. When Nisroch stopped roaring he placed his huge head on his clawed feet looking at the charred body of the young girl. Madame Lilith raised her wand and shouted, "The dragon has accepted our sacrifice, he will grant our wish."

Barbara gasped, "Sacrifice?"

"Yes, these wily little self-important women gave me that young thing. Now if you will excuse me, I have a show to put on for them. I think you'll find this interesting."

Nisroch raised his huge head and turned toward the rock where Teresa lay in a state of stupor. The women and Madame Lilith surrounded her, chanting. Nisroch raised his foot extending the first hooked claw. He held it over Teresa's body while Madame Lilith chanted and the other girls repeated or answered her. The words were gibberish to Barbara. Nisroch took the claw and inserted it into Teresa's body just below her chest. Barbara screamed. The group ignored her, Nisroch winked at her.

"I told you that you would enjoy it."

He inserted the claw deep into her body and slowly ripped Teresa's body open from sternum to pubis. Teresa arched her back and screamed in agony. The women around the rock kept chanting and moaning. Nisroch reached in and pulled out a full-grown newborn baby. He held it up in the air for all to see. The women started dancing and shouting with laughter. The crying, terrified baby wriggled and attempted to get away from Nisroch's claw. It didn't help. The huge dragon held the baby firm in his hand. Barbara jumped up from her knees and attempted to climb up Nisroch's back to rescue the baby. When she touched him, she felt intense heat coming from his body. Falling back onto the ground she looked at the open burning belly of Nisroch. The screaming baby tensed up and his little body turned red with the heat from the hand of the dragon.

Then Nisroch looked down at Teresa and made a strange statement, "Moloch, and I thank you." Then he opened his huge mouth and raised his arm letting the screaming infant roll into his mouth and appear in the flames of his belly. The infant screamed and writhed in pain until his life burned out of him.

Barbara stood behind the dragon and watched the faces of the women dancing around the torn body of Teresa, her blood dripping onto the rock. The dragon raised his claw to his mouth and licked her blood. The fire in his belly disappeared.

Nisroch looked down at Barbara. "Where is your God, now?

Barbara collapsed. She didn't know what to do. "Is there any hope?" Her question remained unanswered. Madame Lilith's deep gravelly voice broke the silence.

"Tonight our workings serve the dragon god as he sent the goddess Freya to us to answer Teresa's question." The group moaned, rocked, and touched Teresa's blood flowing over the rock.

Barbara heard the pounding of drums and the lone whistle of a flute. Madame Lilith looked at Barbara.

Smiling she said, "Tonight there is a gathering of dragons giving us their power."

She raised her arms in the air. Nisroch stood behind her and breathed a little fire over Teresa.

"He's here," Madame Lilith said as she dropped her hands and bowed her head.

Again a little puff of fire. The girls all groaned in appreciation of his little display. He looked at Barbara and winked. She tried to scream. She remembered how a gigantic serpent mimics pure evil with only his horrific appearance. More atrocious creatures gathered around him. Among them stood the orange man. She couldn't look away. A creature lurked behind every girl there, orange man stayed next to the dragon and watched Barbara. The women stood and waved their hands in the air, chanting and lighting candles. The creatures behind them laughing. Nisroch looked at Barbara, "If they knew what you are seeing you would be their new queen and high priestess."

Barbara didn't answer. She wanted . . . she wanted . . . her daddy. He would know answers and tell her what to do. She felt safe in his presence, but then she remembered his warning to her that she would have to fight this battle alone. She dropped her head and groaned with pain, "I don't want to do this."

"My daughter, has your spirit guide spoken?" Madame Lilith said as she waved her wand over Teresa's body and the apparition of Teresa's butchered body disappeared. She offered a hand to raise Teresa from the altar. The blood remained covering the rock altar, yet yielded up an intact Teresa.

"How?' Barbara stammered.

"Nisroch laughed, "Remember my greatest power is to trick you."

Barbara turned and saw the young girl's charred body lying on the ground. She groaned in pain.

"What about her? Is that an illusion?"

"Sometimes I just show off." Nisroch laughed.

Barbara bent over the young girl and started talking to her in soft tones about Jesus.

Nisroch growled, "Leave her, she's mine."

He rolled her over with his claw and raised her up. She stood on her feet and looked around. Her body still burned. "This is the appetite of demons." Nisroch snarled.

"You mean to burn them alive?"

"No, we devour them." He lectured Barbara. With that he opened his maw and consumed the young girl in one bite. "Delicious," he taunted.

Barbara gasped and her hand went to her mouth. Another young woman walked up to her, "He took our sacrifice, we are blessed today."

Barbara looked at the young girl speaking to her and responded, "But what about her parents. . . the people who loved her?"

"Only the dragon loved her. She won't be missed on this earth."

"Everybody's loved by someone," Barbara admonished.

The young girl laughed. "I'm next. I hope he takes me with him."

"He didn't take her! He ate her!" Barbara screamed.

Nisroch stood in front of Barbara, "Tsk, Tsk."

"Leave her alone," Barbara pleaded.

"I can't, they give themselves of their own free will," Nisroch licked his lips.

The second young girl waltzed up to Nisroch and began dancing in front of his face.

"Can't you see him?" Barbara stuttered.

"In a way; I feel him. Don't you feel him?" She asked Barbara as she danced in front of Nisroch.

"I see him and he's vile." Barbara said with authority. Nisroch laughed at her effort to be strong.

"Watch this," he invited Barbara.

He reached out with his forked tongue and licked the young girl delivering his vile poison to her skin.

"Are you alright?"

"I am blessed, he chose me."

"He tortured you," Barbara yelled.

"I know and the pain mingles with the pleasure." The girl smiled and started to walk away.

"Wait," Barbara called out to her.

"Do you know Jesus?" Barbara blurted out hanging onto any hope.

The girl looked at her and laughed, "You serious?" She shook her head and rolled her eyes. With a chattering laugh, she walked toward the circle with the other girls.

Almost as if in a trance Teresa sat up and spoke in a dull voice,

"The parasite within my body must be removed. It's an infestation of the enemy."

Barbara watched in amazement as Teresa approached her. There were no wounds on her body.

"What did I just see?" She asked Teresa.

"I don't know what your spirit guide showed you, but mine told me this baby will be cut out of me and I will be free of it. What did you see?"

"I don't want to talk about it," Barbara answered.

Teresa joined the circle. Barbara stepped back into the shadows. Madame Lilith invited the girls to join the sharing of the energy. A gold goblet passed from one woman to the next, each one taking a drink. Barbara knew the contents of that goblet. Madame Lilith gather its contents from Teresa's body when she lay on the altar. Some deceitful representation of Teresa's blood. The goblet held Teresa's life blood and each of them drank it.

16

The Awfulness Of Idolatry

'Only acknowledge your iniquity, that you have transgressed against the LORD your God and have scattered your favors to the strangers under every green tree, And you have not obeyed My voice,' declares the LORD.

---Jeremiah 3:13(NASB)

SHARON ANSWERED THE knock on the door. "Come in Michael. She's in the living room."

Barbara sat on the couch with her legs pulled up in front of her wrapping her arms tightly around them. Her feet were bare in spite of the coolness of the room. She shivered and rocked back and forth.

"Thank you for coming." Sharon murmured.

He studied Barbara as he answered Sharon. "You sounded urgent. I didn't figure you would call me at three in the morning if it wasn't." Michael explained.

Barbara had not yet acknowledged his presence. She stared into the space in front of her. He spoke to her, "Barbara."

She didn't answer but pushed her unruly hair behind her ears and wiped her tear-streaked face. She nodded and made a quick glance at him.

"What's going on?" He asked as he sat down beside her. He noticed her pale and drawn face, smeared mascara and red eyes.

"Blood, so much blood," Barbara answered. Michael didn't understand what she meant but he did understand her befuddled state of mind must be the result of some kind of trauma. He put his arm around her shoulders.

"Sometimes talking helps; sometimes being comforted helps; which do you want?"

"I want the truth," she sobbed.

He held her a little tighter and she released her legs, letting her head fall on his shoulder. She began to wail and mutter unintelligible words. Sharon sat across from them.

"Do you know what's wrong?" Michael asked her.

Sharon shrugged her shoulders. "She's been like this ever sense I found her about an hour ago. I have no idea what happened."

"Did you see the dragon?" Michael said in a soft voice.

Barbara nodded and her face wrinkled up holding back tears.

"He burned a young girl alive. Then. . . then. . . he ate her." Barbara wailed with the words revealing the horror she witnessed only a few hours earlier.

Michael pulled her a little closer, and his tears melded with hers. "I know little one, I know."

"Have you ever seen anyone burn alive?" She fumed.

"Yes, but I called the dragon, napalm." Michael testified.

Barbara shuddered, "I'm sorry, I should have known."

The two of them sat still in their knowing embrace. Sharon joined them on the couch. Michael reached over and patted Sharon's hand. The three sat in silence for a long while, gaining strength from each other.

Through sobs Barbara asked Michael the question crowding her heart, "Am I. . . ?" She couldn't finish the statement. Her body jerked causing her head to fly back and her eyes revealing only the whites.

"She's convulsing," Sharon screamed.

The emergency waiting room was filled with people, moaning and groaning in their own private agony. Michael and Sharon knew Barbara was in one of the treatment rooms. The overworked clerk sitting behind the glass window would not open it. They stood there waiting for her to provide information. Finally, she opened the window. "Name?" Was all she said.

"Barbara Troye." The girl thumbed through some papers. Finally, she said, "no visitors, you can wait over there." She pointed at the waiting room. Before the girl could close the window on them Sharon blurted out, "Is Dr. Holloway working tonight?"

The girl nodded. "You want to talk to him?"

Sharon nodded.

"He's with your party. I'll get him."

"No, that's okay we'll catch him later." Michael reported. The girl shut the window. Michael and Sharon found seats and sat down.

"At least we know she'll get the best care possible." Michael said. Sharon nodded. It was two hours later before Daniel came to talk to them.

"Her temperature rose beyond the boundary of the human body tolerance, so she went into a seizure." Daniel explained. He sat down across from his friends and brushed his hands over his face, "She'll be okay."

"What about you?" Michael asked. Daniel shook his head.

"What did she get into . . . I mean . . . her emotions haven't been very stable for a while, but now---"

Michael prodded, "Did she tell you anything?"

"Not much, but the things she described were so strange, I encouraged her not to talk. I didn't want anyone else in the room to hear her story. It could---you know." He paused and looked up.

Michael completed Daniel's thoughts, "cause problems?"

"Yeah." Daniel answered.

"Do you think it would be alright if I go back and see her?" Sharon asked Daniel.

He nodded, "That would be good. She's being dismissed. My shift is over so I'm going home too, but I'm going to go with you to take Barbara home first, if it's okay."

When they returned to the apartment, Barbara leaned heavily against Michael.

"Why did my temperature go so high?" Barbara groaned as she lay down on the couch and Daniel covered her with a blanket, placing a pillow under her head. She smiled at him and patted his hand. "Thank you." He sat down in the chair beside the couch and stared at her.

"I'm okay," Barbara assured him with a smile. "You don't have to stay with me."

"I'd like to stay if you don't mind."

Barbara nodded and closed her eyes.

Daniel joined Sharon in the kitchen, "What did she tell you?"

"She went with Teresa to a meeting, she called clandestine, whatever that is?"

"You know don't you?" She asked him. "Did she tell you?"

"No, I've seen other girls come into the ER from those meetings. They are usually wounded pretty bad. Barbara had no wounds, other than in her mind. Scuttlebutt at the ER is that a witches' coven is soliciting in the area. The police haven't been able to find any clues or get any testimony. The girls are usually at odds with their parents or wards of the state."

"Clandestine and witches; makes sense. It must have been pretty bad. All she has talked about is the blood." Sharon handed Daniel a cup of coffee and took one to Michael. They sat around the couch for a few minutes. Barbara stirred and almost fell off the couch.

"We need to put her in bed." Michael said as he rose and picked her up. He carried her to the bedroom where Sharon tucked her in.

"Why do you think she went?" Daniel asked Michael when he returned to the living room.

"Who knows why, maybe because she wanted to be a friend to Teresa? She's gullible and sensitive to other people."

"Is she asleep?" Daniel asked.

"Yes, and no longer tossin," Sharon answered.

"I gave her a sedative; she should sleep for a couple of hours. Maybe when she wakes we can learn what this is all about." Daniel assured them.

Sharon nodded. "I remember when I first met Barbara, I thought she was the strongest person I knew. She was my rock."

Daniel related his own special memory. "She thought I bumped into her accidentally at the end of assembly. If she only knew how detailed I planned that little meeting."

Sharon teased, "I remember your tongue hanging out."

"She's a different type of girl, you know," Daniel mused. "I fell hard that day I saw her; and it only gets worse, in spite of her efforts to shoo me off." Daniel smiled.

"She's always been different," Michael added to Daniel's thought.

"Why?" Daniel asked.

Sharon piped in behind Daniel's question, "and since I've known her, she's strong?"

"It was her dedication to the Lord. From the time she confessed her desire to be a follower of Christ, she was different. But not always in a good way. She was obnoxious in a sweet way."

"How so?" Daniel prodded Michael to keep talking.

"She became so righteous and good. Nobody wanted to be around her because she would tell us everything we were doing wrong. She was always saying, "God told us what to do right, if we do it wrong, well, justice will come.""

Daniel and Sharon both laughed at Michael as he mocked Barbara as a young pre-teen.

"She's right you know." Sharon quipped.

"One Sunday afternoon I took all the cousins to town for a coke in my brand new red Chevrolet convertible. She didn't say much until we started to order our drinks. She didn't want anything. We knew this was out of character.

Finally, she said, 'It's not right to make people work for you on Sunday.'"

"What happened? Daniel asked.

"Nobody ordered anything, we left and rode around town a bit, then back to Granny's house where we indulged in the homemade desserts our mother's had made."

"I told you she was strong; she could influence a whole group of kids." Sharon said.

Daniel nodded.

"So why is this orange thing, getting a grip on her and tearing her apart?" Michael addressed the obvious.

"I don't understand how she has become so involved with the women's lib when it has so much wrong with its anti-family philosophy," Daniel added.

"I think the two things are related." Sharon interjected

"Her daddy is one of the strongest Christian men I've ever known." Michael decreed. "I would think she would have enough knowledge of the Lord to flee from a devil."

"I knew her when she couldn't get enough Bible study. The more she learned the more she wanted to teach," Sharon added to the argument.

"She's broken. The experience in her hometown is still very much a part of her heart." Michael proposed.

"I would think that experience would have made her stronger in the Lord," Daniel emphasized.

"We forget the dragon came to Church Creek Falls with false teaching in the church," Michael started to explain when Sharon interrupted him.

"The reason she wanted to be a Bible teacher was to teach truth."

"What happened?" Daniel entreated the two people who knew her at that time.

"If she learned from false teachers, she didn't have truth. Her religion failed her," Michael explained.

"Instead of understanding she developed anger when her 'sacrifice' went unrecognized. She was proud of her knowledge. She turned against the male gender when she was passed over and acknowledgement given to insincere boys." Sharon mused.

"I think those meetings must have made her feelings legitimate." Michael added.

"As she focused more on herself she forgot her Lord. She has basically become her own god." Sharon concluded.

"She knew what she wanted and it wasn't keeping me close or happy." Daniel smirked.

"Mr. McCord put an arrow through her heart when he told her to be content to be a pastor's wife." Sharon said.

"That was like throwing a wrench in a clothes dryer; a lot of noise and ripping of clothes." Daniel added. "I probably haven't helped telling her I want her to be my wife."

Barbara stirred. *Where am I?* She rose from the bed and sat on the edge. She buried her groggy head in her hands and moaned as the memories flooded her mind. She went to the bathroom, and caught a glimpse of herself in the mirror. "Ugh." She said and moved away. She washed and dried her face. She could hear voices muttering from the living room. Opening the door to her bedroom she tiptoed down the hallway to see Michael, Sharon and Daniel sitting around drinking coffee, talking and laughing.

"What are you guys doing?"

Sharon laughed, "Talking about you."

"You guys need better subject matter."

"You're right. I guess we're worried about you." Michael answered as the group turned more serious.

She gave him a smirk, "I'll show you what's wrong with me."

She went to the bookcase and picked up her Bible, opened it to Jeremiah seventeen and read out loud.

"The sin of Judah is written down with an iron stylus; With a diamond point it is engraved upon the tablet of their heart And on the horns of their altars, As they remember their children, So they remember their altars and their Asherim By green trees on the high hills. O mountain of Mine in the countryside."

"It's God's message to the people that were worshiping idols in the woods by throwing their children in the fire." Barbara shouted with a red face and angry attitude. "That's what I saw last night."

Barbara closed her Bible, dropped it on the coffee table, and slumped down on the couch crossing her arms in front of her pouting.

Daniel pulled her close attempting to bring some comfort. Barbara snuggled closer to him. "I'm confused." She said.

Daniel kissed her forehead. "We are too." Barbara pushed away from him and sat up.

"You guys will never understand. I prayed and asked God to help, and He didn't, He let that girl die."

She jumped up but Michael grabbed her arm. "Sit down little one. Listen!" His authoritarian tone of voice took her by surprise. She sat down. Michael spoke.

"If what you describe is the same as this scripture, you need to understand God's heart, not your head." Michael scolded.

"I do understand." She argued as she pulled her arm from his grasp.

"Then explain." He stood in front of her unmoving.

She fumbled and muttered, "I'm not sure."

"Then listen to me," Michael instructed her.

"That scripture is a picture of people intent upon worshiping an evil god. That sin of turning to another god and away from the one true God, is a life-threatening matter. When the deception of a false god captures one, God can't reach them, which means, He can't save them. Do you understand?"

"No, I don't. God can do anything."

"Your right, except make people love Him. That has to be the choice of the person." Michael explained. "It's called free will."

"In other words, they couldn't hear Him because of their desire for the dragon's promises of power." Sharon said.

"Are you saying God couldn't save that girl?" Barbara moaned with the memory.

"God let you see the depth of evil the dragon is capable of performing."

"Yes, that's exactly what I saw." Barbara sat down on the couch again shaking her head. She looked up at her roommate, best friend, her cousin and . . . and Daniel; a man she wanted in her life.

"Your saying God will let them have what they think they want." Barbara realized. The group nodded.

"You know what the dragon said to me?"

The group shook their heads.

"He said, 'you're in my church now,'" Barbara groaned.

"From what you have told us, I would have to agree," Daniel responded.

"I still don't understand. What about the girl he ate? Why did God let that happen if He is a good God?"

"He ate her?" Sharon asked bewildered.

"Yes, first he burned her, she lived through that and then he ate her. But that wasn't the end of it. Another girl offered herself to him. She was happy he wanted her. What's wrong with them?"

"God gave us the freedom to choose, evil does not, when we choose evil, it will consume us." Michael said quietly. "The Bible tells us Satan travels around the earth looking for someone to devour. You saw the literal interpretation of that."

The group sat silent for a few minutes. Daniel broke the silence with a tearful statement, "Barbara you are choosing evil and we are watching it destroy you."

The rest of the group nodded.

"What do I do?" Barbara asked, pulling her robe tighter around her.

"Fight," her friends said in unison.

"With all your might," Michael instructed.

"I don't know how." Barbara answered.

"Yes, you do. Don't let this demon win." Daniel kissed her on the cheek. She smiled at him and leaned into him. He brushed his lips against her ear. "Please, fight for our sake," He whispered.

She looked up at Daniel and asked again, "How?"

He stroked her cheek and with a tender voice he gave her the only possible answer to her dilemma, "Trust Him."

17

Murder

> They have built the high places of
> Topheth, which is in the valley of the son
> of Hinnom, to burn their sons and their
> daughters in the fire, which I did not
> command, and it did not come into My
> mind.
>
> ---Jeremiah 7:31 (NASB)

THE MEETING STARTED as another "poor me" session. One speaker offered an endless story about the unfairness of being a wife and mother. She spoke of her husband as the "jailer" and her kids as her "cruel guards." The major portion of her endless speech bragged of her talents and the things she could do for society if given a chance. In the middle of the woman's tearful plea to abandon her family,

Teresa leaned over and whispered into Barbara's ear, "Let's get outta here. I need to talk to you."

Once the girls were back at the car, Teresa blurted out, "I need your help." Alarmed by the sudden plea. Barbara answered, "Sure, what for?"

"I need you to drive me to the clinic."

"Why don't you ask the baby's father or Madame Lilith?" Barbara snapped at her in disgust.

Teresa ignored it and responded, "He won't do it, and it's not a baby; it's a blob of tissue, nothing more."

Barbara bit her lip trying to keep from exploding on Teresa. Right now she hated her because of what she wanted to do to her innocent baby. The vision of the dragon eating the baby kept playing across her mind.

"Teresa responded. "What's wrong with you?"

"You." Barbara retorted.

"What did I do?" Teresa demanded in an angry voice once they were outside.

"Do you have any idea what happened to you at that coven meeting?"

"Yeah, my spirit guide gave me instruction." Teresa answered rather puzzled.

"No, it didn't! You were cut open with the claw of a dragon."

Teresa laughed.

"And that's not all! That madam took your blood, and put it in a cup and then they all. . ." Barbara couldn't finish the statement.

Teresa stared at her stunned. "I don't know what you saw, but that's not what happened."

"You're blind." Barbara quipped. "You can't murder your baby. Put it up for adoption. Don't let the dragon have it," Barbara pleaded.

Teresa let out a full belly laugh. "You're something. You know it. You're entertaining like a good movie."

Barbara didn't say anything. She stared at her hands, folding them over each other.

"Listen friend, I have to do this thing; I don't want to be connected for the rest of my life to the ---." Teresa stopped looking for a word.

"The father? Don't you like him?" Barbara questioned. Teresa ducked her head and didn't say anything.

"I don't understand you." Barbara quipped.

Teresa leaned in close to Barbara and whispered, "Just trust me. I don't want skuz bucket messing up the rest of my life. That's why I need your help."

"No way, it's your decision. I don't agree with it. Sorry, I can't help you."

"Just take me to the clinic. My parents won't do it, and they won't do the abortion if I come alone. Please." Teresa pleaded. Besides, it will be more comforting with you there. At least I know you care."

Barbara relented, "Okay, I'll drive you there, but that's all."

Teresa smiled. Barbara thought she saw an orange glow over Teresa's head. She ignored it.

Barbara arrived at Teresa's house in the afternoon. When Teresa got into the car stuffing a check into her purse, Barbara questioned her.

"Didn't your mother give you cash?"

"She wrote a check," Teresa answered.

"They won't take a check; you're dealing with murderers, remember?" Barbara scolded.

"Okay." Teresa went back in the house. Barbara waited in the family's circle driveway admiring the beauty of their home.

"It's good to have nice things," a low voice spoke into Barbara's thoughts.

"I guess," she answered the voice and shrugged her shoulders.

"You know, if you do things right, you can have anything you want, even that religion degree. Maybe consider medical school with Daniel. Just think about doing late night study dates with him." A chilling laugh followed.

"You bat-crazy, orange thing," she sneered.

The orange glow filled the interior space of the car like smoke. It took the shape of a man. She could feel her heart racing and her hands growing clammy. She raised her arms in the air to stretch, hoping this figment of her imagination would disappear. As Teresa opened the door, Barbara screamed out.

"What's wrong?" Teresa asked as she climbed back into the car.

"I stretched and pulled something," Barbara answered between groans of pain. "The pain is going away now, but it felt like my shoulder pulled out of its socket."

The voice spoke in Barbara's head. "That's exactly what I did."

Barbara answered, "Why?"

A snicker followed with a most obscene answer, "Because I can."

Teresa heard Barbara ask her the question.

"Why what?" Teresa responded.

"Why---did you take so long?" Barbara groaned with the effort of covering up the real why.

"Mother had to find the cash. I'm ready now."

"I think you better drive," Barbara said as she climbed into the passenger seat rubbing her painful shoulder. Even with her eyes closed, the orange glow surrounded them.

"See what I can do if you try to go against me."

Barbara tried to ignore it. She turned her head and looked out the window, but the face followed her.

"I've got a friend you'll meet when we arrive."

Barbara answered in her head so Teresa wouldn't hear. "I don't want to meet a friend of yours."

"Oh you'll meet him whether you want to or not; he's the god of child sacrifice, and he loves children," The orange glow in front of her face smirked with a fang-like toothy grin. It made Barbara gag. "See my dear you have no choice. Since you chose to come with Teresa, you will see the fine work of my friend." The orange man sang out.

They pulled up into the rear parking lot of a forgotten clinic. It looked abandoned, dirty and creepy. Once inside the door they saw a modern clinic.

"Hello, you must be Nichole?" Sang out the receptionist as they entered the foyer.

Teresa answered, "Yes." Barbara looked at her funny. Why would Teresa use a different name?

"We don't use real names around here," the receptionist explained, as if she could read the puzzled look on Barbara's face. "My name is Fancy; you know like the song by Bobbie Gentry. I just love her music, don't you?" Barbara nodded. She didn't want to get into a conversation about something so frivolous. Fancy didn't give up easily.

"I like to dance too; soon as we get this sweetie taken care of, that's where I'm a goin'; me and my honey. Do you dance sugar?" she asked Teresa. She nodded. "Well, you will be out of here and on your dancin' feet before the night is through. This is easy stuff you know."

"Really!" Barbara said with a drawn out tone of disgust.

"Really." Fancy answered with a deeper authoritative voice. She turned her attention back to Teresa.

"Do you know how long it's been since your last period?"

"Almost six months." Teresa answered.

"Oh!" Fancy said. Barbara noticed she grew a little pale. "It's okay, you may have to wait till tomorrow to go dancin', but' it's okay. You and your boyfriend will be free as the birds' tomorrow night."

"I don't have a boyfriend." Teresa snarled.

"Whatever you say sugar, ain't none of my business if you is in it for entertainment or love. My business is to get you out of it." Fancy chuckled. "I guess you could call us the clean sweep business."

Fancy changed the topic again and asked Teresa. "You ever had any health problems?"

"No."

"Ever had any surgeries?"

"Does appendicitis count?"

"Why yes ma'am, if you been cut, I wanna know about it."

Teresa looked at Barbara and raised her eyebrows. Barbara nodded.

"I think we are ready now sugar. If you will go back to the room and take off your clothes from your waist down and get on the table, the doc will be with you in a minute."

"Can I have something to cover with?" Teresa pleaded.

"Sure, there's a sheet in there just help yourself."

Fancy turned to Barbara, "You comin?"

"No!"

Barbara waited for three hours in the foyer. She tried to read the outdated movie magazines in the waiting room. Screams and moans from behind the treatment doors assaulted her ears. With each cry she heard a cackling laugh in her head. She covered her ears but it didn't help. Orange man spoke in her mind.

"Listen," he whispered in her vexed mind.

"Go away." She demanded even though she knew he wouldn't.

"It makes the Supreme One weep when my friend Kokopelli is at work."

At that moment a couple walked out of the treatment area. The young man held her arm and supported her back. Barbara sneered at him and thought, *You should have been more thoughtful of her before you violated her, you fiend.*

The girl swayed from side to side while her eyes rolled around unfocused. Drool ran down the side of her mouth. With each step she groaned.

"See, he does good work." Orange man's voice sounded in Barbara's head. She turned her eyes toward the inside of a magazine and answered, "Who?"

"I told you: Kokopelli."

"He's a character from cave drawings."

"Oh, baby, he's the god of fertility. He loves little babies. It fact he's been taking child sacrifices ever since he was called Moloch."

"What?"

"A demon's appetite carried out in human form," Orange man answered.

Barbara remembered Nisroch's statement at the coven meeting, "the appetite of demons." He said it after he swallowed the infant. Barbara didn't want to talk to that crazy cloud. She wiped her sweaty hands on her pants leg.

"Kokopelli 's picture shows how he sucks up life before it begins. I think it's funny how people made it look like's he's playing a flute. He's a fine one, he is." Orange man said the words in a sing song celebratory voice.

"Ol' Moloch had a fire in his belly,
drums and flutes begged for young tender deli,
mommas placed upon his arms;
God's gift of their newborn charms.
Then Moloch sang with leaping flames,
while babies cried in screams of pain. "

"Go away." Barbara tried again. Orange man continued.

"An infant makes a small small bite,
but in grand numbers their a demons' delight
For when they eat the flesh of babes,
the Holy One weeps with tears of heartache."

"That's awful." Barbara groaned.

"It's deception, young one. Even you so-called Christians give your precious gifts of life from God to us. You're so easy to manipulate, but the best is yet to come; wanna hear it?"

152

"No!" Barbara yelled. "Why are you telling me these things?"

"Because I need to educate you before you become---" He stopped short of finishing his sentence.

"Become what?"

"Never mind," he said and picked up his soliloquy. "It's easy to build up more victims for Kokopelli. We just tell gullible girls how much their boyfriends love them, and we tell brain-addled boys that she's willin' and you need some tension relief."

"Stop it!" Barbara yelled and put her hands over her ears.

"They say, 'We love each other, nothing bad can come from something so beautiful.'" Orange man danced around the room as he laid all his deceptions in front of Barbara.

"Then the next thing you know, Kokopelli is performing his chaos and you humans are committing murder." Orange man fell on the floor laughing and holding his sides. "But you know the best part?" he taunted.

Barbara didn't respond. She felt sick at her stomach, she looked around for a bathroom as the taste of vomit filled her mouth.

"Aww, come on, you're stronger than that."

Sobbing at the horror of Orange Man's mocking and the seriousness of this place of murder, she blurted out, "God wouldn't let that happen!"

Orange man released a roar of laughter and Kokopelli joined him. The louder they laughed, the more visible they became. Kokopelli didn't present as a cute little flute player. Instead he appeared as a dragon of unspeakable ugliness. His face looked flat on one side while the other side bulged like a lump. His eyes drooped, knives protruded from his skull like tufts of hair. Barbara's hand went over her mouth as she gasped at the ugly monstrous creatures standing before her.

Kokopelli spoke to Orange Man, "Her eyes are opened since she went to the tree grove last night; otherwise she might not see how happy we are." They both laughed. "Unlike the Supreme One." Orange man jeered.

"Barbara, did you know He once told His prophet Jeremiah, 'Why would my people do such a horrible thing? I didn't ask such a thing, nor would I have even thought of it?'"

Orange Man stopped speaking for a minute and stared at Barbara. Then a toothy vicious grin split his face and he said, "We dragons came up with that idea."

Orange Man and Kokopelli danced around Barbara, surrounding her with the stench of sulfur and the repugnance of the gathering of two large dragons. Barbara pulled her arms around her body attempting to stop her shaking. She lowered her head and closed her eyes, hoping the nauseating vision would go away. It didn't. "Leave me alone!" She screamed.

"Not before we kill and maim all you image bearers. Today and every day in this building, we get our revenge on Him and pitiful humans like you."

Barbara wanted him to be quiet and go away. She shuddered and turned her head toward the window trying to ignore his jabbering. Again Barbara called out, "God, please get rid of them." The dragons kept dancing. Barbara didn't expect anything less. Her prayer proved useless. They faded from her vision and from her hearing, although she could smell their presence in the room.

Suddenly orange man spoke to her, causing her to jump. "I never told you the best part. We make you think you're smarter than the Supreme God." He became visible again pointing and laughing at Barbara. She put her hands over her ears and yelled, "Stop it! Stop it!"

A nurse dressed in surgical scrubs rolled Teresa into the waiting room. She didn't move. Her body draped over the wheelchair like a worn blanket. Her head bobbled to one side. The nurse asked Barbara, "Are you okay?"

Barbara took Teresa's hand and responded to the nurse, "I'm okay, just having a bad dream."

"Teresa," Barbara called her name. She looked up at Barbara and then dropped her head again. She attempted to hide the uncontrollable shivering of her body. The nurse nodded and continued with her practiced speech of aftercare and discharge instructions, ignoring the pitiful state of Teresa.

She handed two pieces of paper to Barbara and said, "Don't leave her alone for the first twenty-four hours. She will have some heavy bleeding. If the bleeding becomes excessive, call your doctor."

"Here's some pain pills. She should be more alert and active in forty-eight hours or less." The nurse walked away but stopped and turned, "No aspirin." Two young girls stood alone. One drugged and bleeding and the other one shaking in terror.

Barbara knew exactly what she intended to do; return Teresa to her parents. When her mother came to the back door, Barbara helped Teresa stumble into the house and into her bedroom. Barbara handed the instructions to her mother and hurried out. She wanted to block the whole awful scene from her memory.

"You look like you've seen a ghost," Sharon said as Barbara ran into the kitchen and gulped down a glass of water.

"Nope, just dragons."

Sharon gave a weak knowing chuckle. "How'd it go?"

"Oh, Sharon," Barbara moaned as she took her refilled glass of water and fell into the nearest chair. "I witnessed a dreadful thing."

"Tell me."

"I can't explain it, but once they got the money, the sugar sweet caring disappeared. I don't know what they did to her, but I could hear her screaming. At one point I swear I heard one of them slap her and tell her to shut up."

Sharon sat on the couch opposite Barbara. "I'm sorry."

"I should have talked her out of it." Barbara groaned.

"It's hard to be in a situation when someone wants your help to do something immoral," Sharon counseled.

"She said she needed me and I cared about her. I wanted to help her when she said that."

"I know." Sharon reinforced.

"You sound like the voice of experience."

"I guess I am; I found myself in a similar situation not too long ago."

"Tell me, I need to know I'm not alone," Barbara pleaded.

"Dr. Prewitt, you know the one we student nurses call Dr. Quack asked me if I wanted to make some extra money."

Sharon opened her story. "He needed help in his private clinic. The hours were short and the pay good---no, better than good. I could make as much in one brief shift with him than I make in the hospital all week."

"Did you know what kind of medicine he practiced?"

"I had an idea, after all, we nursing students hear all the gossip, and if we don't hear any we make it up." Both girls gave a slight knowing chuckle.

"Did you ever see an abortion?"

"No, I cleaned up afterwards. I wouldn't have taken the job if I hadn't been so broke."

"Care to elaborate?"

"Not really, but the truth is they run people through there like a cattle auction. I cleaned as fast and as decent as possible, but I never did a good job. They would bring a patient into the room before I finished. I seldom had time to sterilize the instruments. It horrified me that no one complained."

Sharon stopped and took a drink of water. She gazed into the air. "I turned my eyes away, but I couldn't turn my ears. Those poor girls would be wide awake and alert. I suspect, Dr. Quack's greed kept him from using much anesthesia, if any. It had to be painful with that power vacuum they used. I could almost hear the poor baby screaming as the thing ripped off the infant's arms and legs"

"Eww. Why rip off the baby's arms and legs?" Barbara asked rubbing her temples.

"That's how an abortion works; it literally sucks the baby out of the momma, tearing the baby to pieces. Then they crush the baby's skull with forceps so it will come out easier. Once I picked up an eyeball." Sharon whispered and wiped a tear away from her cheek. She continued, "After the second day I worked, Dr. Quack asked me to empty a bucket. I made the mistake of looking inside before I dumped it."

"What did you see?" Barbara drawled.

"Baby parts, tiny perfectly formed baby parts. There were tiny little hands and feet, and then I saw a head. Sharon shuddered. "It looked at me." Sharon wiped away the tear. "That's when I quit. No amount of money was worth helping someone kill those innocent babies."

The girls sighed. Barbara patted Sharon's hand. The subject matter too intense to discuss further.

"I'm exhausted. If you don't mind, I'm going to take a hot bath and go to bed." Barbara broke the awkward silence.

Before she lay down she took one of the pills from Teresa's bottle. She had forgotten to leave it with her mother. Teresa took one earlier, so she would be okay till morning. Right now, Barbara needed one to wipe away the emotional pain in her heart. Just one wouldn't hurt.

The persistent ringing of the phone invaded Barbara's dream. Opening one eye she looked at the clock; 7:30 A.M. She thought she had woke up, instead she rolled over. The medication wouldn't let her rise.

"Barbara, Barbara!" Sharon called and shook her awake.

"What!"

"The phone . . . it's Teresa's mother. I think you need to take it."

"Why?" Can't you take a message?" Barbara said through her drugged haze.

Sharon tried to stir Barbara again, without success.

"Do you need some information or help from Barbara?" Sharon asked into the phone. Barbara heard Sharon talking and made herself get up and listen. She needed to see about her friend. While listening to Sharon she tried to wake up enough to talk to Teresa's mom, she heard another familiar harsh voice. "Sit up!"

Barbara recognized the harsh command. She didn't argue, but obeyed in spite of the drug-induced disorientation. Somehow, she knew there would be pain if she didn't obey.

"Hello." The somber bass voice came from the corner of the room. She looked there and saw him. A full-grown blond man dressed in an orange suit and shoes with a blue tie. His orange fedora hat exposed the trim in turquoise blue to match his eyes. His mouth curled up, but it wasn't a smile, more like a smirk.

"You learned a lot today."

"Who are you? What are you?" Barbara screamed.

"You can call me Jorkphat."

"Jerk Fat?"

"No, Jorkphat, like jor fa."

Barbara raised her groggy head and looked for him. He appeared in front of her. "Jerk Fat!" She screamed.

"He stepped closer to her ignoring the perversion of his name.

"I'm proud of you."

"Why?" Barbara wrinkled up her nose. She didn't want Jorkphat's praise.

"You didn't spill any of that Christian crap on Teresa. You were a good friend. You said you couldn't do it, but you didn't try to talk her out of killing that vile parasite."

"I would've, I just didn't know what to say."

"You're growing. Soon you will be like God," Orange man divulged.

Barbara curled her upper lip but didn't respond. His statement made no sense to her drugged mind. She didn't have the strength to argue and she really didn't care. She jumped when she saw a glimpse of the dragon Nisroch behind Jorkphat.

"What are you looking at?" Jorkphat screamed.

"The dragon behind you," Barbara smirked. Jorkphat turned and became smaller. His face displayed the same fear Barbara felt only a few minutes earlier.

"What's taking you so long?" Nisroch growled.

"I can't get a full grip on her. There's that other thing blocking me," Jorkphat said

"What other thing?" The dragon roared in anger.

Jorkphat shrunk under the roar. He stood as tall as he could muster and held onto his stance of authority.

"Well." Nisroch roared again, waiting for an answer.

"A prayer covering."

The noise disappeared from Barbara's head. She saw the little Orange Man become an orange blob again and the dragon moaning as if in agony as his huge body sauntered off into nothingness.

With the dragon gone, the orange blob snapped in front of Barbara's face.

"If you have to be drugged to see me and obey me, then you better prepare. I'm introducing you to one of my favorite tools, legal pharmacology." The orange blob disappeared.

"Ow!" Barbara screamed as she woke up. Her head pounded with a terrible headache as she sat on the edge of the bed holding her head.

Sharon heard her scream and burst into the room. "What's wrong? Are you okay?"

"I don't know; I've never felt headache pain this bad.

"It's probably a hangover," Sharon said.

"No, I don't drink," Barbara said.

"Alcohol isn't the only thing that causes hangovers, ya know," Sharon answered.

"How'd you know?"

"I saw you with a pill bottle last night. I reasoned it out."

Sharon brought her a glass of water and some aspirin. "Take this and see if it will help." Barbara took the pills and leaned back on her bed.

"What happened last night? I feel like I've been in a tornado."

"You were pretty beat up about Teresa's abortion."

Barbara looked at her and smiled. "I guess you're right."

"I have to go to work. We can clean the car tonight. Then you can put it all behind you, but first you need to call Teresa's mother," Sharon instructed.

"Hello," the answering voice said softly.

"This is Barbara. Is this Teresa's mother?"

Barbara could barely understand her.

"Yes, I called. I'm so sorry for disturbing you, but I thought you would want to know."

"Is Teresa okay, I have some pain pills here for her, I can bring them over right now." Barbara started dressing.

"The pills won't help, she had a bad night."

"What happened?"

"There was so much blood, and we couldn't stop it. I called an ambulance and rushed her to the hospital."

"Which one?"

"University Medical Center."

"I'll be right over there; tell her I'm coming."

"Barbara, don't come," Teresa's mother said through gulps of tears.

"Why not?"

"Teresa died early this morning. She bled to death. The doctors couldn't stop it. My baby girl, she's gone, forever."

Barbara's legs buckled under her and she cried out, No!

18

Saying Good Bye

The heart is more deceitful than all else And is desperately sick; Who can understand it? I the LORD search the heart, I test the mind, Even to give to each man according to his ways, According to the results of his deeds.

---Jeremiah 17:9-10 (NASB)

BARBARA WANTED TO see Teresa's parents, Sharon and Daniel took her. On the way Daniel asked, "How'd you meet this girl?"

"At the conscious raising meeting."

"What's that?"

"Meetings designed to share ideas for promoting the ERA to state leaders and urge its ratification as an amendment to the constitution," Barbara answered him.

"It's already passed congress but it has to be ratified by thirty-eight states before 1979. There isn't much time left."

"What's ERA?"

"Equal Rights Amendment."

"Why add an amendment to a constitution that already states all men are born equal?" Daniel asked with a raised eyebrow.

"Exactly," Barbara raised her voice, "Men are created equal but women---now that's another story."

Daniel turned and looked at Sharon, "What's she talking about?"

Sharon shrugged. Barbara didn't give her a chance to answer, "Equal pay, equal opportunity. Women can do anything men can do."

"And more!" Daniel exclaimed.

Barbara took a deep breath and realizing what Daniel had said, "What?"

"Women display the best of God."

"Explain yourself." Barbara's ready defense for women's rights fell flat at Daniel's comment.

"Just that women give new life, like Jesus."

"I don't get the connection?" Barbara queried with a raised eyebrow.

"We are new creatures in Christ, not just saved, but created new," Sharon completed the thought.

"Yes, and God chose woman to bring new life, including Jesus. Women project the glory of God, in her beauty, her softness, her caring, her nurturing---"

"Okay, I get the idea," Barbara interrupted.

Barbara couldn't think of any response to Daniel. She just looked at him and shook her head, "You make me admire you, and at the same time make me mad at you." She really wanted to argue for women's lib and the ERA, but after Teresa's death it all felt so. . . pointless.

Daniel continued, "That's why Teresa's death is so sad and useless. She exchanged God's greatest blessing for a painful horrible death."

"Both Teresa and her baby," Barbara added.

Silence pervaded the car as each mourned for the loss of both lives in their own way.

When the trio arrived at Teresa's home, Barbara remembered the night she had sat looking at the house when Jorkphat visited her. Today, the house looked plain and simple even in disrepair. Barbara wondered why she thought it looked like a mansion.

Daniel opened the door for the two girls. Sharon carried a cake she had made. Barbara fidgeted with her empty hands.

"Thanks for coming." A friend of Teresa's mother greeted them with red swollen eyes. "Come in." She pointed toward the kitchen for Sharon to take the cake. Groups of people sat around speaking in whispered tones.

Horror overcame Barbara when she saw the old man, the one she called skuz bucket sitting there.

"Who is he?" She asked Teresa's father.

"He lives next door. Do you know him?" Teresa's father asked.

"No, but I've seen him around Teresa before." Barbara suppressed the growl that she felt in her heart but her voice still came out harsh. Teresa's father quickly walked away. She didn't blame him. Barbara's anger grew visible in her demeanor. She knew that revealing what she knew to Teresa's parents would not help their broken hearts, but then she wondered, *did they know?*

Barbara hugged Teresa's mother. "I'm so sorry. I should have stayed that night."

"It's okay, I should have been with her. She said she needed your strength. She often spoke of how much she admired you."

"Admired me?" Barbara asked, "Why?"

"She said you were a free thinker. She claimed you had been brainwashed by religion but still had an open mind."

Barbara blushed at Teresa's false assessment of her. However, it did display the true measure of the persona she presented to others.

"I guess neither one of us wanted to be a part of ---you know---the abortion." Barbara offered in an attempt at comfort.

"Your right. I didn't want to have the baby . . ." She stopped and looked at the old man. Barbara noticed her brow furrow along with the clinching of her jaw. Teresa's mother knew what had happened. Did she know before or after Teresa's pregnancy and death?

"What did Teresa see in him?" Barbara stared at the grisly old man.

"Nothing. I didn't know until after she became pregnant." Teresa's mother broke down in tears, "We didn't know."

Barbara took her hand. "Neither did I."

"I think that's why she became a witch. . . she wanted the power to make him stop."

"I guess it didn't work."

"I think she inflicted some physical health problems on him. After all he's only forty-eight years old."

Barbara turned and looked at him again, "That one? "The old man that looks to be ninety?"

"Yes, he aged quickly when Teresa cast spells on him."

"I wonder why he kept showing up at the women's lib meetings if she put a curse on him?"

"He begged her to stop and to reverse the damage," Teresa's mother answered. "He often came here. She wouldn't see him, so he went there to see her."

Sharon and Daniel listened from a distance. "Sounds like demons at work to me." Daniel whispered to Sharon in a whisper so Teresa's mother wouldn't hear.

Teresa's mother continued to hold Barbara's hand as she wept quietly. Wiping her nose with her handkerchief, she looked at Barbara with a sorrowful smile.

"I have a box of Teresa's clothes and jewelry for you. I think she would want you to have them.

Teresa's mother turned to another woman and asked her to retrieve the box from Teresa's bedroom. The trio stayed for a few more minutes before making a graceful exit.

"Barbara what's wrong?" Sharon asked.

"You remember that conversation we had about God's glory portrayed in woman?"

"Yeah."

"It's stupid."

"What happened to you?" Daniel asked.

"Did you see that old man hanging around the food table?"

"The gray headed one with the mustache?"

"That's the one."

"What about him?"

"I think he's the one that got Teresa pregnant. Her mother said he's been molesting her for years."

"Why did they let it go on." Daniel asked.

"They just found out."

"How could a parent let that happen to their little girl?" Barbara made the redundant statement each person thought.

"She enjoyed it." Came the familiar voice from the orange cloud floating outside the window. Barbara ignored it. She sputtered under her breath where no one could hear. "No! she didn't."

As people passed the casket, some stopped and looked, while others simply walked on without a glance. Barbara wanted to walk past, but she knew she had to look. She needed to see. The last time she saw Teresa, was the night they stumbled into her house with blood pouring from her body after her abortion. As she stared at the empty shell that once held the person of Teresa, she shuddered. She looked peaceful, like a painted china doll.

During the service, Daniel took Barbara's hand and helped her stand. Daniel put his hand on her back to gently guide her outside. He could feel his heart becoming more tender to her each day. This vulnerable state of mourning made his desire to protect her even greater.

Barbara didn't stop and wait for the family. She kept walking toward their car. "Let's go!"

"Why the urgency?

"I need. . . I just need to go, now," Barbara said as she headed toward the car at a brisk pace.

Barbara needed to tell Daniel everything. She felt herself depending on him more and more. She wondered if he knew about her secret if he would still want her for his wife. If she wanted to commit to a relationship with him. She knew she wanted to share her life with him. First, she needed to tell him about the demon, Jorkphat. She needed to tell him all the details about the clandestine meeting--- *oh,* she thought *call it what it is, the gathering of dragons,* the night before Teresa died. She wanted to tell him the details on the night she shot a man. She feared he wouldn't want to be with her any more. The very thought of losing him made her stomach lurch. This may be a good time to let it all out. She didn't want any secrets between them that could stifle the development of their relationship. Love for this man found a crack in her heart. She felt a twitter in her belly thinking about his claim on her as his wife. "Daniel, there is something I need to tell you."

"Okay."

"You know that man that broke into my apartment?"

Daniel chuckled a bit, "I remember."

"When he fell in front of me, I looked at his face and. . . ."

Just as Barbara started to tell her darkest secret to Daniel, she heard a deafening sound. Daniel shouted "Barbara!"

Screech! A car ran a red light. It hit them square on the front of the driver's side of the car. They spun around in the middle of the intersection. The force threw Barbara over on Daniel. When the car stopped she saw blood pouring from his head. He didn't respond. She wrapped her sweater around him. Looking at the other car she saw the orange man in front of it. She screamed. "Why can't you leave me alone?"

At that moment the orange cloud surrounded them and she heard a distant but clear voice say, "Neve, you belong to me!"

Sharon greeted the ambulance at the emergency room. "What happened?" She cried when she saw Barbara covered in blood. The hospital personnel whisked Daniel to a treatment room.

"A car. It came out of nowhere and hit us," Barbara stammered an explanation. "Daniel? Is he okay?" Barbara sobbed. Sharon nodded, although she had no idea about Daniel.

She took Barbara to a treatment room and prepared a tub to wash the blood off Barbara. "Daniel's unconscious." She answered Barbara as she observed the EMT's shuffling the gurney with Daniel toward another room.

"I'll let you know about him as soon as I can. Right now, let's see about you." Sharon picked up Barbara's arm cleaning the blood. "It's not mine. It's Daniel's."

"I'll check you for injury anyway."

After several hours of people coming and going, Sharon came back into the exam room with Barbara.

"You're both good. No serious injuries, although you may be sore. Daniel's head injury proved to be a puncture wound, not serious. The doc is signing dismissal papers right now and then I'll take you home."

"What about Daniel?"

"He's made other arrangements."

Barbara felt her stomach tighten. She had seen the orange man. She wondered, *what did he do to Daniel?*

"Okay, let's go," Barbara responded in a whisper.

Taking a strange route home, Barbara asked Sharon, "Where are you going?"

"I want to show you what you survived." They stopped in front of the car salvage place where Barbara saw Daniel's car, completely demolished. "There is no way either one of you should be alive. Look at the front seat."

Barbara stared in disbelief at the twisted hunk of metal with the front driver's seat pushed to the back of the car. She felt her heart beating in her temples.

"Your guardian angels were watching over you both tonight."

"You're right." Barbara answered still gazing at the wreckage. "but I only saw a demon."

19

Mother Knows Best

> O Daughter of my people, put on
> sackcloth and roll in ashes; mourn as for
> an only son, a lamentation most bitter.
> For suddenly the destroyer will come
> upon us.
>
> ---Jeremiah 6:26 (NASB)

BUSTER AND MERILEE arrived at the girl's apartment a short time before dinner. Barbara hugged her parents. Both she and Sharon felt comfort at their presence.

"I'm so glad you're here." Barbara welcomed them. "I know things will be okay now." She smiled at them, knowing they would come as soon as they heard about the car crash.

They sat down at the dining table and enjoyed a hearty meal. Barbara related the car crash incident, but left out Daniel's absence in her life since then.

"I saw something," She finally muttered with her head down afraid to look her parents in the face.

"Is it Nisroch?" her dad asked.

"I don't think so, although I know he's present and watching."

Barbara mustered up her courage and exclaimed, "I've been seeing an orange man and I think it's a demon that's working for Nisroch."

"How?" Merilee exclaimed as she returned from the kitchen.

"I see an orange man, and sometimes Nisroch is behind him." She opted not to tell them about the coven meeting she attended with Teresa. It would only worry them.

"Remember when the mask pricked you?" Merilee asked. Barbara nodded. They rose and took a more comfortable seat in the living room.

Merilee continued, "Your shoulder swelled up."

"I didn't know that." Barbara said.

"It wasn't deep, but it turned red and feverish."

"Well, I think I know why." Barbara answered her mother and took her hand. "I think that's the moment the demon found me."

Buster came into the conversation, "That makes sense if the mask is Nisroch's idol, then what you are seeing could be. . . what?" Buster shrugged his shoulders.

"Nisroch's spawn?" Sharon queried as she entered the living room. Her listening ears had caught most of the conversation while she loaded the dishwasher.

"How?" Barbara asked and wrinkled up her nose. "Can a dragon have a demon son?"

Buster laughed at Barbara and tweaked her nose.

"There are many things we don't know, but some things we can guess and that's one of them."

"Upon what are you basing your guess?" Merilee chided.

"If Nisroch's one of the fallen angels that mated with women in Genesis six, then the children they had would be half spirit and half-human." Buster stated. "And it very clearly says the sons of God had children with human women."

"How do you know the sons of God are fallen angels?" Sharon reasoned."

"The first chapter of Job, among other scriptures." Buster responded. "The first century preachers and the church fathers taught it. Those who heard Jesus or one of the disciples teach."

"Makes sense." Barbara replied.

Buster continued, "The human part will die but what about the spirit part? It's immortal."

"Then wouldn't it stand to reason the idol would have the spirit of Nisroch's offspring or a demon behind it?" Merilee asked.

"Michael said there's a demon spirit behind every idol." Sharon retorted.

Buster nodded. "Paul made that statement in 1 Corinthians 10:20."

Barbara reflected on her father's statement, "Are you saying a demon is. . . what?

"After you." Sharon reasoned.

"What does that mean?" Barbara pondered.

"I think it means the demon is attempting to take your body over as his habitation. You know Jesus said if you remove one demon but don't bring in His righteousness, then that demon will return with seven more vile than himself. They want a place to live."

Barbara shook her head.

"Mom, that day on the couch, when the thing stuck me it felt like something dripped into my soul," Barbara said. "Where is it now?"

"I threw it in the incinerator."

"Why?"

"To keep it from harming others."

"Do you think I'm protected." Barbara moaned in a low voice.

"From what?" Merilee asked.

Barbara didn't speak for a while. She pondered how much to tell her mother. She wanted to tell her everything she knew. Barbara looked at her mother straight on. She decided to share her trials with her but not all the details. "I'm being tormented." She blurted out.

"Why?" Merilee pondered.

"Because I'm a girl." Barbara exclaimed. Merilee grinned and squeezed her.

"My girl, you're trying to find your role in life as a woman of God."

"I don't believe God cares about women." Barbara rose and stomped off to her room slamming the bedroom door. Buster sat down on the couch beside Merilee comforting her. "This goes beyond normal parenting. I don't understand what makes her so angry."

"It happens when she gets on the subject of the unfairness of being a woman. She's really hardheaded on that topic. I don't think Daniel is getting through to her either and if ever a man deserved better treatment, it's Daniel." Sharon interjected.

Buster nodded. He really liked Daniel and could see the man loved his daughter. He pondered why Barbara couldn't see and accept his love.

Merilee sipped her almost cold coffee, she didn't notice. How could they direct their daughter through this? After a few minutes she spoke up, "I read an article in *Time* Magazine about this."

"What did it say?" Buster asked.

"Mostly gibberish about a woman named Betty Friedan who had written a book," Merilee stopped and slugged the last of her coffee before she rose to go wash her cup. "I can't remember the name of it."

"Could it have been *The Feminine Mystique?*"

"Yeah, how did you know that?"

Buster raised a book for Merilee to see.

"Oh no! I think I understand a little better."

"Explain to me."

"This woman, Freidan, is a discontented lost woman who is miserable and wants everyone else to be miserable with her. If Barbara is reading this book I can understand the confusion. Approaching adulthood is hard enough without taking on the problems of a confused activist."

"How do you know she's confused." Buster looked over the book jacket, "Although, I can see why her husband would be discontent, she looks miserable in this picture."

Merilee sat down beside Buster and took the book. She opened it to a passage and showed it to Buster. "I think this is the root of Barbara's problem. Look at the woman's personal story."

"I felt a strange uneasiness; there was a question that I did not want to think about. "Is a wife and mother really what I want to be?" I felt the future closing in---and I could not see myself in it at all. At seventeen I had the wide horizons of the world and the life of the mind had been opened to me. I had begun to know who I was and what I wanted to do. I couldn't go back now. To the life of my mother and the women of our town, bound to home, bridge, shopping, children, husband, charity, clothes. But now that the time had come to make my own future to take the deciding step, I suddenly did not know what I wanted to be."

"Remember she's determined to get a religion degree?"

"Why? She is so far from the Lord." Buster asked.

"Probably stubbornness. She wants to prove she can."

Buster nodded but said nothing. Merilee rose and pulled pencil and paper from her purse. She scribbled out a note and put it in the book.

"What are you doing?" Buster asked.

"I'm putting the real answer to that question in this book, the answer God gave in Proverbs thirty-one."

"You don't think that will make it worse?"

"Maybe at first, but at least it will bring her to me where I can explain it. If she doesn't bring it to me, then I'll know she isn't reading it."

"You're a smart woman," Buster said as he patted her on the back.

"More like a concerned mother."

"There is one thing that bothers me."

"What's that?" Merilee asked.

"The dragon, what's the connection?"

Barbara came out of her room and sat down opposite her parents.

"Tell me one thing, Mother," Barbara demanded.

"Okay."

"Why did God make us subservient to men?"

Merilee smiled at Buster. He rose and filled his ice tea glass and prepared to listen to one of the greatest Bible teachers he knew---his wife.

"My sweet daughter, that's a beautiful question that can only come from a thinking mind. A mind given to you by God. He gave us a clear and useful answer. But He made the answer such that we must search for it. That way, when we find it, we know that we know for sure, and nothing will sway us from the answer."

"That's what I want mother. I want to know how I'm supposed to live my life as a woman wanting a career like a man, and still be a Christian.

"Let's look at how God created the earth and mankind. If you look at Genesis 2:7 you see that God picked up a lump of clay dirt and formed the body of a man, and then He breathed life into that body."

"Yeah, I guess that's why men are supposed to be the head?" Barbara said with a sneer.

"Not really, let's go back to Genesis 1:27, what does it say?"

Barbara read the verse, "'Let Us make man in Our image. . . He created him; male and female, He created them.' Sounds awkward."

"Not if you use punctuation."

"What?"

"He, God, created one man to represent all mankind and in that realm he made both male and female."

"What are you saying?"

"I'm saying God created us in His image. When God looked at His Creation He saw a problem."

"Aww, you got me now, God doesn't make mistakes."

"You're right, but He did notice a problem, not a mistake. Adam, was all alone. God said, that's not good. So what did He do?"

"Made Eve." Barbara answered with confidence she had the right answer.

"No, He gave Adam a task."

"A task?"

"Yes, look at verse 18; He said, 'it is not good for man to be alone, I will make a suitable helper for him.'"

"What do you think suitable means?" Barbara asked her mother.

"Perfect for Adam in every way. A helper is someone human like him, but different. By making a woman different He revealed His whole image. He is both strong and single minded like a man providing and protecting his family, but soft and nurturing like a woman, noticing every need of His children."

"Does it tell us how He created Eve." Barbara asked.

"In a way. He told Adam to name all the animals."

"What does that have to do with Adam being alone?"

"When Adam named all the animals they passed by him in pairs. By the time Adam named the zebra, he noticed no other creature in the Garden looked like him."

"Then God made Eve." Barbara interrupted.

"No, then God told Adam to take a nap."

"I don't understand." Barbara wilted a bit.

"God saw the problem long before Adam did, but God didn't want to fix the problem until Adam knew the problem."

"I don't think I understand," Barbara moaned.

The task of naming the animals revealed no other creature in the garden looked like him, in other words no other human bearing God's image."

"You mean we are the only creatures that look like God?" Barbara mocked her mother.

"Yes, but it goes beyond that, we are the only creatures that carry the life and breath of God. Look at Genesis 2:7. Man is the only creature God made with his hands and breathed life into him. All the other creatures he brought up from the ground. They too are made of dirt, but only man was formed by the tenderness of a loving father. This means only mankind was given God's breath."

"So then God made Eve after Adam had his nap?"

"Not exactly, God brought Eve from Adam's rib while he was asleep." Merilee tried to explain.

"That's how He created mankind as male and female."

"Why?"

"Remember the helper, Eve is the perfect complement to Adam. She is equal to him, but God made her physically different to accomplish different tasks. By their differences God revealed a complete picture of His image."

"How?"

"Since no one witnessed the event, not even Adam, remember he was asleep, this is apparently one of God's mysteries he wants us to discover for ourselves. We only know he opened Adam's side and removed a bone. From that bone he fashioned the body of Eve."

"So women are one of God's mysteries?" Barbara repeated.

"I'll say!" Buster chimed in with a big toothy grin while staring at Merilee. She blushed and coyly ducked her head.

"What happened next?" Barbara pulled her mother back into the story.

"He woke Adam and brought the woman to him."

"That's pretty neat," Barbara said smiling.

"Yeah, and the neatest part is yet to come."

"What?"

"When Adam woke up and God brought the woman to Adam, he said, 'Wow, this beautiful creature came from my bone and my flesh. I will call her woman."

"That sounds like another mystery," Barbara groaned.

"I guess it is because God said, 'For this reason, a man shall leave his father and mother and cleave only to his wife and the two will become one.'"

"What reason?" Barbara pondered.

"Marriage between one man and one woman for a lifetime, according to God's instructions. It is the picture of our relationship with Him. When a marriage is built on God's instruction, it gives the couple companionship, security, financial prosperity and an inheritance of children raised in the security of love. All the things God gives us."

"What *does* God give us?" Barbara wrinkled up her nose as she asked the question.

"A picture!"

"Of what?"

"A man sacrificing all he knows to build a new life with his helper, his wife."

"What good is that?"

Merilee shook her head at the antagonism of her daughter. "Listen, if you can't see God you can't understand and you will never see God if you don't understand the mystery of marriage."

"That's a good fairy tale mom." Barbara snickered.

"God's word is not a fairy tale. It has deep significant truth. God gave us marriage to see a picture of our relationship to Him as children and our future with Christ, who will be a husband to God's children." Merilee became stern.

"Okay mother, don't go ballistic on me. I enjoyed the story, but even if it's true, that still doesn't answer my question; Why does God hate women, especially me?"

Merilee looked at Buster and sighed. Then she reached over and patted Barbara on the leg. "Some things you have to learn for yourself, like Adam."

"How do I do that?" Barbara's question dripping in sarcasm.

"I think you have a task to do."

20

The Games Of Demons

> Every man is stupid, devoid of knowledge; Every goldsmith is put to shame by his idols; For his molten images are deceitful, And there is no breath in them. They are worthless, a work of mockery; in the time of the punishment they will perish.
>
> --- Jeremiah 10:14-15 (NASB)

BARBARA SLUMPED IN the nearest chair at her weekly psych meeting. Today she didn't want to be with the wounded and damaged.

"Funny"

"What's funny?" Sid asked as he sat down beside her.

"Us."

"Yeah, we are. Wanna' talk about it?"

Barbara looked at Sid and with a smile remarked, "I'd like to, but what you guys have been through makes what I'm thinking pretty silly."

"Your feelings and thoughts are as important as ours."

Barbara patted Sid's hand. "You guys really are a different breed. I didn't want to come to day. Probably because today's the anniversary of my friend's death."

"That's not silly," Sid responded. The others nodded and muttered in agreement. "You want to talk about it?"

"I think so. It was a such a tragic and useless death. She died from a botched abortion." Barbara waited for a reaction. She saw tightened lips and the wringing of hands.

"We saw the death of so many innocent children," Michael paused and rubbed his eyes. "It's hard for us to understand," Michael explained. It helped Barbara digest the men's reactions.

"I hurt because I didn't try to rescue her baby." Barbara ducked her head. "I said nothing except, 'it's your choice.' I didn't feel like I had the right to say anything."

"Believe it or not we can relate," One of the men said.

Nurse Young asked, "Barbara, why do you think that's silly?"

"I didn't want to come today. It seems the more I need to be here, the less I want to be here."

The men all sat back in their chairs, and chuckled or made little cackling noises.

"That's not silly, that's reality. I feel that way every week," said Russ.

"Me too, in fact I start talking to myself hours before time, but it does get easier each week." Paps added.

The other men nodded with understanding.

"All of you?" Barbara looked around the room.

"We don't know what to do with our lives. Most of us have lost careers, girlfriends, and wives," Michael said. "Even the American culture we knew before we left no longer exists."

Sid added, "And some of us have lost pieces of ourselves. We don't know who we are or why we're alive." He held up the metal hook on his right arm. "At least I can say I have an awesome right hook now." Sid said with a smile as he hit the air making Barbara smile and giggle.

"That's better." Russ winked at Barbara.

"So if we need it and we want it. . . we even know it's the best thing for us, why do we not want to come?" Nurse Young asked the group. Barbara watched each man's face grimace at the question.

"I know here I have to face facts. I killed people. I did some of the awful things those Vietniks say we did; you know the ones protesting the war. I wanted to come home and be greeted and loved so I could forget; instead I'm reminded every time I go out. When my countrymen hate me, I hate me."

Another man picked up the rant, "That's the hardest part. Our own people don't want us and . . ." He started crying. The two men on each side of him patted him on the back. No words were spoken. They weren't needed.

After a while, Barbara said, "See, you guys have an understanding I don't have. I have no one to comfort me."

The men stared at Barbara. "Why do you need comforting?" Young asked her in blunt terms.

"I killed a baby." She waited for the men to react. No one did.

"Did you have an abortion?" Nurse Young prodded.

"No!" "I ran over a child with my car and killed her."

Michael could see the effort it took for her to force the words out, so he stepped in to help. "A three-year-old ran in front of her car. There's nothing she could have done to stop it." Michael explained.

"That's the way it was with us. We didn't set out to kill women and children. Their government had no respect for them or their lives. That's one of the reasons many of us went insane."

"I killed a man who broke into my apartment." Barbara winced as the confession left her lips.

"Self-defense?" Jerry said in his deep baritone. Barbara nodded.

"You are more like us than you realize." Jerry added.

"Barbara, can you talk about the man?" Nurse Young asked her.

Barbara nodded and took a drink of water offered her by one of the men. After a long pause, she spoke, "I feel ashamed talking about my little problems."

"It's okay Barbara," Paps said. "So do we, but we need you to help us readjust."

"I don't understand?"

"The war changed us---"

"Nightmares: awful nightmares," Russ said as he ran his fingers through his hair.

Barbara watched them, they were. . . different. No, that's not the right word. They were haunted. Barbara looked up at Nurse Young and with a steady voice asked a question.

"Why am I here? Who is responsible for putting me here? I'm the only one that didn't serve in Vietnam. I don't think I want to do this anymore."

Barbara headed toward the exit and tried to open the locked door. Nurse Godfrey came up behind her.

"Unlock this door, I'm quitting the group," Barbara demanded.

Godfrey didn't say anything but stood there with arms crossed and legs slightly apart. Mr. Young approached, "That's not an option for you."

"What do you mean?" She demanded. The other men turned their backs and ignored the outbreak.

"You are here by court-appointment."

"Why? I don't understand? When did I go to court?"

"Your doctor submitted a request for you to be in the group. The judge granted the request. You'll have a review with Dr. Greenstein, and she will determine whether you will go to court. Till then you have to finish this class."

"Why?"

190

"You claimed to have killed a man." Young stated without taking his eyes from her.

"I know, I told you that. He broke into my apartment."

"There are some questions that need to be answered, that's all."

Barbara paced around the room flaying her arms in the air. Her face glowing bright red as her voice escalated to a screech.

"What's happening?" She fell into a chair and clutched her abdomen. She rocked back and forth and screamed, "I'm the victim!" Jorkphat stood nearby whispering to Barbara's mind.

"Please tell me, who put me here?" Barbara screamed at Nurse Young.

"My doctor? My parents? You? I don't believe a judge put me here."

"Why do you want to know?" Nurse Young asked her.

"Because there's a reason someone, somewhere thinks I share something with these returning soldiers. What is it?"

"Barbara," he said, leaning over and cupping his hands around hers and speaking calmly, "tell me about yourself." Barbara responded to his gentle touch and relaxed.

"Not much to tell. I grew up in a loving family, in a small town, and then went to college before I ended up here."

"What happened in your small town?"

"It got blown up."

A collective gasp went around the room and Russ said, "Church Creek Falls?"

"Yes, how'd you know?"

"It made national news, everyone knows."

"But you were in Vietnam."

Michael interjected, "The Vietcong used the information as negative propaganda. We all heard it, multiple times. I prayed for you and your family every day after that."

"Propaganda?" Barbara queried.

"The communist continually played their national radio with a sweet female voice telling us we were murderers, and we came from a land of murderers." All the men nodded their heads.

"Continue, Barbara," Young said.

"I enrolled in the nursing program at the hospital. First week here, I got shot."

Nurse Young leaned into Barbara, "Tell us about it."

"He broke into my apartment, rifled through my things, turned around saw me. That's when he shot me. I blacked out and woke up in the hospital."

"Okay, let's take it a step at a time. How did he break in?"

"I don't know. I heard something in the living room, so I walked down the hall and saw him."

"Did you notice a broken window, an open door, anything?"

"No, but I wasn't thinking about how he got there."

"Why not?"

"I don't understand your question," Barbara said.

"If someone invades your privacy don't you want to know how?"

Barbara closed her eyes, "The front door was open."

"Kicked in?" Young asked.

"No, partly open, and a key was hanging in the door knob. He must've had. . ." Barbara stopped.

"Had what?"

"I don't know, a key?"

"Did you see the door open?"

"I guess so, but . . ."

Young interrupted her. "What happened next?"

"I stood in the hallway and watched him. He went through the things on my desk."

"Why do you think he did that?"

"I don't know; I couldn't figure it out. I didn't have anything of value. Only papers cluttered my desk, nothing of significance to anyone, but me."

"What made him stop?"

"I don't know, I... guess I made a noise, and he turned around and saw me. Then he held his gun in my face, and I pulled my gun and started shooting him."

"What kind of gun?"

"One that goes bang and pushes a bullet out." She said with sarcasm and an attitude of dismay.

"Describe it, tell me about his gun."

"I don't remember." She pleaded.

"What happened?"

"Something pushed me, and I fell to the ground, and so did he. I looked at his face and felt his last breath blow on me, then I passed out."

"What did you see?"

Barbara wrapped her hands around each other. She could feel heat rising to her face. "I don't want to say."

"You must. Tell us, what you saw?"

She started rocking back and forth, "I can't."

"Yes, you can."

"We have learned to talk about our traumas or they control us." Michael interrupted. "We don't like to talk about it either. We *need* you to talk."

Barbara stopped rocking and looked around the room. They all stared back at her. Red, misty eyes belied the hurt of each man. She decided to tell for their sake, but only because she loved these broken men.

"I saw blood and orange slime coming from his head."

"Did you hear anything?

"Only that same phrase I saw on the paper my mother had, '*The planting of seed is singular but the harvest comes in multiples.* I have no idea what it means other than the obvious. Plant one seed and it will produce many seeds." She let her hand go to her head.

"Tell me about your wound." Young prodded.

"Here on my head. Can you see a scar? That's why the ambulance brought me to the hospital."

"No, Barbara. They brought you here to the psychiatric pavilion because you were hysterical and screaming about an orange man."

Barbara slumped back in her chair and cautiously asked Nurse Young, "Was he orange?"

"No, he wasn't. In fact, he wasn't in the hall."

Barbara looked up in surprise, "What do you mean?"

"The ambulance attendants didn't find evidence of a body. The only weapon was in your hand."

"But. . . but. . . I saw him. I shot him."

"There was no one there," Young grasped her hands a little tighter. "But you did see something, and that's what I want you to tell us. What did you see? What was there in your apartment?

Barbara decided she had nothing to lose, so she took a deep breath to reveal at least part of the secret she had been hiding. Michael put his arm around her. "Tell him what you saw?" he urged.

"I saw an ugly dragon, like the one that was on our farm at Church Creek Falls." She burst into tears. "I'm afraid. . ."

"Afraid of what?" Young encouraged her to express her thoughts.

"Of what it will do."

The men leaned back in their chairs and sighed.

"Now you know why you're here with us?" Sid answered.

She looked at him, "Did you know?" He nodded. She looked at the other men, and they all nodded.

"You've seen ---" Barbara stammered unable to say the word.

Jerry finished her thought for her. "We've seen the dragon. "We've all seen dragons."

Michael pulled the full whiskey bottle from his coat pocket. All of the other men did the same thing. "That's why we carry this."

"I don't understand?" Barbara pleaded.

"Yes, you do. Look in your purse, what do you have in there?" Young prodded.

Barbara ducked her head. "Nothing."

"Barbara!"

"Oh, all right." She fished in her purse and brought out the pill bottle half full of Valium. "But I need them to sleep, that's how I forget." She moaned. The men all picked up their whiskey bottles and raised them toward Barbara, "Salute!" They shouted.

"You drink for the same reason I take pills." They all nodded and said in unison, "Dragons!" They all smiled through the collecting tears. Barbara knew then she belonged here.

Sid stood up and walked over to Barbara. He came down on one knee in front of her and took her hands in his left hand. "Honey, the dragons are real. They are the ones who don't want us here. If we think we are the only ones fighting the dragons, then we submit to them. Look how full our bottles are. We carry the whiskey, but as long as we come here, we don't drink it."

"But I have smelled it on you." Barbara retorted.

He held up her half-empty pill bottle, "When do you take them?"

Barbara thought for a while, "When he's tormenting me; when he's hurting me."

"Uh hu." Sid kissed the back of her hand and rose from the floor and went back to his chair.

"He's a strong man. We can't defeat him. Together we are strong. We sharpen our sword and fight him. We have a weapon that wounds." Paps said as he held up his Bible.

Barbara scowled, "I don't believe the Bible anymore."

"We know. We all have a hard time believing what we've been taught. The simple answers we learned in Sunday school failed us when we needed first-hand knowledge with understanding." Michael said.

"What do you mean first-hand?" Barbara asked.

"You have to know for yourself, not what someone has told you," Michael answered.

Nurse Godfrey stepped into the conversation, "Jerry, tell us about the dragon you saw?"

He nodded stood up and began to pace around the circle. "Yes sir, I want to talk about that conniving evil snake."

Barbara watched this big hulking confident man slap his fist into his other hand and work his jaw. "I hate him, oh how I hate him."

"At first, I just saw these two cartoon character like dragons made of wood. They had one paw resting on a ball. They had blue bodies and white clown faces with a row of pink around those faces. Behind them stood tall pillars supporting the building made of gold dragons. It seemed harmless enough. My unit waited on that street. As I watched this clown show, I pulled out a cigarette and lit it. Before I threw down the extinguished match those two clown dragons jumped off those balls and in a split second they were both in my face hissing and flicking a split tongue at me. I pushed back. They slinked around me, eyeing me. One of them wrapped his huge blue tail around me and started squeezing. The other hissed. While these two held me one of the dragons from the pillars came over. He stood three times the size of the clowns. When he walked around me I think I wet my pants.

Another young man name Ronnie told his story. "It wasn't just the North Vietnamese. The villagers helped whoever was helping them. They struggled to survive. The women and children . . . they helped. . ."

Ronnie stopped talking and as he sat down. Marvin picked up the discourse. "They helped build weapons, horrible weapons. They would dig holes in the ground and put sticks they had whittled to a sharp point, cover it and then we would step on them. It would be impossible to walk." By this time Ronnie had gained his composure, "And those were the kind ones."

"Cross-bows and spears were their main weapons. The traps. . ."

Barbara sat still and listened to the stories the men told. The dragons gathered in the places where they were worshiped to carry out their ultimate destruction – death! She realized in this group she registered *normal*.

Russ stood up and started talking. "I was on the Forrestal. I watched that fire breathing dragon belch from an airplane, then---." He choked up but wanted to continue. "Then he blew the jet plane fuel toward the bunkers, where the men on the last shift lay asleep and unaware of the tragedy about to unfold above them. That flaming fuel slipped into the cracks and poured onto those sleeping boys." Russ stopped and let out a wail of pain and agony. "I heard them screaming, I tried. . . I tried to get them out." He pulled up his long sleeves and revealed the burn scars on both arms. "That dragon laughed and blew the fuel toward the men. If it wasn't lit, he breathed fire on it." Russ sat down and sobbed deep gut-retching sobs. Other than the sound of tears, the room remained silent.

The old man known as Paps, always sat by himself in his wheel chair near the back. He listened more than he talked. This time he spoke up and made a surprising announcement, "I've seen the dragon's lair."

Paps took a deep breath and looked around. The room waited for Paps to continue telling his story. The pain of his words deepened each time he tried to speak. He opened his mouth but the scars of memories prevented the words from forming. He shook his head and buried it in his hand. After a few minutes he raised his head and blurted out,

"Just a baby and I deserted her. I left her. . .with. . .a dragon."

Sniffles could be heard as Paps kept trying to tell his story. Finally, he shook his head and rolled back to his corner of the room. The words would not form.

Nurse Young spoke up. "It's time to apply the balm of healing to our souls." All the men pulled their metal covered Gideon Bibles out of their coat pockets.

"This is the other thing we carry with us." Michael said, as he pulled an extra from his briefcase and handed it to Barbara. Michael held his up, "It saved many lives in more ways than one." He put his finger through a bullet hole. "I carried this one over my heart."

Barbara looked at the Bible, knowing it probably saved Michael's life. She heard a small whisper in the back of her head, "It will save your life too."

Barbara reached over and put her arms around Michael's neck. "For that Bible I am grateful." She stood up, "I love you guys, but this balm has no answers for me. Nurse Young may I be dismissed?"

This time Carl Young allowed it. The message had been delivered to a heart too hardened with disappointment to receive it.

21

Vision Or Nightmare

Thus says the LORD, "Do justice and righteousness, and deliver the one who has been robbed from the power of his oppressor. Also do not mistreat or do violence to the stranger, the orphan, or the widow; and do not shed innocent blood in this place.

---Jeremiah 22:3 (NASB)

BURLINGTON UNIVERSITY HOSPITAL, 1974

DANIEL FELL ON his bed in sheer exhaustion. Each time he relaxed his legs and arms they jerked as the tense muscles released their strain. He had completed a brutal twenty-two hour shift in the emergency room. This one took a heavy toll on his body and his mind. Tonight, this one felt personal to Daniel. His soul distressed him beyond anything he had experienced in his life as an intern.

Every time he closed his eyes searching for sleep, a horrible vision played upon the darkness of his eyelids. He could see beautiful bodies mangled in their last moments of life. He saw the angelic face of a toddler and the smooth young face of the child's mother. The child's body looked as though he could get up and run away. It had no blood or scratches upon it. However, the slight bruising that grew upon his body told the ER staff, his insides were bleeding. The ashen color of the mother's skin highlighted deep blue eyes giving her a peaceful look in spite of the trauma which ripped her lower body half away from the upper.

The trauma team focused on the tormented and still breathing father struggling to live. He kept insisting the team care for his wife and baby. At one point he rose slightly from his gurney and saw the blood-covered body of his wife. "Help her!" The father demanded. Then the reality of her death plagued his tortured mind. "My wife?" He muttered as he lay back down in compliance and let the team continue to work on him. Daniel saw a look of resignation come over the man's face, as he asked, "My son?"

Daniel carried the responsibility of telling the man his son had expired. Hours after the event he could still see the light of life fading from the man's eyes. Still the father needed to talk, to explain what happened. Daniel and the

ER staff listened as they continued to give their full attention to the man's wounds.

"I took a wrong turn, my wife wanted to turn around. I kept assuring her we could make it back to our road. Our young son sat between us in a car seat designed to give him better vision, not keep him tethered to a stable base." The man groaned and turned his head at the memory of his child. He sighed, coughed and continued his confession. Daniel looked at the blond, blue-eyed toddler with dimpled chin and pudgy legs lying on a gurney out of the father's sight. Daniel could imagine the boy walking and laughing; but never again. He felt his throat constrict with the strain of holding back his emotions as he listened to the father's final words.

Once at home, Daniel scolded himself. He had seen tragedy before. Never before did his patients overwhelm him with so much grief. Daniel climbed into the shower and stood under the running water. He hoped his lingering under the water would wash away the horrible vision of a family lost forever just because they followed the wrong road. He kept wondering why the parents didn't consult the map. The one thing that could have put them on the right path.

Walking to the kitchen after a shower he poured himself a glass of milk. Searching his cabinets for something to satisfy his ravenous hunger, he found a box of crackers and a jar of peanut butter; not what he wanted, but good enough. He really wanted something to ease the pain in his heart and the horror from his memory. Sitting at the dining table with only the moon for light, Daniel said out loud, "Dear God, My Father," he muttered. The words comforted his hurting soul. His thoughts returned to the confession of the father.

"I didn't see the wall; it was . . . invisible." The father moaned.

"Our baby begged me and his mother to stop fighting. He didn't understand we were arguing about the best way to resolve our dilemma. She took him out of his seat to comfort him."

Daniel thought about his efforts to comfort Barbara. Had they ended up similar to this family? Daniel could not erase the father's last words from his memory. "When we hit the wall, my son's body was crushed between the dashboard and his mother. She screamed and held him up close to her, then the front of the car folded on top of her. I reached for them but couldn't touch them. I couldn't understand why? It was a mistake made in the dark."

Daniel knew the man needed to explain, understand and find forgiveness all in the one statement. The memory invaded Daniel's mind beyond the point of sanity. The mangled bodies were tragic but not a personal bother to a well-seasoned intern. Daniel had seen worse tragedies. This tragedy pierced his heart as none other. It lingered in his mind and made his heart ache. Although he didn't want to admit it, he knew why this tragedy impacted his heart. Even now in his own bed, it continued to haunt him. He couldn't shake the memory of the spattering of a glowing orange slime over the bodies.

After much tossing and turning, Daniel climbed out of bed and tried to read. The words didn't make sense to him so he rose and paced around his bedroom. He sat down on the edge of the couch, bowed his head and confessed, *I need to know why. Is this a vision? A message? What? Why? What do I do with it?*

A strange peace settled over him as the Holy Spirit wrote upon his mind exactly what he was to do. He needed to see Barbara even though it was the middle of the night.

The knock on her door at two in the morning surprised Barbara. She yawned and stretched while the knocking continued. When she reached the door, she looked out the peephole and saw Daniel. She opened the door and turned her face away from him to wipe the sleep from her face.

"Getting off work?" She asked him with a sleepy yawn and a raking of the fingers through her baby fine hair that stood at attention in the middle of her head like a Mohawk haircut.

"No, couldn't sleep. I'm sorry to bother you. I had a horrific night at the ER. I needed to be with someone, and I wanted that someone to be you," Daniel said. "I think I can understand the temptation to drink. I want to wipe away the memory of last night," Daniel began his confession to her.

"What happened?"

"I can't get the scene of an accident out of my mind. Every time I close my eyes, I see it."

Barbara slipped her arm through his. "I'm sorry."

She felt grateful for her last minute decision to skip the Valium for the night. She needed to break the drug habit and endure the same as her fellow patients at the psych meeting. This may be a good start. It had been hard to go to sleep without it, but now she could give her full attention to Daniel.

He shook his head and continued talking, "It was bad enough to see that kid and his mother. Death claimed them so they felt no pain, but that poor father." Daniel stopped talking.

Barbara noticed a mist building in his eyes. "Did the father live?"

"No, he died a couple hours later. Probably a blessing. He suffered a great deal in those last hours, both physically and mentally. He lived long enough to tell us about the accident. He needed to confess. I guess that's the same thing I need."

"What?" Barbara asked.

"I need to tell you not only what I saw but how I keep thinking about it. It's driving me crazy."

"I'm no stranger to crazy, so I guess you came to the right place."

The corner of his mouth turned up in a grin, "I know, that's why I'm here."

"Okay, tell me why you think you're joining me in the crazy club."

Hesitant at first, Daniel spoke, "There was orange slime spattered over the bodies."

Barbara sat up and looked at Daniel, "Where did it come from?"

"I don't know. I do know that no one else saw it."

Barbara stood up as if coming to attention. She moaned and paced around the apartment.

"What's wrong with you?" Daniel asked.

Barbara grabbed a book. "Like this?" She asked him.

"Like what?"

"The orange slime. . . did it look like that?" Barbara pointed to the book as she danced from one foot to the other.

"What are you doing?" Daniel set the book down and put his hands on her shoulders. Barbara started crying. "Can't you see it on the book?"

"No, I see nothing but a book. What do you see?" Daniel asked.

"I see a book covered in orange slime," Barbara whispered as she settled onto the couch. She pulled her hands through her hair.

"What's going on Daniel?"

He sat down beside her and took her hand in his. "I don't know."

After a few moments of silence, Barbara spoke up. "I think we need to talk about it, you see orange slime on dead bodies, and I see it on imaginary dead bodies and books."

Daniel nodded his head then rested it on the top of Barbara's head. "What do you mean imaginary bodies?"

"I learned in my psyche group there was no body in my apartment. I shot a man but there was no one there but me."

Daniel held her tight. "Now I know why I came here. There's more to this than being crazy."

"Explain."

"It's not our imaginations. What I saw on that family tonight is more than a coincidence."

"What do you think it means?" Barbara pondered.

Daniel stroked her gently. "A spiritual battle! It appears it's our battle not yours alone."

"I don't understand."

"Do you still study your Bible like you did when you thought you were going to be a Bible teacher? "Daniel asked.

"No."

She turned her eyes from his view and admitted, "I'm not sure I believe it anymore. I don't study." Barbara answered as passion grew in her voice, "I don't believe God is real. He's just a creation to keep people in line. I wanted to be His servant, and then when I did the right thing, I was mocked and put in my place. . ."

Barbara stopped talking, but her mouth remained open.

"And?" Daniel encouraged.

She turned and looked at him as if she had forgotten he was in the room with her. "Sorry, I was thinking about the meeting I had with Mr. McCord. Daniel, you've seen terrible things in the ER before, why did this one have the orange and not the others?"

"I wondered that too. I remember they came in after a lull in emergency room patients. I went to the lounge and got a soda. I had taken my first drink of it when I thought about me and you as a family." Daniel ducked his head as he said the words. "I do that often, you know, think about you as my wife and how we will build a life together. When I saw the bodies, I thought of us. What if we started a family and then something dreadful happened? That's when I saw the orange slime."

Barbara tilted her head, "You think about us? Often?"

Daniel nodded but felt too much embarrassment to look at her.

"I do too."

"Really?" Daniel couldn't believe his ears. "How do you think of us?"

"Let's just say it isn't exactly the same as your thoughts."

"I thought so. Since I embarrassed myself, my thoughts were focused on you then I saw the orange slime."

"What do you think it was?"

"My imagination, or exhaustion. I think I saw it because you were on my mind." Daniel answered.

Barbara sighed, "What are we going to do?"

"We are both in a state of tired, I'm going home and get some sleep." Daniel answered as he headed toward the door, still holding her hand.

Barbara agreed. She moved her head when he started to kiss her. He laughed and kissed her on the cheek. "Silly girl," he said. She missed his kiss with her awkwardness. He didn't try again. He winked and headed toward the door.

After he left, Barbara picked up the book. It came open and the inside pages were pristine. She sat down and started reading. It made sense. She turned a page and a slip of paper fell out.

She recognized her mother's handwriting. She opened it up and saw a reference to Proverbs 31. "Oh, mother, I don't need to read about shopping and washing clothes and cooking breakfast." Before she closed it, she saw the sentence Merilee had written below the biblical reference, "The heart of her husband trusts her."

I'll ask her about that next time I see her. Closing the book, she swallowed the rest of her milk. Pondering the statement, she thought, *If I want Daniel to trust me, it may be time to tell him what the dragon did in my apartment that night.*

The next morning Barbara struggled to wake up. She realized the night visitation by Daniel left her short a couple hours of sleep.

Sharon came into her room. "What's up, Chap?" She asked.

"Tired to the max."

"Worried, thinking, what?"

"All of the above," Barbara said. "I feel like there's someone else living in my skin with me."

"That's weird, why?" Sharon muttered.

"Because I'm confused. Why am I seeing strange things and going to a psyche class? Why did a judge order me to go to those meetings? I feel like everybody knows my story but me." Barbara answered.

"Quit going to those women's lib meetings. They mess with your head." Sharon said in a flat tone.

"Why would they not let me major in religion?"

"Girl, not only are your thoughts all over the place, you're still moaning over something that wasn't that big a deal when it happened three years ago. Get over it."

"You make it sound easy."

"It is, concentrate on your new career as a nurse. Just think we will be graduating at the end of this year, Daniel will start his residency and we can begin living an adult life."

"I want more," Barbara argued.

"Of course you do. You want power over your own life. That ain't gonna happen. Look at where my dad is. He had money, prestige and power." Sharon said.

"Do you think that's what I want?"

"Sure, that's why you got involved in those meetings."

"You remember the meeting about power?" Barbara chuckled.

"Yea. The speaker said we should use sex to get power," Sharon mocked and gave Barbara a long look. "It still sounds stupid."

"Yeah, I want to spit in the face of those people who told me I couldn't take religion because I'm a girl."

"So you going to have sex with Mr. McCord?" Sharon said sarcastically.

"Eww, no." Barbara grimaced. "That's not an answer."

"I agree. And you don't have a problem!" Sharon chastised Barbara. "You have an inflated ego."

"You don't know, you've never been shamed," Barbara retorted.

Sharon glared at Barbara with downcast eyes. "That's a stupid statement too, I'm an authority on shame. You weren't shamed, and sex is not an instrument of power over another, that's called bullying. Barbara, I'm going to tell you the truth, even though you don't want to hear it." Sharon said and began a lecture.

"Sex is the symbol of a committed relationship between a man and a woman for a lifetime and you know it! It is not power or recreation! So quit listening to those people who are doing all they can to destroy the most beautiful gift God gave to mankind when it is used properly."

Barbara had never heard Sharon speak so bluntly. It took her by surprise.

"I try to keep my opinions to myself. Now I'm going to tell you the truth about that women's lib group, their goal is to destroy the family by destroying the God-given role of women."

"What is that role? "Barbara stopped and stared at Sharon waiting for an answer.

"You want to know what that role is? Just look at yourself, you are pushing Daniel away so you can be 'an independent woman' when he is the best thing that has happened to you and his love makes you independent, but you are too blinded by vengeance to see it." Sharon reprimanded. "He won't wait forever and you'll lose the most valuable gift God has given you. A husband to love you even as Christ loves you."

Barbara sat down, "I need to think about this."

"You think too much; you mull over the things Mr. McCord said to you. He's living in your heart and tromping all over your soul." Sharon said as she walked over and took Barbara's hand. "Your need for vengeance is destroying you and you don't even know it."

Barbara leaned in to Sharon and hugged her. "You're right. I don't know how to stop it. I try to fight the crazy ideas but I'm a wimp," Barbara moaned. "I should've tried to stop Teresa. My tongue tied, when she told me she practiced witchcraft."

Barbara stopped talking and shook her head and grimaced. She held her head as if in terrible pain. She squealed, "Go away."

"Barbara, look at me!" Sharon said with loud affirmation. Barbara complied.

Staring into Barbara's eyes, Sharon listened as Barbara spoke strange words in a deep monotone voice, "A *work came into my mind with great stealth. It was a spirit that passed by my face; the hair of my flesh bristled up. It stood still, but I could not discern its appearance; a form was before my eyes; There was silence, then I heard a voice, 'Can you stand just before God?'*"

Sharon stepped back, "Barbara? Is that you?" She said with a trembling voice.

"No, my name is Jorkphat." Came the words from Barbara's mouth.

"Scared? Little girl?" The words came from Barbara's mouth but not in Barbara's voice. "Call now, see if anyone will answer you. Man is born for trouble."

Sharon backed as far away from Barbara's body as possible. Realizing she faced an evil spirit, her legs became weak like they were made of wax. She remembered Michael's instructions to use scripture. She stood up and repeated the only verse she could remember from her recent study of second Peter. "*God is not slow as some consider slowness but He is patient wanting that none should perish.*"

With the words Barbara put her hands over her ears, shook her head, then looked at Sharon again and with a smirk continued, "*Against his angels He charges error, so how much more those who dwell in houses of clay?*"

Sharon stood stunned for a few minutes. She silently asked the Holy Spirit to reveal the meaning to her. A vision flashed across her mind. An angel stood over a courtroom. In that courtroom stood Barbara before God the Judge. He was stern as He studied the file of offenses Barbara had committed. A man stepped up behind Barbara before God spoke, held up his pierced hands and said, "She's mine." God slammed the gavel and announced, "Forgiven!"

Sharon smiled. She understood what the demon was doing. He was making an accusation against God's children using God's words.

The spirit of deception in Barbara complained. "God gave His Spirit to humans when angels should have received it."

She stood firmer, using her sword to fight this spirit with a fierce swash across him with words from Peter. "*For if God did not spare angels when they sinned, but cast them into hell and committed them to pits of darkness, reserved for judgment: and did not spare the ancient world;*" Sharon used her sword to make the final jab, "*then the Lord knows how to rescue the godly from temptation and to keep the unrighteous under punishment for the day of judgmen*t."

A terrifying scream released from Barbara's mouth which turned into a whimpering of fear. "Sharon!" She cried.

"It's okay, honey, He's gone. I told him his future.

Trembling Barbara asked, "Did you . . . see him?"

Sharon nodded and put her arm around Barbara. With a deep sigh she said, "We need to prepare for battle."

22

The First Battle

> Thus says the Lord, "What injustice
> did your fathers find in Me, that they
> went far from Me and walked after
> emptiness and became empty.
>
> ---Jeremiah 2:5(NASB)

WITH ONLY BLACKNESS around her, Barbara couldn't see the owner of the voice. It didn't matter, she knew the owner. As a result, she clenched her teeth.

"What do'ya want?" Turning her head from side to side she could taste the bile of fear rising in her throat.

"Why Barbara, I'm your best friend," The voice sang.

"If you're my best friend, then you won't mind telling me your name." Barbara announced.

"Smart girl; Nisroch told me you wouldn't be an easy conquest."

"Nisroch? The dragon at my family farm. The one that cut ---?" Barbara choked as she attempted to stand.

"Finish your statement, I love to hear it," The voice cooed.

"No!"

"Then I will; the dragon who cut your friend Teresa open from stem to stern."

"Why? Why did you kill her?" Barbara screamed out. She felt a pool of sweat collecting in the nape of her throat.

The voice ignored her question and proceeded on with his enticement.

"You call him a dragon. I call him master."

Barbara looked up as she sensed the voice coming toward her. She saw the now familiar orange glow approaching. It changed from a star shaped blob to the form of a man. Upon his approach, she could see an orange suit, orange fedora, and a turquoise blue tie. He carried a cane and his orange shoes had blue spats. His face came into view. His strange dark eyes exuded a yellow glow revealing a smooth almost feminine skin. His facial appearance presented a human face with an illusion of perfection, the same way an actor in a film is made up to cover human flaws.

"Master?" She questioned while planting her feet firmly in place. She would not let him see any signs of her fear or anxiety.

"He's my boss. He sent me after you."

"After me?"

"Yes, I am to train you."

"Train me for what?" Barbara sneered, not really wanting an answer, she changed the subject.

"What's your name?"

"You know my name, we met in your drunken stupor. My name is Jorkphat."

"Jerk Fat. You sound like your proud of that name."

"I am. It means 'Sky of God, and it's pronounced Jorgpha.'"

"It's too hard to say. I'll call you Jerk Fat," Barbara said with a silly and condescending grin.

"No, that name stinks and has no class."

"Okay, Jerk Fat, what do you want? I'm not afraid of you."

With a scowl he came and stood over Barbara almost touching her body, he growled, "You have no idea what it means to insult me."

Barbara stumbled back and hit a wall. Still Jerk Fat kept coming pushing the breath from her. She extended her hands to shove back, yet she didn't connect with anything solid. The pressure on her chest increased and something stung her arms

"What are you doing?" She screamed, trying to contain the growing terror she felt.

He said nothing. She let her body go limp and slip away from his invisible grip. It didn't help, even with the disappearance of the orange form she could still feel the pressure and the stinging increase. Tossing her head from side to side she attempted to free herself from his bondage and get away from his acrid breath. She raised her arms to her head and started screaming letting all the fear come rolling out from the pit of her stomach to the megaphone of her mouth. The sound panicked her, still she could not stop. The blackness enveloped her. She heard a thump as she fell on something solid. In the distance a sound penetrated her own screaming. A distant voice reached her ears. It built within her a strength to press toward it. Suddenly, she felt the weight of Jorkphat on her chest again bashing the air from her lungs.

She knew the unseen orange man engaged her in hand to hand combat. How could she fight an orange cloud that didn't even penetrate the darkness surrounding her hateful adversary.

The encouraging voice drifted though the one-sided massacre to her ears again. Turning her face toward the sound of safety she recognized a refuge, her shelter. The place she needs to go, if only she can reach it. At the same moment an agonizing pain ripped through her skull. She turned back toward the smell of Jorkphat. She slumped in submission, with no escape.

From the pounding in her head she felt an idea rising. Concentrating all her attention on this shred of hope, she heard the voice of her daddy in her mind saying, Sing, just sing praise."

Her daddy's oft told fairy tale about his escape from Phillip Donnigan made her smile. Jorkphat administered another slamming blow to her head. "You have nothing to smile about." He screeched at her. She didn't listen to Jorkphat. She listened to the memory of her Daddy's story, "It's a simple act, but the enemy cannot tolerate praise or sacrifice to the Holy One."

How can one sing when pain lashes out at every body cell? She cleared her throat and let a few raspy notes come out. Jorkphat stopped her, but not before she heard him gasp. He's afraid of praise songs. The only song of praise coming to her battered mind came out in garbled tones as her body gave way to the encroaching finality of death.

She saw an orange fist, with knobby knuckles and pointed nails like a claw come at her. Slamming into her solar plexus she grunted and doubled over. The clawed hand remained in front of her face. She could see nothing else. The hand grew and curled into a fist. Barbara tried again. She took a deep breath and released all the sound she could with the limited air in her lungs, "Yeeee ua." The claw kept coming, and she knew if it touched her she would be. . . She really didn't know what would happen. Her intuition told her she would be gone either in mind or body, or both. Trying again she forced the air from her lungs and cried out again. "Yees. . .u. ..a" Her voice grew stronger, she felt hope.

Taking a deep breath, she put all she had into it, "Yeesus Luv mew."

"The clawed hand shrunk and moved back. She kept the momentum and did it again, "Yeesus Luv Me!" It took all her strength but she didn't take a breath before she shouted out, "Bi -bla tell mew."

The hand returned to a normal size and there stood Jerk Fat behind it. She pulled up her shoulders in spite of ripping pain from her legs to her head, "Yesus Love Me I know Bible tell me so."

She kept singing and watching the orange man shrink and fade. His words became more muffled and distant. In the place of his growling commands, Barbara heard another voice, a loving voice, the voice of Daniel, he sang with her. Then he stopped singing and spoke, "Jesus Loves You and so do I." She heard the voice of Daniel. Jerk Fat no longer occupied her space. She opened her eyes and saw Daniel over her with Sharon. They were both singing and crying.

She and Daniel planned to have a date this afternoon. Jerk Fat showed up uninvited. "Bad dae I am."

Sharon heard thumps and bumps in Barbara's room. She ran to check out the commotion. When she opened the door a shirt swirled onto her head. The room danced with swirling clothes and various other objects. Barbara stood up against the wall with a look of terror on her face. Sharon quickly closed the door and called Daniel.

"Barbara, Barbara," Daniel shouted while he wrestled with her right hand holding an open pair of scissors. She scraped the blades deep into her forearm flesh. With Daniel holding her arms tight, Sharon managed to get the scissors with only a minor injury to herself. Daniel let go of her arms. She continued to fight and pull out several fist full of hair while letting out a blood curdling scream.

Finally, she let go of her hair and slumped to the floor against the wall. Her body slid down to the floor like a rag doll. Sharon kneeled beside her. Barbara slung her head from side to side. At one point it appeared someone or something slammed her head into the floor. Daniel held her close and noticed one of her arms spurting blood with each heartbeat.

"Sharon, hand me my medical bag, quick." Daniel exclaimed as he held his hand tight around her arm.

"She's cut an artery; we've got to hurry." Sharon opened the bag and pulled out scissors, thread and a needle. She poured alcohol over it, threaded it and handed it to Daniel. They only had seconds to get the bleeding stopped.

Barbara moaned and tried to speak while he worked. Her body became more limp due to the loss of blood. Daniel worked swiftly. She sounded as if she had no tongue. Her words didn't make sense.

"She's trying to say something." Daniel and Sharon listened as Barbara continued to groan and writhe.

"She trying to say Jesus," They both said "Jesus." Barbara's garbled language took on meaning.

"She's trying to sing, 'Jesus Loves Me' Sharon noted.

They sang with her. Daniel broke the song and said, "I love you too." At that declaration, she opened her eyes and grabbed Daniel by the neck. He pulled her arms away from him.

Daniel dressed the sutured artery while Sharon pulled clumps of hair from her fists.

"Your palms are bleeding," Sharon groaned.

Daniel took a quick look. "Shallow, will be painful but not threatening. As he bandaged the arm, Sharon remarked, "Good job for an intern." He chuckled and responded, "Emergency room experience."

"God equips His servants for His work." Sharon mused. Then her thoughts focused back on the self-inflicted wounds of Barbara. At least only one proved life-threatening.

"Why would she do this?" Sharon asked Daniel. He shrugged his shoulders and with a trembling voice answered. "I don't know."

Sharon picked up Barbara's bloody hand. "My dear friend, what is happening to you?" Suddenly Barbara's eyes opened and she sat up alert, "Jerk Fat!" She screamed. The she lay her head back down again still in a stupor.

"Have you called Michael?" Daniel asked Sharon.

"No. But I will."

He arrived in a few minutes. "What's happening?" He looked at Daniel for an answer. Daniel held up the bandaged arm to show Michael the extent of her injury.

"Jerk Fat!" She said again.

"Do you know what she's saying?" Sharon looked at Michael.

"Yeah, I'm afraid I do."

"Care to let us in on the plot?" Daniel implored.

Michael shook his head and ran his fingers through his hair. He turned back toward Sharon. "Let's get her to bed," he said.

Daniel carried her toward the bedroom. Sharon spoke up, "Put her in my bed."

"What's wrong in there?" Michael and Daniel both asked.

"Go look," Sharon pointed to the room.

The two men entered. "Did she throw all this stuff around?" Daniel implored Sharon. She nodded and shut the door behind them.

"I don't want her convulsing like she did the last time, let's get her some water." Daniel instructed Sharon.

Barbara stirred and muttered, "Jerk Fat. Beat me."

Daniel picked up her hand and kissed it. "My sweet girl, what is. . ."

Michael interrupted, "The demon."

The rest of the group looked at Michael. "How'd you know?" Daniel asked raising his voice.

"I recognize his methods of torture because I've seen him too."

"Now what?" Daniel demanded.

"Barbara said you saw people covered in orange slime in the ER." Michael addressed Daniel.

"Yeah, I did."

"You saw the demon too."

"Why would he reveal himself to me?"

"He wants you to know he has control of her. Your vision proved he could infiltrate your mind too."

Daniel moaned, "Can it get to any of us?"

Barbara heard Daniel's question and struggled to answer him, "Yh know."

Since they couldn't understand her, no one addressed her statement, but tried to encourage her. Sharon came over and put a cold washrag on her neck to cool her down. "It's okay, darlin, we're not going to leave you."

With Sharon's statement, Barbara relaxed and didn't try to talk anymore. She closed her eyes and listened to their conversation. Sharon related the battle she had with the demon to the two men.

"We're all in this battle," Michael muttered.

"Why Barbara?" Daniel moaned. She looked at him when she felt his touch. She smiled.

Michael continued, "Barbara is most susceptible to his deception since she's rebelling, but he can come after any of us."

Barbara looked around at her faithful friends. She saw her bandaged arm. She looked at Daniel. With drooping eyes, she said, "Jer Fat. Pease believe."

"I do," Daniel whispered. He could feel her body temperature rising.

Barbara spoke up, "Give water and time," then she interjected, "food!. " Her speech slowly returning to normal.

"That has to be good news." Daniel took her hand and held it. Michael stepped away and went into the other room. He started out the front door. Sharon chased after him. "Will you stay, please?" She pleaded with Michael.

"Thanks, but I've another mission to complete."

Sharon nodded her head. "I trust you, but know I'll miss you." She shouted after him.

"The feeling's mutual." He waved good bye. Sharon returned to the apartment and went into the kitchen to prepare food."

"Tell me how this. . . horror show started?" Barbara asked between gulps of food. She stuffed her mouth full and chewed with the ferocity of a grinding machine.

Sharon answered, "The day we went to that rally."

"No, it actually started with Mr. McCord." Daniel countered.

"Truth is, it started before I met any of you. It started in my hometown."

"What happened there, I mean other than a bomb." Daniel caught his statement before the obvious answer.

"It started when I was fourteen. I've told you the story about how I wanted to go into special service." Barbara looked at her friends. They nodded. "That's when my anger started building"

"So you took that anger to women's lib meetings?" Daniel queried.

"No, the meetings found me. That must have been part of Jerk Fat's plan."

"So what about Mr. McCord?" Sharon asked.

"I think he's one part of the puzzle."

"What are you going to do now?" Daniel asked her as he rose to refill his water glass.

Barbara spoke with a more serious tone, "I don't know. The things that happen and words spoke still hurt my spirit."

"Why did it hurt you so bad?" Daniel asked.

"See you're a man; you can't understand what a woman thinks or feels or even what she has to go through. You want a woman by your side to look pretty in public, be available for sex and cook a hot meal. You men can't even pay us a decent wage." Barbara stood up as she ranted, at least for a little while. Her weak body wouldn't hold her up. Daniel caught her as she melted toward the floor.

"Sit down, and finish eating. You're too weak to give any rants tonight," he lectured.

Barbara didn't argue with him. She still felt hungry. The three of them sat quietly for a while. Barbara broke the silence after she finished her meal

"Daniel, how does a demon take over a person, especially a Christian and make me get angry at my friends like I just did?" She asked.

Daniel choked a bit at the question, "Do I look like a theologian?"

Barbara smiled at him, "You're a doctor, you should know the body. How can a demon invade a human body?

How can he physically hurt me and cut me and make me pull out my hair?"

Daniel pondered the question. Then he thoughtfully said, "I don't know. Most often those unexplained things are thrown into the general category of mental illness. There is a difference between a true mental illness and the unexplained.

"Maybe we should become theologians," Sharon added.

"That's why I wanted to get a religion degree, so I would be considered a reliable source." Barbara stated with emphasis on reliable.

Daniel jumped at her comment, "You're right. If it's supernatural, then the answer is supernatural."

Sharon set up a place in the living room for each of them to have a comfortable seat, allowing for Barbara's stitched up arm.

"You don't have to fuss over me so." Barbara argued.

"I know but I don't' want any more surprises. We're too close to graduation for you to break a stitch."

"Why do you think that demon happened to me?" Barbara pondered. About the time she made the statement the front door opened and Michael came in with her parents following him. Barbara started to get up but Sharon pushed on her shoulder and pushed her back down.

Merilee came over and hugged Barbara on one side while Buster gave her a kiss on the other. Then she squealed when she saw her brothers come in behind them. After the greetings, the group gathered around the table.

Merilee broached the unspoken topic, "I want to know what's going on?"

Barbara stared at her mother. "What makes you think something going on?" She smiled.

Merilee returned Barbara's smile, "don't try to hide it from your mother, sweetie, we have extra help for our children. A birdie sent from the Lord tells us."

"I've been thinking a lot about what happened. Daddy, I did battle with the demon and won. I won it by singing."

Merilee rose and pulled Barbara's collar back exposing her neck and shoulder. She touched Barbara's shoulder.

"What are you doing?" Barbara asked her mother.

"Looking for the place where that mask pricked you. Remember?"

Do you think the demon entered me then?"

"It's a possibility, he saw your vulnerability and took advantage." Merilee said.

Barbara sat back, "Well, I'll be a monkey's uncle. I was scared, depressed and... vulnerable."

"So when Mr. McCord made the comment to you about being a pastor's wife, your demon became active." Buster explained.

"I think you are on to something, but that's not when he became active," Barbara said to the group.

"So when did he become active?" Sharon asked.

"The night Mr. McCord broke into our apartment."

23

The Trap of Beauty

Can a virgin forget her ornaments, or
a bride her attire? Yet My people have
forgotten Me days without number.

---Jeremiah 2:32(NASB)

PAPS WASN'T AN old man, he was an old soldier. Military service aged his body beyond his years. His military career started at the tender age of fifteen in the World War II Pacific theater and ended at the age of forty-seven in Vietnam.

After the Japanese attack on Pearl Harbor December 7, 1941, he and many other young boys lied about their age in order to join the military. He lied about his age again when he signed up for his second tour of duty in April 1968. He joined the military again after the Tet offensive in Vietnam. During his last year of service, he trudged through the swamps of the Mekong Delta. There a North Vietnamese booby trap sliced off both of his legs in a second.

Michael entered his hospital room and saw Paps sitting up eating.

"Looks like you're doing better." Michael said to him.

"Compared to last night? Yeah!"

"Any idea what happened?"

"Doc will be in soon. If you have time to stay, we'll find out together," Paps encouraged Michael.

Michael sat down and told Paps about Barbara and the demon cutting her. Paps shook his head. "That sweet girl shouldn't have to be fighting that kind of battle."

"I agree. But we both know she's going to fight the same battle we did." Michael mused.

"Doesn't make it any easier to watch."

Paps stopped eating and stared out the window for a moment. Michael interrupted his solace, "What 'cha thinkin'?"

"I don't know. I guess I think only men should do things like that, we're supposed to protect our women folk, it's the way God made us. It's why we go to battle."

Michael guffawed.

"What are you laughing at?" Paps said as he stared at Michael.

"You're so right, and yet that's the very thing causing her problems."

"What do'ya mean?"

"The difference in the sexes."

Paps smiled, "Yeah, she's a bit of a tiger when it comes to men. So Mr. Guardian what are doing for her?"

Michael shook his head, "Watching, praying."

Paps leaned his head back and sighed, "If only we could tell her."

"You know we can't. She's not ready yet. Besides she has to find out for herself. I'm not sure she would believe me and you. If she discovers on her own. . . ." "Then she will know. . . first-hand." Paps finished the statement.

"The journey toward that knowledge is so tenuous and dangerous."

Paps pushed his tray of food away, half-eaten.

"What's wrong Paps, I've never saw you turn down food."

"I know; but I don't feel so good," Paps said as he sunk into the bed.

"He suffers from septicemia," The doctor explained to Michael as the medical crew worked on inserting IV's. "That means he has an infection in his whole body." The doctor stopped talking and pointed to Paps legs. "It's always been local. I'm not sure he's going to be able to fight it off this time."

Michael looked at the flat sheet below Paps knees. He remembered the night Paps lost those legs. A volley of bullets zinged past them when Paps hit the booby trap. It ripped both legs off in a second. Michael pulled their belts around the stumps, slung Paps over his shoulders and ran. The adrenaline pumping through his body moved his legs with inhuman speed. He carried Paps out of the jungle to the waiting Huey helicopter, Paps kept shooting. It took both of them to get out, carried by an angel and chased by a dragon.

"How long will he stay in the hospital?"

"Until his body gives out or he recovers," The doctor answered.

"You mean. . ."

"His body is getting tired. This man has proven himself a fighter over and over. He may just be tired of fighting."

Michael nodded, "That he is!"

Michael went back into Paps room, sat down beside his bed and looked at his friend. War made the two men more than friends. They had been to hell and back and survived it together. They shared nightmares even though they were both given a second-chance at life. That common moment of terror and escape, bound them for a lifetime. Michael felt a tear trickle down his cheek. "I'm not ready to give you up buddy." He said to his sleeping friend.

Paps heard Michael but feigned sleep. With his face turned away from Michael, he could hide the tears. He was ready to go home with the Lord, and be free from the pain and night terrors. No, his tears were for Michael, all the other guys, Barbara, and Patti. The he realized the task of giving the message to Barbara belonged to him. He couldn't leave this world until he delivered it.

Paps jerked toward Michael. "I've got to tell her."

"Are you sure?"

Paps gasped for his breath. "Yes, It's time."

"We decided she wasn't ready to hear it.

"I know, but it's my mission to tell her before I croak. Can you bring her here?"

"I'll sure do my best. In the meantime, we better both be praying, it's not going to be easy. What about Patti?" Michael softened his voice when he said the name.

"I don't know. Is there any hope?"

"There's always hope," Michael answered his old friend. "In Christ there is always hope."

Barbara recalled how her friends gasped out loud when she revealed the intruder was Mr. McCord, they laughed in disbelief.

"Why would he break into your apartment?" Their argument made sense, but now in retrospect she felt more confused. Did she really see him? After all, years have passed since it happened and she has been holding on to this bit of information secretly during that time. What could his motive possibly be?

She didn't reveal all the details of the intruder's activities to her friends. She feared their reactions, if they knew it all. The questions lingered in her mind and soul since that night, how could she share something she didn't understand. She groaned and sat down on the edge of her bed. At that moment, her feet bumped something.

She looked down and saw the box Teresa's mother had given her. How long has that been there? She took the time to trace it back to the day of Teresa's death. More than two years had passed since that dreadful night when she placed the box under the bed and forgot about it.

Pulling the dusty box out she determined to donate it somewhere. The clothes would be out of style by now and she and Teresa didn't share the same taste. She really didn't want the clothes then or now. Curiosity led her to open the box. There would surely be some comic relief in the styles. However, when she spread the dresses out on the bed, she gasped at the beauty of the two dresses.

Never had a piece of clothing appeared so exquisite. Holding the most magnificent of the two dresses in front of her she danced around the room. Stopping to look in the mirror. The crimson velvet dress flowed to a short train, with off-the-shoulders long sleeves. The petal shaped ruffle around the bottom of the skirt drew her attention and amazed her. It rested on the floor like a flower blossom. Barbara had never seen anything so beautiful before in her life. She couldn't help herself, she slipped it on. It fit. She stood straighter with a sense of power and importance. She glanced at the open box and realized it contained more treasure. She dove into it and found a diamond necklace that fit the dress neckline perfectly.

After adorning her body with the jewelry, she admired the dress and twirled around like a dancing princess. *Where did Teresa wear this? Where would she ever wear something so elegant?* Barbara picked up one of the small boxes and saw a necklace that would have cost a full week's salary. A brilliant gold chain held a stone with streams of fine gold threads hung from it. Behind the necklace in the exquisite box lay an embossed scripted note, *Stone of the higher self and of our spirit guides! Blazing like a comet, this cabochon of clear, quartz crystal (associated with all the body's chakra centers!) Trails a tail of fine, golden chains all in fourteen karat gold.*

Barbara slipped it over her head and let it hang delicately between her breasts. She went to the full-length mirror and gazed upon herself. Her heart grew with pride as she observed her own beauty. Even the dark circles under her eyes presented a smoky mysterious look. The mirror revealed a goddess staring back at her. The reflection captivated her gaze. A little tune she learned at the women's lib meetings escaped from her lips, "I am woman, hear me roar."

Barbara continued to sing the song until it reached a fever pitch and she belted it out with enthusiasm. As she sang, she pulled each little box out to find high quality pieces of jewelry, each with their own description in fine embossed paper and words that flowed with intensity. A bright orange and blue box caught her eye. She opened it.

On the cover, in orange lettering outlined in blue, it read, "ENTER THE DRAGON."

The impressive bracelet revealed brown diamonds surrounding a center cluster of topaz gems, all in a serpentine shape which wrapped around her wrist. It sparkled with the spectacular beauty of encrusted diamonds along both sides.

The paper in the box presented a simple message, *A symbol of good fortune blazes in fiery scales of bright orange rubies and diamonds.* This piece included a price tag. Barbara pulled the price tag up and looked at it. It read, "Your soul!"

Barbara jerked and dropped the box when she read the words on the tag. With a racing heart she looked at herself in the mirror. Her reflection calmed her. She had to admit the dress happened to be stunning, and it made the diamonds in the dragon bracelet sparkle. She kept looking at her reflection noticing she had changed to a shapelier, sculpted perfect woman. The jasmine smell of the dress wafted up to her nostrils. She inhaled deeply. *This can't be bad, if it makes me look this good.*

Jorkphat watched Barbara as she admired herself. He smiled. Nisroch stood beside him. "Good move," he said to Jorkphat. "In spite of that vile little exercise in the book of oracles, she will soon be ready. How are you going to get her there?"

"I have a devious plan using one of our own." Jorkphat told Nisroch.

That night restful sleep would not come to Barbara; she tossed and turned. Jorkphat entered her sub-conscience and gave her a most pleasant dream of a handsome man waiting to rescue and care for her. He made sure she felt secure in her dream. He also gave her a vision of her wedding dress, a crimson red flowing gown with a diamond necklace and a perfect bracelet in the image of himself, her bridegroom.

24

Pap's Story

The words of his mouth are wickedness and deceit; He has ceased to be wise and to do good. He plans wickedness upon his bed; He sets himself on a path that is not good; He does not despise evil.

---salm 36:3-4(NASB)

THE PSYCHE MEETING day served as the highlight of Barbara's week. She sat in her usual place, but Pap's wheelchair space sat empty. Nurse Godfrey came in alone. As he started the meeting, he announced the group had fulfilled their obligations and the group would be disbanded. A sadness permeated the room. The last step would be their individual evaluations with Dr. Greenstein.

Once the completed evaluations are submitted the participants would receive credit for the class and a stipend.

"This ten-week course is now ended three years later." Godfrey snickered. The rest of the group laughed with him. "There will be a new group starting next week. You are all now qualified to lead a small group if you desire."

The final meeting turned into a party overshadowed by an unspoken fear of being alone again. Most of the men made arrangements to lead a new group of returning vets. Barbara sat next to Nurse Godfrey.

"What am I supposed to do now?" She whined.

"Nurse Young will send a letter to the judge who required your attendance as well as a letter to Dr. Greenstein," Nurse Godfrey informed her. "This has been an experiment in psychological treatment, she's the doctor overseeing the study."

"Oh."

"You do have an appointment set up for your exit interview tomorrow afternoon." Godfrey informed her.

"At least it will be over quickly." She responded. "By the way, I noticed Paps is not here," Barbara put forth the statement hoping for some information about him.

"He's suffering from an infection. He's in room 312 if you want to see him," Michael answered when he overheard Barbara' statement.

"Oh Paps," Barbara wailed when she saw the pale man wasting away in the hospital bed.

He reached out to her. "I'm good now that you're here."

He held her hand in both of his and took a deep breath, "I have to tell you something."

"Sounds serious," Barbara consented.

Paps pursed his lips in a tight grimace. "It's a matter of perspective."

Barbara didn't understand, but she sat down beside him on the bed.

"I was on the Mt. Olympus." Paps said and nodded his head.

Barbara had no idea what that meant. He had made that same statement in meetings several times. She continued to listen.

"I know. I saw. I was young, and scared out of my wits, but I know."

"Paps, I don't know what you're talking about."

Paps let go of her hand and wiped a tear from his face. "I couldn't stop it," he moaned.

"Stop what?"

"Any of it, and then it . . . it." Paps choked up. After a few minutes he continued.

"The dragon. . . I saw it. . . I know where it came from."

Barbara listened.

"Not symbolically. Literally," Paps warned.

Barbara nodded. "I know; I saw it too." She didn't tell him she saw a gathering of dragons at the witch's coven.

This wasn't new information. Why was Paps displaying such anxiety?

"Ya don't understand. What I saw in Nam, I saw around you."

"Paps, I wasn't in Nam."

"Yes, you were!"

Barbara looked at Michael for an explanation. "Do you understand?"

Michael nodded. "We both saw you while we were there.

"I don't remember being there?"

"No, we saw you while we were there, in a vision," Michael restated.

He shook his head. Barbara looked at Paps, hoping he would pick up the explanation. She noticed his face had no expression and his eyes were fixed and staring. She touched him. His cold skin told her his body had been vacated by his soul. She picked up his hand and held it. "Michael," She called to him in quiet repose. "He's gone."

Michael studied the form lying on the bed and walked toward him. He touched his body on the shoulder, "Oh, Paps, not now. I can't do this without you."

They both stood there looking at the empty shell of their old friend. "At least he's at peace. Look at his face," Michael said.

Barbara turned to Michael, "What do you mean, you saw me in a vision?"

"Not now, little one, not now."

Pap's memorial proved to reveal a life filled with as much mystery as love.

"Michael, where is Paps' family?" Nurse Young asked as he entered the restaurant where Paps' wake took place.

"As far as I know he didn't have a family," Michael reported

"He talked about his little girl often in group," Nurse Young countered.

"I know; she was the daughter of his true love He claimed the child even though he never had the opportunity to be a father to her. I'm not sure of the details." Michael related hoping the little tidbit of information would stop any further inquiry. In reality, Michael, knew every thread of Paps life, and for that reason, he protected his memory with a facade of ignorance.

Michael stood at the door and greeted each person coming in and making sure they signed the register. At the appointed time to begin, Michael walked toward the front of the room and called for everyone's attention.

"This is the time we tell our memories of Paps, who wants to go first?"

Sid sauntered up on the podium and told of some funny antics during their group meetings. Barbara knew he searched for antidotes because he didn't want to remember their friend in the solemn way they actually knew him. They knew there existed a sadness deep in Paps. In truth no one in this room actually knew the man, his history, his dreams, his hurts or his loves.

Barbara sat near the door to greet anyone who came in. Grateful for the job since it kept her out of the mainstream of conversation. A few of Paps old Navy buddies had come to the service. However, no other Vietnam Vets came, except those in the psych group. There were neighbors and friends gathered to celebrate a life well-lived. Where ever, he went, people who knew him loved him. It seemed that only Michael had any grasp on the real life of Anthony Patrick O'Bannon. Many spoke of the deceased, but when Michael started his speech the crowd hushed and listened.

"Paps O'Bannon, a man of incredible mystery. Each day I knew him a new life event revealed itself. Each time he would tell me a tale, he taught me a lesson. None of Paps words were ever spoken without depth of beauty or meaning. He lived for all seasons of life. All who knew him loved him well and all who thought they knew him, loved him still. To those lives he touched with grace and gospel, I lift my glass and say, 'Goodbye, dear friend, you will be missed.'"

The crowd cheered and raised their glasses. "To Paps O'Bannon a man of courage and love."

Barbara felt a tear trickle down her face. She wasn't the only one who loved him. As the audience swallowed their drink in memory of his life, a small voice approached Barbara from behind.

"Is this the wake for Patrick O'Bannon?"

Barbara turned and saw Patti. "Patti, so good to see you. Please sign the guest book."

Barbara watched the crowd while Patti wrote in the book, beside her name she wrote--daughter.

"I didn't know you were Paps daughter."

"Neither did he," Patti demurred.

Barbara raised an eyebrow at the comment,

"Okay, I need you to tell me what you mean. Paps didn't know you were his daughter, if that's so how do you know?" Barbara confronted the young woman.

She wiped her eyes and sniffled. "My grandmother raised me and when I reached fifteen she took me to see him. I started to run toward him, then she grabbed me and said, 'He must never know you exist.'"

"Why not?"

"Her explanation seemed strange at the time and now I wish I hadn't listened to her," Patti continued.

"What did she say?"

"She said, he's too sensitive. She explained to me that he thought I died with my mother. 'A greater love never existed than those two,' she said."

"I should think that would be reason to reveal yourself to him."

"I thought so too, but grandmamma said it would break his heart to know I lived and he had not cared for me all these years."

"Why didn't she let him know you were alive as a baby?"

"I asked her that and she explained he joined the army."

"I thought he served in the navy," Barbara retorted becoming a bit wary of Patti's elaborate story.

"He was. He finished his tour with the navy, and after my mother died, he rejoined in the army. That's how he ended up in Vietnam during my childhood."

"Gosh, I'm not sure I could have kept from telling him. I adore my daddy; I can't imagine living without him."

"I didn't. I made friends with him. He called me his little China doll." Patti sat down at a nearby table. She put her purse up on the table and pulled out a simple brooch. "It was my mother's. Paps gave it to her. I wore it one day, hoping he would recognize it."

Barbara smiled, "Did he?"

"If he did, he didn't speak of it."

"You never told him?" Barbara asked.

"No, I wanted to honor my mother's memory as my Grandmamma asked of me. Still I also wanted to know my father."

"Who did he think you were?"

"The librarian, a job I applied for so I could see him every day. He came there and read the newspaper. After he finished I would join him. He told me his topic of the day and ask for recommendations for books. Then he would invite me to the nearby coffee shop for my break."

"It's hard to imagine you never told him."

Barbara noticed Patti didn't seem upset.

"He told me about you. That's why I came to your barbecue party." Patti said as she nibbled on a snack and looked around the room.

Barbara's eyes enlarged, "What did he say?"

"He said, he saw you in a vision.'

Barbara's ears perked up. Maybe Patti knew the content of the vision. She responded hoping for more information.

"He mentioned that vision just before he died, do you know what the vision was?"

"Just that he saw you in Vietnam."

Barbara gulped, "Is that all?" She gave a sarcastic reply with a smirk.

"It does sound rather fantastic." Patti acknowledged.

Barbara leaned in close to Patti. "Patti, did he tell your grandmother the vision?"

Patti leaned back as if pulling away from Barbara.

"I don't know. Come to my house and ask Grandmamma yourself."

Barbara shrunk back, "I'm not sure I want to do that. Why would she tell me anything?"

"I understand, but if you don't come and talk to Grandmamma, then you may never know about Paps vision of you. What have you got to lose?" Patti encouraged Barbara to come.

She thought about it. She wanted to know all she could. Even though Michael could tell her, he wouldn't. This way she could get the story and maybe more information from two people.

"Okay, I'll come, when and where," she answered.

"Tomorrow night, can you meet me at the library around 8 p.m.?"

Barbara didn't know Jorkphat whispered curiosity into her mind.

"Good job, Jorkphat," Nisroch growled.

25

Visiting A Mansion

'Your dwelling is in the midst of deceit; Through deceit they refuse to know me, declares the LORD.

---Jeremiah 9:6(NASB)

SHARON CLAPPED AS Barbara twirled around in the red dress. "It's gorgeous. Where do you think Teresa wore it?"

"I don't think she did, it doesn't appear to have been worn."

Sharon gasped when Barbara held up her hand. "That bracelet is stunning."

"Yeah, I thought so too. But I do wish it wasn't in the shape of a dragon."

"It's the shape that makes it so interesting," Sharon noted as her fingers inspected the jewels.

"It's just a thing, it's not an actual dragon, so I put it on and I felt . . . comfortable," Barbara explained.

"What else did you find in that box?"

"Not much besides a few pieces of jewelry, a snow globe and another dress. You want to try it?"

"You need to ask?" Sharon's voice lowered an octave with the obvious answer.

As the girls admired themselves in the mirror, the doorbell rang.

"Oh, my gosh, I forgot about the time," Barbara said as she rushed to the front door where Patti waited.

"I thought we were meeting at the library," Barbara blurted out when she saw her new acquaintance.

"I got off work early. Wow! What a dress," Patti exclaimed.

"A friend passed away and her mother gave me this dress. Give me a few minutes and I will change into something more appropriate.

While waiting on Barbara to change clothes, Patti spoke to Sharon. "Would you like to go with us?"

"Where?"

"We're going to visit my grandmother's house." Patti answered.

Sharon shuddered.

"Are you cold?" Patti asked.

"No, I just felt a chill." Sharon complained. "And thanks for the invitation but I don't think I will be going."

The musical strains of a Rachmaninoff Piano Concerto hit Barbara's ears as soon as she entered the elegant building behind Patti.

"Is this your grandmother's home?" She asked as her head swung from side to side, taking in the opulence.

"Yes," Patti answered.

"Is she royalty or something?"

"Something," Patti answered with a sly smile enjoying Barbara's fascination with the surroundings. Soon a gentleman in a suit joined them.

"Is this one your guest?"

Barbara's mouth dropped. "A butler?"

"No, he's my uncle, he lives here."

"Anyone else?"

"We have many guests." Patti droned in a monotone voice. Barbara caught the air of redundancy in her voice and didn't ask any more questions, although they bounced around her head like a basketball.

The girls entered a sitting room appointed with rich brocades and original oil paintings by such artists as Jackson Pollack and Andy Warhol as well as a few creations of women in gardens with flowers in their hair and little else. Barbara gasped out loud when she saw the familiar face of Gloria Steinem among the paintings.

"What is it?" Patti asked.

"What does your grandmother do?" Barbara asked in curious fascination. Whatever she did, Barbara wanted the same job.

"She's a businesswoman."

"What kind of business?"

"She doesn't like to say."

"Is she ashamed?"

"No, more like careful. Many people have attempted to scam her and others have tried to shut down her business, so she trusts no one." Patti explained.

"Smart woman." Barbara replied.

A tall gray-haired, woman entered the room with an air of nobility around her. Her clothing as impressive as her home. In a strange display Patti bowed before her and then kissed her on the cheek. "Hello Grandmamma."

"Who is this pretty one?" Grandmamma pointed to Barbara.

"She attended Pap's funeral."

"Ahhh!" She nodded her head.

After tea and cookies and banal conversation, Grandmamma spoke to Barbara. "I understand you want to know more about Paps." She glared at Barbara over her teacup.

"Yes, especially a vision he had of me. Do you know anything about it?"

Grandmamma put her teacup on the coffee table and tented her fingers in front of her face. She stared into space. Barbara felt she was searching for something or attempting to ignore the question. She wasn't sure which. She never answered her. Instead, she stood and said to Barbara, "Thank you for coming. Uncle will take you home."

The assertive statement dismissed her without further conversation or explanation.

26

Demons And Creatures

And thorns shall come up in her
palaces, nettles and brambles in the
fortresses thereof: and it shall be a
habitation of dragons, and a court for
owls. The wild beasts of the desert shall
also meet with the wild beasts of the
island, and the satyr shall cry to his fellow;
the screech owl also shall rest there, and
find for herself a place of rest.

     ---Isaiah 34:13-14(KJV)

DANIEL WALKED HOME from his shift in the early morning
hours. *Walking was a dumb idea.* He had left in the beauty of
a crisp afternoon, not considering his walk home would be
in the wee hours of the morning. While the rest of the
world slept, Daniel Holloway walked through their dreams
and nightmares.

He shivered as the moisture sank through his scrubs onto his skin. He wouldn't do this again. The mile between his apartment and the hospital exposed Daniel to all weather elements, both good and bad. With his head bent down to avoid the mist hitting him in the eyes, he heard a slight noise. *Some other idiot walking home.* The scuffle didn't sound like footsteps, it sounded more like something being dragged. Daniel looked up expecting to see a beaver pulling a tree toward the creek. Instead he watched a person hunched over a large object, pulling it between two apartment buildings. Stepping behind a tree, he stared for a few minutes. He inched toward the alley hoping to see the source of the noise. A deep growling voice startled him. He couldn't understand any words. He felt the need to keep his distance from the strange acting people.

He saw two figures, one appeared to be a large man dressed in an orange shimmery coat. A petite raven-haired woman stood beside him. She turned toward Daniel and he could see piercing blue eyes and smooth luminescent skin. The big man turned toward Daniel. His fedora hat covered much of his face.

He put his arm around the woman and said, "Let's go, it'll be daylight soon." He growled.

"What do we do with that?" She pointed toward the large sack.

"Leave it."

Daniel decided to keep going to his nearby apartment.

The dreariness of the morning made Sharon's bedroom darker than usual, or so she thought. When she opened one eye to look at the clock she saw the time. Two in the morning, no wonder it's still dark. She yawned, rolled over, and settled in to return to sleep when the sound of people talking outside her bedroom window alerted her.

She sat on the edge of the bed and listened for a few minutes. Trying to control her heavy breathing, she inhaled slow and deep. The male voice sounded almost like a growl with a hiss at the end of the words. They must be right by her window. She opened the curtains a bit to look.

Two people communicating in a hostile manner stood over a large sack. She could hear their muffled voices, yet could not discern any intelligible words. She had never seen them around before and wondered why they would be in the alley on a rainy night. She shrugged her shoulders, hugged herself for warmth and headed to the bathroom. It wasn't her problem, but a call to the police might be prudent.

Michael's apartment on the first floor coexisted under Daniel's efficiency on the second. The two men could hear the other's coming and going. However, their developing friendship and common love for Barbara Troye made them more like family than neighbors.

It wasn't odd to hear Daniel's door open as he came home from work, often at strange hours. Michael rolled over to go back to sleep. Tonight he found himself wide awake. He went to the kitchen and made himself a cup of cocoa. He sat down in the living room, waiting for sleepiness to revisit him. In the meantime, he recognized the call from his Lord.

"Okay Lord, you have my attention. Talk to me." He said aloud and picked up his Bible. He knew a sleepless night often meant a spiritual appointment with God's Word. The times served as precious learning experiences. In addition, they often provided an urgent message.

He opened his Bible to the page he had read the night before, Mark 1:23.

"Just then there was a man in their synagogue with an unclean spirit; and he cried out, saying, what business do we have with each other, Jesus of Nazareth? Have you come to destroy us? I know you. You are---The Holy One of God! And Jesus rebuked him, saying, "Be quiet, and come out of him!" Throwing him in convulsions, the unclean spirit cried out with a loud voice and came out of him."

Michael pondered the passage; he recognized God's voice speaking to him. Meditating on the message would give the Holy Spirit time to interpret it. He read it again noticing it said *"we"* so more than one evil spirit resided in the man or the spirit referred to the entire demonic kingdom. Either way it indicated that all demons seek to avoid any contact with Jesus – The Holy One of God. Jesus told him to be quiet and not to speak.

Michael sipped his cocoa and leaned his head back, "Holy Spirit, you are my teacher. Teach me your truth. I know when you speak you speak only truth."

At that moment Michael heard a noise outside. He slipped on his shoes, grabbed his rifle and went outside toward the noise. He came upon a huge man dressed in an orange coat standing beside a petite dark-haired woman. They were talking as they looked at the ground. Michael followed their gaze and saw a strange animal lying there. Too big for a dog and too misshapen to recognize. He wondered if the couple had lost a pet. As he inched closer, he could hear their words.

"We have to get rid of it," The man said.

"I know, but how?" The woman asked.

"Dig a hole; put him in it."

Michael walked up to the couple to offer some assistance. When the big man turned around and faced him, Michael knew he faced a demon, not a man.

"Can I help you?" Michael squeaked out the words knowing he couldn't leave without being seen.

"I know you." The orange hulk growled.

"Yes, you do!" Michael trembled with the recognition of the creature before him. His mind returned to the most horrific moment he had experienced in Vietnam. He knew the Holy Spirit prepared him with scripture for this event.

"How'd you escape?"

Michael replied with a stutter, "The. . . Ho. . ho. .ly one of God. . .

With that proclamation, the couple covered their eyes.

"Leave us," the man moaned as he fell to his knees. "We have nothing to do with you."

Michael watched as the couple ducked their heads and backed away from him. In only a few seconds they disappeared behind a building. Now that they were gone, he took time to look at the object lying on the ground they were dragging. He gagged at the ugliness of the strange creature.

"What do I do with this?" Michael's words hit the cool morning air and dissipated with no reply.

Hearing the commotion, Daniel came out and joined Michael. They both stared at the strange object lying before them.

Daniel lurched, "Ew. Any idea what it is?"

"Ever heard of a satyr?"

"No, what is it?"

"Usually depicted as a lion with a goat body and the head of snake coming from the top of its head."

"For real?"

Michael pointed to the creature in the bag, "Not exactly the same but it's for real."

Daniel nodded and spoke the obvious, "We can't leave it here, even if it is partly covered. We could call animal control to come get it," Daniel suggested.

"Do you want to explain what it is or how we found it?" Michael chastised him.

Then Daniel had an idea, he opened his eyes wide, "I know, Dr. Winegren might be interested in this. . . whatever it is. It appears to still be alive." Daniel pointed to the wriggling sack around the strange body.

"Do you want to look?" Michael mocked.

"No way! Let's get this thing over to the lab."

Dr. Carl Winegren met them at the door with their strange bagged specimen. He took one look.

"Good thing you brought this to me," Dr. Winegren remarked when he removed the covering to reveal the stubby body of a goat with the grotesque unhinged jaw of an ugly misshapen serpent like dragon head. "He bit off more than he could chew." Dr. Winegren chuckled.

"That's some kind of nightmare." Daniel said.

"You're right," Michael confirmed.

Dr. Winegren looked at the macabre mess, "Let's get it in the cage."

Michael invited Daniel to come to his apartment for a while when he saw him shaking. Michael's Bible lay open on the couch. Daniel read the passage and remarked, "you know, Jesus wouldn't let the demons declare who He was. Did you ever wonder why?"

"Yeah, it didn't fit with the message of proclaim." Michael sat down across from him.

"I wonder if it's because the demons know Jesus is God." Daniel pondered.

"They know Jesus came to render them helpless."

The two guys sat there for a few minutes and let their cold weary bodies relax. They mulled over the ideas in the scripture mixed with the vision of a strange creature in the night. Then Daniel sat up.

"They know! Michael! Listen! They know!"

"I think you are trying to say something."

"Without faith it is impossible to please God. They don't need faith because they know."

"Okay, go with it." Michael encouraged Daniel to pursue further understanding.

"Their goal is to destroy God's creation, us." Daniel rose from his chair and started pacing. "Not only are humans the creation of God, they are the image of God."

Michael smiled as Daniel revealed the work of the Holy Spirit's teaching in his heart.

"When we disobey God's commandments, we distort His image and curse His creation."

"You're onto something," Michael affirmed Daniel's thought processes.

Daniel sat down and pondered in silence. Michael picked up the soliloquy, "If the demons lie to us, they can make us forget about God as the creator then we believe them. Humans are part of that creation. Lies create confusion and that makes us susceptible to the lies."

"Like destroying the family by making fathers a curse instead of a blessing?" Daniel shouted as he stood.

"Yes." Michael confirmed and allowed Daniel to finish the concept.

"If we can't see creation then we can't see Jesus. If we can't see Him then we cannot see what He did for us when he went to the cross." Daniel's face exploded in a smile with the jewel of truth he discovered. A second later he realized this lie captured his beloved.

At the same moment Michael felt a tug on his heart. The two men, reaching the same realization, shouted in unison, "Barbara!"

27

A Gathering Ensues

Behold, everyone who quotes proverbs will quote this proverb concerning you, saying, Like mother like daughter. You are the daughter of your mother, who loathed her husband and children. You are also the sister of your sisters, who loathed their husbands and children.

---Ezekiel 16:44-45

PATTI MET UNCLE at the front door. He held a towel and a robe. She stripped down and handed him her wet clothes.

"How'd it go? Did you erase our mistake?"

She wrinkled her brow and scowled at him, "No! It escaped, we had to chase it. Then one of the Holy One's saints showed up. We couldn't scare him. We had to leave."

"Are you saying a holy man has the creature?" Uncle paled even more than usual as he confirmed Patti's details.

She scorned him with a look of anger. "Yes. Jorkphat called him out."

"What happened?" Uncle rubbed his hands together.

"He called on---" Patti pointed up. Uncle gasped and his hand flew over his mouth.

"You know that means we have to advance our plans."

"Yes, and my subject is not ready yet."

"The young lady you brought here to meet the madam?" Uncle asked.

"Yes, she's the one."

"So what now?"

"Consult with Grandmamma."

Uncle moaned, "I don't envy you."

"Oh no you don't. You aren't leaving, you're coming with me."

"Please Ms. Patti, don't make me, you know I . . ."

"Oh, shut up and come on."

The two walked down the long hallway to the sitting room where Madam Lilith sat reading. Without looking up she confronted them.

"Come in you two, I can hear you breathing."

"It got away," Patti stated.

"Where is it now?" Madam Lilith scoffed.

"In the university lab," Patti let her head drop and she stared at the floor, hoping to miss the inevitable slap coming. It didn't help; the slap connected firmly to Patti's cheek knocking her to the floor. "Now they have evidence."

Patti stood to her feet, but still didn't look up. Uncle pressed against the wall, looking down.

"Get the girl ready, I'll set it up for tomorrow night. It's a full moon."

Patti nodded and left to prepare, Uncle stepped in behind her.

"Put on your chauffeur suit, and let's dazzle our prey," Patti instructed him.

The loud, persistent knock on the door aroused Sharon and Barbara followed close behind. Without looking out the peep hole Sharon opened the door. Barbara swatted her and whispered, "not a good idea." Sharon let the door close before she fully opened it. Then a voice from the other side spoke.

"It's Michael and Daniel."

Sharon opened the door, "You scared us."

"What's going on?" Barbara asked them.

"Did you see the activity outside your building?' Daniel asked them as he peeked out each window.

"We did, and we called the police. What do you know?"

Michael related their recent activity to the girls. "The animal was taken to Dr. Winegren's security lab. There is no danger, but wanted to make sure you knew that."

"Okay guys, something isn't adding up with your story. What else is going on?" Barbara demanded.

Michael started with a warning, "The people out there, one of them was Patti and the other was the orange man Barbara calls Jerk Fat."

"You saw him!" Barbara stood up and whispered.

"Both of us saw him, I ran, Michael confronted them. That's how we know it was Jerk Fat" Daniel added.

"What does this mean?" Sharon calmly asked. She took Barbara by the hand and guided her to sit back down on the couch.

Michael pondered the Bible scripture he had read and decided not to share it with the girls. Sharon would be able to accept it, but Barbara would make fun of the message. He looked at Daniel and nodded. Daniel nodded back ever so slightly. They both knew there were many demons working together, even the black clouds revealed evil forces gathering.

Michael opened his explanation with a plea, "We need prayer covering, all we can get. I think there are seeds of a spiritual nature being planted."

Barbara didn't understand his last statement, but she didn't want to go there. She wanted to be rid of Jorkphat, and if Michael had a plan, she would support it.

"Zay and Rance will be here this Sunday," Barbara announced.

"I'll call Buster and tell them to be in prayer, they don't have to be here."

Barbara rolled her eyes and stood up. "You guys." She laughed.

"A dog or some animal wanders onto campus and you guys act like hell landed. I'm going back to bed. This will seem foolish in the morning light."

Sharon, Michael and Daniel watched her amble back to her bedroom. "She doesn't know, does she?" Daniel moaned.

"It will get much worse before she knows," Michael added.

"Why?" Sharon prodded.

"The animal we took to Dr. Winegren's lab was a small dragon," Michael answered. Sharon gasped at the announcement.

Daniel completed the details. "Grossly malformed, with the body of a goat and the head of a dragon."

Sharon stared at the two men and said one word, "Satyr."

28

The Vision

> While Peter thought on the vision,
> the Spirit said unto him, Behold, three
> men seek thee. Arise therefore, and get
> thee down, and go with them, doubting
> nothing: for I have sent them.
>
> ---Acts 10:20 (NASB)

MICHAEL CAUGHT UP to Barbara. "Are you through for the day?"

"Yeah, what are you doing here near the science building?

"I came to visit Dr. Winegren," Michael explained.

Barbara didn't understand his answer. She asked, "Why?"

"To ask him about the creature we found the other night."

Now she understood. "What did ya learn."

"Nothing, lab was locked, so here I am walking home and I run into you." Michael explained as he opened the door to his apartment. He motioned for Barbara to enter.

He took a deep breath. "I think the time has come for me to tell you how Paps and I saw you in Vietnam."

Barbara sat down, anxious to hear Michael's story.

"Listen with a heart trusting God, not yourself."

"I'm not sure I can do that," Barbara conceded.

"That's why we didn't think you were ready. The appearance of that creature makes me think you need to know. It may help you understand that although you have turned your back on God, He has not abandoned you."

Barbara nodded and gave Michael her full attention. "It was before Paps lost his legs. We were on patrol and somehow got separated from our unit. We saw VC or Vietcong as the North Vietnamese were called. They took us prisoner. We had heard tales of their horrific torture routines, so naturally, we were scared out of our wits."

Michael stopped for a moment. Barbara saw him shutter. "It's a fear that grips your soul like a thick chain." Again he stopped. After gathering his courage, he continued.

"The goons led us to a hidden grove. We couldn't understand anything they said. Through grunts, groans and pointing, we figured out we needed to sit. So we did. They didn't tie us or even guard us. Fear chained us to the ground."

"What kind of information could you give them if you couldn't understand each other?"

"Oh, this war didn't care about gaining land or power. Victory was calculated in the number of kills. The one with the most bodies won. We were booty. We didn't know why they were keeping us alive though. We figured they wanted to torture us before we died, just for the fun of it."

"How awful on your - - -" Barbara wrinkled up her nose.

"Soul, is the word you're looking for." Michael said softly as the memory flooded him.

"I guess so."

"You're right, we were dying minute by minute. Then Paps said, 'let's pray.'"

"The only weapon available to us, so we used it. We prayed out loud and fervently for hours."

Michael stopped and a smile crept across his face. "That's when we saw you."

"What?" Barbara furrowed her brow.

"You were standing about ten feet in front of us, smiling, peaceful and beautiful. You were a mature woman."

"Was it . . . you know like a dream?" Barbara asked.

"No, you were solid, just like you are now. I believe time is all-inclusive to God. He is outside of time so he sent you in your later years to us in our younger years." Michael admitted.

"How did you recognize me?"

"We both knew who you were and Paps had never met you. But he called you by name first."

"By name?"

"Strangest thing I ever saw. His face glowed and he said, 'Barbara?'"

"What did you do?"

"Crazy thing, I looked at my hands to see if I had grown older. If you were older, then I had to be too. I decided then we were both dead. I turned to Paps and said, 'meet my cousin.'"

"What did Paps do?"

"He said,' I know, she told me.' He heard somethin' I didn't."

"Did I say anything?"

"Yeah, you did, the most beautiful words I ever heard."

"What were they?"

"Fear not, for the battle is not yours but the Lords."

"Wow!"

"At that moment we both relaxed. You spoke Scripture to us before you disappeared into the mist. Paps and I looked around and saw, all the VC had left. They forgot about us."

"How?"

"Paps thought the vision of you covered us physically and mentally and they forgot they had us. So we went back to our unit."

"How did you find it?"

"They found us. We ran right into them. But before we did, Paps told me what you told him."

"Well, what did I tell him?"

Michael sighed again and took both of Barbara's hands in his. He looked at her. "Listen carefully, without prejudice."

Barbara nodded as she prepared to receive important information.

"He would be wounded, but we would still come home alive. He would find his daughter Patti."

"Sounds like good news to me," Barbara said.

"It was, except that . . ."

Michael stopped. "I can't tell you now, I don't think you're ready to receive it."

"Why not?" Barbara demanded.

"There was more to the message and I think it is the most important one for you to understand."

Barbara wrinkled her brow realizing he was not going to give her the full vision. She ducked her head and watched her hands twirl a pencil. After a few minutes she regained her composure and asked a question she hoped would let Michael tell her the rest of the vision.

"Why would God send you an image of me?"

"Remember the vision Peter had of the Gentile man, named Cornelius asking him to come to him?"

"Yeah!" Barbara recalled.

"We can't know the ways of God, only that He can reveal Himself any way He desires."

Barbara smiled and nodded. "Yeah, that's a nice thought."

"Your message to me and Paps gave us hope. After the incident we spoke of it often. The form in which we saw you allowed us to discern the message." Michael added.

"What do you mean, the form?" Barbara furrowed her brow and asked.

"You were an older woman, so that told us the message came from your experience and for the future. We decided the message sent was actually for you. We were God's chosen delivery men."

Barbara shook her head in disbelief. "I gave you a message for you to give to me."

"Sounds ridiculous, but yes, we both thought so."

"So what's the message?"

Michael hesitated as he whispered a prayer in his mind. With renewed confidence he related the vision to Barbara.

"It was a message for us at the moment as we faced torture and death but also a message for you after we returned." Michael disclosed.

"I don't understand," Barbara pleaded.

"You may not understand when I tell you the message either."

"Tell me."

Michael looked up and smiled as he recalled the message that had restored him and Paps. I have the honor to deliver God's message to God's intended recipient.

"Hope is found in a child and even a coward can be brave, with hope."

29

A Worthless Life

> If you do not oppress the alien, the orphan, or the widow, and do not shed innocent blood in this place, nor walk after other gods to your own ruin, then I will let you dwell in this place, in the land that I gave to your fathers forever and ever.
>
> ---Jeremiah 7: 6 (NASB)

PHILLIP MCCORD FELT his stomach lurch as he entered the bar. There had been a rift in the middle realm. He didn't like it. He needed to be in a place that was whole, at least wholly evil.

"Hello Phillip," the bartender greeted him. "You don't look so good."

"It's up to you to make me better."

The bartender smiled at him. "You been hanging out with good, moral people again?"

"No, but they are invading my space; Christians everywhere; I hate em."

After a few drinks Phillip began to feel his spirit repairing itself. His grasp on this body grew more fragile each day. With the body coming under the influence of strong drink, the spirit of malice could once again have control over the body, he called Phillip Donnigan McCord.

The old body had its problems but Donnigan repaired them once he took residence in McCord's body. The run with McCoy had been filled with dalliances with beautiful women and the perks of respect. The exchange of Dr. McCoy's persona for Mr. McCord's intolerable personality didn't promote his mission. McCord didn't have the respect of McCoy. But then again, Donnigan didn't inhabit Dr. McCoy's body. When McCoy's spirit filled with guilt over the death of Barry Lawson, the son of his lifetime friend, then Donnigan took over the body .

McCoy's own self-importance made him go to his friend, Jim Lawson with news of his son's infraction of school rules. If he had approached Jim with a helpful, caring attitude instead of a judgmental one, when he found the couple on school property, then Barry Lawson might still be alive. He and the beauty queen would have married and settled down with their new son. Instead, Jim insisted

Barry join the navy. The child was put up for adoption, the mom moved away and Barry was burned alive on the U.S.S. Forrestal.

Phillip Donnigan McCord smiled at the memory of some of his best work. He had successfully destroyed that potential powerful Christian family before it began.

The dragon, also known as Donnigan, put the guilt in Dr. McCoy. It made him easy to inhabit. He had no weaponry. He rejected the Almighty One and depended on his own intellect. This ploy of self-knowledge served as a favorite tool of the dragon since it makes the subject helpless and hopeless. McCord took a drink and laughed at the frivolous attempts of humans to overcome him with their weak resolve. As long as he kept them away from that infernal Bible, the Holy One gave them, then the dragons had free reign over their minds and bodies and possession of their spirits.

After the bomb went off and destroyed the majority of Church Creek Falls, McCoy the man, left town and took on a new identity, Phillip Donnigan McCord. Donnigan, the dragon inhabited both identities. Living in this person of McCord he enjoyed few pleasures of human flesh.

In fact, McCord had failed on all levels. The students hated him, the teachers tolerated him and beautiful women avoided him. He looked around the bar for a possibility of finding a woman, even a plain woman would be better than none. He took another drink to gain a little buzz for this deteriorating human corpse he wore.

He spotted her in the corner. McCord watched her most of the evening. Her face took his breath away. Never had he seen such a dark lithe beauty. He looked around at the bozos in the place and wondered why none of them had claimed her. "Fools, they miss the best." McCord muttered under his breath.

Lucky for me. He kept watch over her until some drunk jerk tried to steal her away from him. She resisted, but the rude man kept on, even grabbing her by the arm. McCord saw his opening and stepped up and distracted the man. "She's with me."

That discouraged the drunk; he ambled off to find other prey.

"May I join you," He charmed her, hoping simplicity would serve as his introduction.

She smiled, and he could feel his heart melting. "My name's Phillip, what's yours?"

The dark-haired beauty let her bold red lips part revealing a tempting smile as she answered, "Patti Pan."

30

Murder And Confession

> Let everyone be on guard against his
> neighbor, and do not trust any brother;
> because every brother deals craftily. And
> every neighbor goes about as a slanderer.
> Therefore, says the LORD of hosts, I
> will refine them and assay them; for what
> else can I do, because of the daughter of
> My people?
>
> --- Jeremiah 9:4,7 (NASB)

MICHAEL KNOCKED ON Barbara's door. Looking and feeling disheveled she still opened it.

"What's with you? You look like you just got out of bed."

"I did."

"I can leave and come back later. Did you work last night?" Michael asked as he turned back toward the door.

"No, I have the next two days off. I just don't feel like doing anything, so I've been sleeping and reading most of the day."

Michael picked up the open book, *The Feminine Mystique.* "Is this what you're reading?"

Barbara turned away from him, "Sometimes, there's some good stuff in there."

"What?"

"Well she says. . .. it's. . . like. . .. well. . . you know. . ." Barbara stammered.

"I think the philosophy of your reading material is bringing you down."

Barbara opened the refrigerator door in his face. She pulled a gallon of milk out and closed it. Michael stood firm even when she tried to push him aside. She had to face him.

"Barbara, how long will you fight this."

"What do you mean?" She walked past him and reached for a glass. She went to the table and sat down. Michael followed.

"I mean your attitude is getting old." Michael tried to explain.

"What attitude?" she countered.

"Sometimes you are the kind, considerate Barbara we all know and love, but then this monster comes out in you."

"Yes, we've talked about him, I call him Jerk Fat. He controls me." Barbara moaned.

"No, you let it control you."

"How do I do that?" She snapped.

"You believe him when he tells you lies."

She nods her head in contemplation. "Okay, but what lie is he telling me?"

"The same ones he told Eve in the Garden." Michael admonishes.

"I don't remember them." She sneered.

"Let me remind you. Lie number one discredited the words God spoke to Adam." Michael paced back and forth while Barbara watched him. "Then he told a second lie when he said she wouldn't die."

"Look, I know I'm gonna die."

"Do you know if that means physical or spiritual."

"What's the difference?" Barbara found Michael's nervous energy rather entertaining. She yawned. She couldn't help it. She rested her head on the palm of her hand.

Michael sat down across the table from her and pleaded, "Do you know whether you are going to live your real life with or without Jesus?"

"Probably, without." She retorted and rose from her chair. She went to the sink and rinsed the milk residue from her glass. She sighed deeply then turned to Michael.

"I want to believe He is real, I really do."

Michael quietly spoke, "But Jerk fat has convinced you that you can be like God. His third and most treacherous lie."

Barbara didn't respond at first, she stared at Michael as she stood in front of the sink. "I can be like God?" She pondered the statement.

"No Barbara, you can't; it's a lie," Michael announced.

At that moment, Rance and Zay burst through the door, laughing.

"What are you two doing?" Michael said with a contagious laughter.

"We just enrolled in the University."

"And we got scholarships; both of us." The two boys did a little dance while singing, *Stayin Alive* by the Bee Gees. They both laughed with delight.

The discussion may be over between her and Michael, but the words lingered in Barbara's mind and tried to worm their way into her heart, her hard heart.

When Rance and Zay completed their little dance, Barbara ran her fingers through her hair and straightened her robe. She went to the kitchen and pulled out the milk carton and pastries for them. "How'd you get scholarships? Ole' Mr. McCord doesn't give them to anyone."

"Well Ole' Mr. McCord isn't there anymore, and the new dean of admissions gave us a hardship scholarship since we were from Church Creek Falls."

"Wait a minute, Mr. McCord is gone?"

"Yep, dead and gone."

"What are you guys talking about?"

"Seems he got into a fight at a bar, and they pulled out guns. Poor Mr. McCord stopped five bullets with his heart. Fell to the floor like a lead balloon."

Barbara's jaw dropped, and she slumped onto the couch. "I can't believe it, Phillip Donnigan left."

"Whoa there sister, I didn't say Phillip Donnigan; I said Mr. McCord," Rance stopped dancing and clarified the statement.

She cleared her throat, "Yea, Phillip Donnigan McCord."

"So does this mean Donnigan is dead?" Rance asked Barbara.

"Don't be silly, Donnigan's a spirit. He can't die, it just moves on." Barbara lectured.

"When a spirit loses human habitation, Jesus says, they are cast into the desert where they thirst until they can find rest. . . which is another body. . . which they call their habitation. Jesus even said, if you rid yourself of one demon and do not fill your house with something else they will come back from the desert and bring seven more demons viler than themselves," Michael added.

Barbara watched him in amazement, "How do you know all this stuff?"

Michael shrugged, "Life is a great teacher."

"You're twenty-five!" Barbara said with a note of sarcasm.

Michael smiled, "I know; I learned really quick to find truth."

"Where's the source of truth?" Barbara ranted.

Michael gave her a stern stare before he answered, "You know. God's Word, the Bible."

Dr. Abby Greenstein looked tired and drawn when Barbara entered her inner chamber.

"Please sit."

Barbara obeyed, "We can reschedule if you like."

Dr. Greenstein smiled, "No, I need to talk to you."

"I feel better than I have felt since this whole thing started," Barbara said. "So maybe . . . you can sign my chart, and I can move on?"

Dr. Greenstein sat down and picked up a couple of charts. "I'm not going to sign off on your chart today."

Barbara felt her stomach drop. She loved the guys in the group, but if she had to attend another class, it would be all new people. She wasn't ready for that move yet.

"I think I'm doing well," Barbara pleaded her case.

"You are doing well, but today's meeting isn't about your progress. Rather, I have called you in as a witness."

"Really? A witness to what or who?" Barbara asked.

"Paps." Dr. Greenstein answered.

Barbara smiled at the mention of her friend's name. "He was a remarkable man. I will miss him. I know he had a powerful influence but I'm not sure he could reach beyond the grave," Barbara noted.

"You're right, but he did reach beyond the grave with a descendant. Did you know he had a daughter?"

"I've seen her a few times." Barbara felt as if she needed to apologize for her acquaintance with Patti.

"I think there is something between you two." Dr. Greenstein said as she flipped through a sheathe of papers.

Barbara nodded. "I guess, we both knew Paps, that's about all."

"Want to talk about it?"

"About what?"

"Your friendship with Patti and her friend," She stopped and opened the chart. . . "Horgfay?"

Barbara cocked her head to one side, "Pardon?"

"This strange name," Dr. Greenstein copied the name on a scrap piece of paper.

Barbara laughed, "Jerk Fat."

"I would never have come to that pronunciation, but okay."

"That's what I call him, he pronounced it Jorg fa."

"It seems you and Patti share knowledge of this guy. What can you tell me?"

Barbara peered at Dr. Greenstein, "Is this a trick question?"

"I don't think so. Why?"

"What did he have to do with Patti?"

"When I interviewed Patti, she kept talking about you and Jorg fa." Dr. Greenstein said. "Ms. Paulsen is being held in county jail. The judge doesn't believe she is mentally stable, so she's been assigned to me. When I read this chart of her arrest, I found your name all over it. Along with this Jorg fa. Why?"

"I don't know," Barbara answered.

"I'm grasping at straws. I have to report my findings to the DA and I am... well let's say your presence in this case confuses me."

"That makes two of us." Barbara countered. Inside she felt fearful this escapade could send her back into another psyche class.

"Do you know Jorg fa?" Dr. Greenstein asked ignoring Barbara's statement.

"I know of him; I prefer not to talk about him." Barbara said and ducked her head.

"Why not?" Dr. Greenstein asked.

"I'm afraid."

"Why are you afraid?"

"Because he's not a person, he's an it." Barbara tried to avoid calling him a demon.

I don't understand. What is he?" Dr. Greenstein put the chart down and leaned back in her chair.

"You'll think I'm crazy, if I tell you." Barbara argued almost in tears.

"'Isn't that why you're here; so we can separate crazy from real."

Barbara relaxed a little at Dr. Greenstein's sympathy. "Do you believe in a spirit world?" she asked.

"Yes." Dr. Greenstein responded flatly. "Is Jorg fa a spirit?" She questioned.

"Yes and a mean one."

"Obviously," Dr. Greenstein smiled.

"I think Jorkphat, or Jerk Fat as I call him, is a demon, he's been tormenting me ever since---."

"Since when?"

Barbara took a deep breath, "When I saw that ugly sculpture on the wall at my home light up. I think that's the first time I saw him." Barbara said as she sat up with wide eyes. "Yes, that's the first time and then he stuck me."

"What?" Dr. Greenstein encouraged Barbara to continue providing an explanation.

"A piece of the sculpture stuck me. I didn't see him again until the night of the break-in at my apartment. That's why he looked familiar." Barbara looked past Dr. Greenstein as she recalled the events.

"Pardon? What do you mean, he looked familiar?"

"I saw an orange cloud surrounding the man who broke into my apartment, and it didn't scare me. Now I know why. That mask stood in front of me. I recognized him".

"Why do you think you recognized him from a sculpture and an orange cloud?" Dr. Greenstein prodded Barbara.

"The sculpture in our house, it had an orange cast to it."

Barbara stopped speaking as she pulled the image of the mask from her memory. Dr. Greenstein waited. Barbara knitted her brow as if she were forming an idea.

"I think he's trying to kill me."

"Go on," Dr. Greenstein said.

Barbara fidgeted in the chair. Dr. Greenstein noticed her discomfort.

"I'm not sure what it has to do with Patti. I haven't been around her a lot, and the demon has never been a part of our conversation. In fact---"

Barbara stopped again and pursed her lips and shook her head. "I don't remember ever seeing the cloud around when I'm with her."

"Tell me about your relationship to Patti; what kind of things did you do?" Dr. Greenstein pressed.

"Patti brought me to meet her grandmother. Only thing we've done together."

"Okay, tell me about that?"

Barbara shook her head as she looked at her hands worrying themselves in her lap.

"I don't know where to start. Patti said her grandmother's a secretive woman. I'm not sure I should be talking about her."

"Are you afraid?" Dr. Greenstein asked Barbara with a soft tone.

"I am, because Patti was afraid." Barbara answered.

"What did you see that made you think Patti felt fear?" Dr. Greenstein asked.

"She bowed her head in submission."

"Why did you make the conclusion she was afraid?"

"Because she trembled, visibly trembled. I remember wondering, why was she afraid? Patti's not a wimp."

Dr. Greenstein took a few notes while Barbara put her hand under her chin and stared at the front of Dr. Greenstein's chair. "Barbara, do you see something?"

Without acknowledging Dr. Greenstein's question, Barbara continued, "It wasn't real."

"What wasn't real?"

"What I saw."

Since Barbara stared intently at the carved images on the arms of her chair she assumed she was talking about them. She continued with her line of questioning,

"Did Patti know Mr. McCord before the . . . incident?"

"I don't know. I only know Mr. McCord from school." Barbara turned her head and looked up at the bookcase. Dr. Greenstein watched Barbara for a while, then said, "Tell me about your relationship with McCord."

"He was a counselor at school; not a very good one either."

"Did he have enemies?"

Barbara chuckled, "Yea, every student. He was a devil you know." Barbara stopped, fearing what she had said.

Dr. Greenstein continued making notes of Barbara's words.

"Did Patti have motive to kill McCord."

"I dunno. Everybody had motive to kill him."

"Do you think Patti is mentally unstable?"

"I don't know. That's your department." Barbara answered curtly.

"You knew Paps. Do you think he abandoned her?"

"No, Michael, my cousin told me Paps wanted her and fought for her, but the grandmother had unlimited funds. Paps didn't. That why the court gave the grandmother custody of Patti."

Dr. Greenstein put her tablet and pen aside and asked, "What are you going to do for Patti?"

Barbara sniffled. Dr. Greenstein handed her a tissue. "I can barely keep my own head straight, how can I help her?"

"Because you know the truth." Dr. Greenstein asserted.

Barbara looked up at her, "What are you saying?"

"You know something. That's why you said they weren't real. You saw something didn't you?"

"I wasn't even there, how would I know?"

"I don't know. Tell me. Did she kill Mr. McCord?" Dr. Greenstein asked as she leaned into Barbara.

"No. Barbara said with firm assurance.

"You sound confident."

"I am."

"Why?"

"Because, now I know for certain who killed him."

"Who?

"I did."

31

Fear

> "And death will be chosen rather than life by all the remnant that remains of this evil family, that remains in all the places to which I have driven them," declares the LORD of hosts.
>
> ---Jeremiah 8:3 (NASB)

DR. ABBY GREENSTEIN stood up and shut her office door. A stack of twelve charts from the first psyche class begged for final evaluations. They were all critical for both the patients and the future of the program. This first class lasted three years at the request of the participants. The continuation allowed for adjustments and improvements to the program. The changes made along the way added to the burden of closing out the charts. Chances are they would never be read, but they needed to be complete and as accurate as if they were being reviewed. The need for readjustment for returning Vietnam soldiers floated to the top as a primary protocol for the program.

Barbara Troye, a civilian, served this first class as the control person to gage the depth of the war trauma as opposed to domestic trauma. She now sat in county jail awaiting her fate. Up until her confession to Abby, the charts were a matter of detail, now Abby would have to research each one in order to reconcile the confession with any statements made by Barbara during group sessions.

The facts didn't support her recollection of the events or the timeline of Mr. McCord 's death. The session with Ms. Troye, regarding her mental stability in the shooting, revealed more than could be seen with human eyes.

Barbara Troye's life and the program were both at stake. Abby hated to admit how much she depended on the outcome of Barbara's recent confession to help fund future groups. This new wrinkle in Barbara Troye's situation would not be ironed out without difficulty. Abby wished she hadn't called the authorities when Barbara confessed to killing McCord. *Did I have a choice?* Right now Abby believed with her whole heart an innocent girl sat in prison. She stood up and walked to the window of her second floor office. She looked down at the street and prayed.

"Lord, you know this girl and her heart. You have placed her in my hand; please give me wisdom to see what I need to see."

After her prayer she pondered the situation. She looked over Ms. Troye's psyche class record along with her school transcript. They revealed a straight A student with a passion for learning.

From all Dr. Greenstein could see on paper, Barbara would be an excellent nurse. The recording of her supervisor exposed personal thoughts not documented. One particular statement played in Abby's mind over and over, "Frankly, she scares me; there's something in her that can't be touched or even imagined."

Abby pondered the statement, 'something within her.' Barbara called it Jerk Fat. Abby walked back toward the window. *I'm missing something.* She went back to her file cabinet and pulled out Patti's folder opening it to the personal data page and made a note. After stuffing the slip of paper into her purse she left her office for her appointment at the district attorney's office.

Barbara sat on the bottom bunk with her three prison roommates. Being the newest one admitted, she watched them to learn the routine of prison life. Her cellmates included one girl about her age, a middle-aged woman, and a grandmotherly older woman. They basically ignored her. Each carried on a portion of a disjointed conversation. The small room filled with the odors of body functions. In a few minutes, she heard one of the women say, 'thank you.' The grandmother had taken a sock and filled it with baby powder. She dusted the air with it. Barbara admitted it helped with the smell.

The middle aged woman climbed on the bunk over Barbara. "Now you know why we want the top," she said to Barbara. She smiled and nodded. Barbara rummaged through the small pack of clothing and bedding assigned to her. She really wanted some socks, her feet were freezing. She discovered the sock used to defumigate the room belonged to her.

The three women chuckled at Barbara's quandary. Barbara ignored them and slipped on the one sock she had left.

"You know your work assignment yet?" The young girl asked.

Barbara shook her head. "Do I get to request?"

"They'll assign you by your skills. Whad cha do before? You know, out there?" The girl pointed toward the wall.

"I'm a nursing student." Barbara answered.

"No, honey, you was a nursing student, your now a prisoner," The old woman on the top bunk opposite Barbara snarled.

"You know what I'm in for?"

Barbara shook her head.

"I'm in for murder."

She watched Barbara's reaction. Barbara surmised this made the old woman the boss of this cell. She stood up, let a crooked smile cross her lips, and looked the old woman in the eyes and announced, "So am I!"

Barbara enjoyed the obvious deflating of the old woman's ego. The woman paled a bit, and the two other women sat up and looked at her. They knew the old woman's story; now they wanted to know Barbara's.

"Who'd ya kill?" The young girl asks with the excitement of a child asking for candy.

"One of the college counselors." She answered them. The room filled with silence. The story had dominated the news media for the last few days.

"You da one?" The young girl whimpered. Barbara nodded.

"Are you a mean person?" The shivering young girl asked Barbara.

"No. He was mean to me." Barbara defended herself.

"They all say that." Snickered the middle-aged woman.

Barbara looked at the old woman, "Who'd you kill?"

"My husband," She groaned.

"Why did you do that ?" Barbara wrinkled her forehead.

"I got tired of his complaining all the time."

Barbara laid back on her cot and pondered some of the things she heard women say in the women's lib meetings. They spoke of killing their husbands. Nonetheless, this was the first time she met someone who actually did.

The young girl spoke in a shaky voice, "My daddy threatened to kill me, but you really did kill a man. Now I'm afraid if I make you mad, you might kill me."

"I'm not going to hurt you." Barbara tried to reassure the young girl.

The old woman snickered and asked the young girl, "Whad ya do that make him wanna kill ya?"

"I don't know, he just hated me."

Barbara felt compassion for this young girl. She thought about the love of her own daddy. How sad it would be if she thought he hated her. He was her security, her refuge, her provider; he loved her and she knew it.

She looked at the middle-aged woman and asked, "What are you in for?"

"Beatin' my baby, stinking no good kid."

"Didn't you love him?" Barbara asked in surprise.

"I tried, but he got on my nerves so bad, wouldn't leave me, just wanted something all the time. He acted like his daddy, I couldn't stand him either."

Barbara sat down and shook her head. "I can't imagine."

"Why not? Smart mommas get rid of 'em before they mess everything up."

"What do you mean?"

"Abortion, sister; it's legal now you know. Been legal since 1973.

The young girl spoke up, "I wish I had my baby, I wanted him so bad, but my daddy wouldn't let me have him."

Barbara still didn't know why the young girl resided with them in here. Her story sounded more like a victim of someone's twisted view of love and hate. There may have been some connection, but she didn't want to know.

Barbara laid back and closed her eyes. She recalled the signs promoting abortion at the women's lib meetings. That led to the memory of the women complaining about their husbands or boyfriends. A tear rolled down the side of her face when a distant voice spoke, "*Listen, I am bringing calamity upon you. Because you have turned away from Me and you have given sacrifices to other gods. You've allowed the place to fill with the blood of innocents.*" Barbara knew the words were from Jeremiah, her favorite prophet, but never had they sounded so personal. She rose from her cot with cold sweat pouring down her body.

"Oh my gosh!" Barbara stammered while the women carried on a diatribe against their husbands and fathers. The women stopped talking and looked at her. The old woman spoke up, "Well, it ain't that impressive."

"That's not what I mean. I'm in real trouble."

"Don't we all think about ourselves? And honey, you're right, if you're in here, you're in trouble," The old woman reiterated.

"No, this can't be right, I killed him in self-defense." Barbara moaned. "I've been so short-sighted, I couldn't see my rebellion, I couldn't hear."

"Honey, they's gonna send you to the crazy place."

"I came from there." She stood up in the middle of the cell looking at the three women in the close quarters with her.

"You got a plan to break us out?" The old-woman snickered.

"In a way, I want to tell you about a man named Jeremiah. He had a message for people going into captivity. I think we may be able to learn from him."

"Sounds good to me." The young girl whimpered. The other two women groaned. "We ain't got nothing to lose. Start teaching, sister."

Barbara landed in the office of an assistant district attorney at ten a.m. The office looked more like a storage room than a legal office. The officer escorting Barbara stood behind her chair. She wondered how they were going to react to her story. *It's either freedom or the loony bin for me when I divulge the details. If I tell them.*

With a sudden shudder, the door opened to the office and a young man entered. He didn't make eye contact even when he spoke. Barbara felt trouble walk in with him. Without any words of introduction, he pulled a form from the desk drawer. Barbara sensed his desire to get through an unpleasant task. Her heart rate jumped about twenty beats. This pressing anxiety brought an appreciation of Dr. Greenstein's advice to hire a good criminal lawyer.

"Ms. Troye, I have some basic questions to ask you as a formality," he droned without taking his eyes from the form. The questions were mostly demographic and non-committal. A strange environment surrounded her. Her feet sweat with the feel of hot water boiling beneath her. In other words, the trouble becoming more intense. *Why did I confess?*

The young man sported a turquoise tie held by a tie tack designed like a dragon. He raised his head but avoided eye contact.

"Thank you Ms. Troye." He rose and exited the room without the form. Barbara pulled herself closer to the desk in order to see a glimpse of it. The officer put a hand on her shoulder and applied pressure.

The action informed Barbara of her captivity. Fear clawed at her flesh. Turning toward the matron, she asked, "May I make a phone call?"

The matron nodded and pointed to a public phone.

"Michael, I need a lawyer, and fast."

Michael instructed her, "Say nothing but be compliant. I'll be there soon with a lawyer."

Two hours later Michael arrived. Barbara felt like the sun rose on a dark night when he entered the room where she sat chained to a chair.

The matron prevented Michael from coming too close.

"We're representing her," the man beside Michael said and the matron allowed them to sit at the table. She didn't leave.

Barbara looked at the strange man waiting for Michael to introduce her. "This is Al Turner from the firm where I work. Tell him everything, and be truthful."

"Even the. . . you know. . .?" Barbara asked quietly.

"Yes, even the dragon," Michael said as he took Barbara's hand and squeezed it. The three of them entered into a conversation which would determine the course of Barbara's life.

"The demons are everywhere in this place," Barbara whispered.

"The Holy Spirit is with you." Michael said as he turned to Al.

Al Turner took out pad and pen and looked at Barbara, "Okay, I understand you confessed to killing Mr. McCord."

"Yes."

"Why are you confessing? I've been told you weren't in the club." Turner asked.

"Because I really did kill him, I put five bullets in him."

The attorney perused a page in the file before him. He turned to Michael, "She's correct. They found five bullets."

Barbara's hands worried each other. She looked down at them. "Are you going to help me or not?"

"Yes, I need all the details and the truth. Can you give that?" Turner asked

Barbara nodded.

"What happened in that bar?" Turner asked Barbara. She didn't look up.

"I don't know. All I know is what Dr. Greenstein shared with me."

"Were you there?"

"No."

"I'm confused how could you shoot him if you weren't there? Tell me what you know about the death of Mr. McCord."

"I killed him years ago. He broke into my apartment and I shot him." Barbara blurted out.

Al shook his head. "Explain."

"There was a dragon following Mr. McCord and an orange cloud followed the beast. When Mr. McCord fell, the orange cloud entered into Mr. McCord 's body. He stood up and walked out of the apartment." Barbara explained. "I think the orange cloud is an evil spirit attempting to destroy me."

"What kind of evil?" Al inquired.

Barbara looked up at him, "Evil! How many kinds are there?"

"I know, but are you saying the bad things people do or ---"

"No, I'm saying demons, devils, dragons are trying to kill us."

"Why?" Al asked.

"Because, their whole purpose is to destroy and kill. They are filled with hate. Just because McCord was the decaying home of a demon didn't mean he would have anything but hatred for him."

Al sat back in his chair and looked at Barbara and then Michael. "Did you know this before you called me?"

"Yes."

"You need a psychiatrist and a lawyer. I'll consult with you as your representative. But know this; I'm not going before a judge with that story." Mr. Turner told Michael.

"I have a psychiatrist, Dr. Abby Greenstein." Barbara inserted.

"I'll speak with her." Turner said. The matron left and Barbara finally had some alone time with Michael.

"I'm sorry." Barbara apologized to Michael.

"Barbara, you've got to put your pride away and return to the One offering true help." Michael pleaded.

"I know. He spoke to me in prison last night." Barbara related to Michael.

"What did He tell you?"

"Calamity is coming on me because I haven't been listening to Him."

"I can't disagree with that evaluation. You haven't been listening to anyone except yourself."

A knock came on the door. "Coming." Michael shouted through the door.

"It's time for us to go. Don't say anything. I'll do the talking," Al Turner instructed.

The three walked down the hall in silence for a while. Barbara leaned into Michael, "Do you think anyone will believe me?"

"I think it's between you and the Lord right now."

"Why did McCord pick me?"

"Your pride made you vulnerable."

Barbara thought, *my pride?*

The same assistant district attorney came into the hall and asked Barbara, Al, and Michael to follow him. When they entered another office much nicer than the last one, she saw an older gentleman sitting behind the desk.

"Please have a seat," the gentleman said. A knock came on the door. "Come in," he shouted. The door opened and Dr. Greenstein came in. Barbara took Michael's hand and sighed. Dr. Greenstein sat next to Mr. Turner. Michael and Barbara sat opposite them.

"Ms. Troye," The gentleman began by addressing Barbara first. "I'm District Attorney Perkins. Dr. Greenstein and your attorney have shared your version of the events with me. The aggressive young assistant you met earlier wants to press charges against you. However, after reviewing the facts of this case, I'm going to dismiss it. It appears there isn't enough evidence to indicate you could have committed the murder of Mr. McCord. The autopsy report leaves more questions than answers, therefore, you are free to go." The man got up from his chair, walked over and shook Michael and Barbara's hands.

Before he exited his office, he said, "May the Lord keep watch over you."

Once they were in the hall Barbara turned to Dr. Greenstein, "You believed me?"

"Yes. We knew something supernatural and evil happened that night. We needed you to tell us the whole story. But we had to wait for you to find the courage to tell it."

"How'd you know?"

"Your supervisor, Carl Young gave me the clue; I think the Holy Spirit interpreted it for me."

"What clue?"

"Paps vision." Dr. Greenstein answered.

"How did that help?"

"Your message to him, 'the battle is the Lord's' I knew then we were looking at a supernatural battle."

Barbara nodded even though she didn't understand. She wasn't going to pursue it. Instead, she whispered a thank you, since she didn't have to go back to that prison cell.

32

Alone

I will make Jerusalem a heap of ruins,
a haunt of jackals; And I will make the
cities of Judah a desolation, without
inhabitant.

--- Jeremiah 9:11(NASB)

THE SUITCASE FILLED up fast as Sharon packed to go visit her mother and her dad. He had been released early from prison and Sharon was both anxious to see him and dreading to see him.

"Strange how the tragedies of life change our future." Barbara mused.

"I know. When I met Billy Sol Estes, he was just my daddy's boss. His scheming and imaginary fertilizer tanks cost my family everything."

"Interesting how fertilizer ruined both our lives." Barbara pondered. Sharon laughed at the comparison.

"Mine were imaginary and yours were explosive, no wonder God brought us together." The girl's laughter soon turned into sorrow as Sharon finished packing and hugged Barbara good-bye.

"I'm only going to be gone a few days," Sharon said.

"I know."

"You know God told the Israelites, if they would just repent he would teach them the right way to live."

"What's your point?" Barbara asked.

"God is teaching you through many people, not just me. Listen to Daniel and Michael, they have words of wisdom." Sharon smiled and said, "I'll be back Monday."

She gave Barbara a hug. "I'll pray for you while I'm gone. Be careful."

"Thanks, dear friend."

Barbara went to the kitchen to clean up their breakfast dishes. Her mind relived her prison days. She looked up and prayed, "Please, dear Lord, let me see and hear You again."

Loneliness overwhelmed Barbara. She slumped in the chair and looked around at the sparse apartment. It felt exceptionally large without anyone else in it. The silence prompted Barbara to take action. She walked across the complex to the building where Daniel lived.

She rapped on his door with a vengeance.

"Need a first aid kit or a doctor?" He asked with a comical smile when he opened the door.

"I need a friend," Barbara answered walking into the apartment.

"You must be missing Sharon."

"Yeah, I am. It's hard to be alone with myself these days."

Daniel pursed his lips at the comment but didn't say anything.

"You know what Michael told me after my release?" Barbara solicited.

"No,"

"He said I needed to trust you."

"Wise man." Daniel smiled at the comment but quickly turned away.

"What are you doing tonight?" She asked as she noticed his semi-formal attire.

"I have a date."

"You do?" Barbara's voice dropped.

"With Clint Eastwood, would you like to join us at the movie theater?'" Daniel asked.

Barbara laughed, "Yes, please."

After the movie, Daniel noticed Barbara's furrowed brow. "Hey, it's not philosophy. It's a western." He mocked her as he gave her a little squeeze around the shoulders.

Barbara released a suppressed snort at Daniel's analysis. "I guess all the events of the last few days are getting to me; I even think a movie is real."

Daniel pulled her hand through his arm and gave her a little pat. "It's been a firestorm." Barbara stated.

"I feel it too." Daniel responded. "You know Satan has a plan for our lives and it's not a good one."

"That's a new concept, you usually hear about God's plan and it's a plan for good, not for evil."

"That's right, even God points out that there is plan for your life that's evil."

"Do you think I'm following the evil ---"

Daniel interrupted her, "Let's not go there again. I don't think I can. Let's just enjoy the walk home."

Barbara wanted him to pursue the quote but he didn't say anything more. She changed the subject, hoping he might elaborate some more on his feelings.

"There's an anxiety in me since I heard that young girl's cry about her daddy hating her."

"That must have been tough."

"Almost as tough as the old woman proud of killing her husband."

She tried to give Daniel a hug of appreciation, but he pulled away from her; subtle, but evident. She removed her hand from his arm and walked beside him in a tense quiet. His jaw set firm. She opted to leave it alone.

Ever since the death of the family in the car wreck, Barbara sensed Daniel pulling away from her. She didn't understand it, but she had a sense she didn't want to know. Just as the truth of her rebelliousness was beginning to sink in her hard head, it seemed Daniel was growing more distant. "Lord, please don't let me lose him now." She whispered.

Daniel walked Barbara up to her door and unlocked it. He took a quick look inside to make sure all was well.

"Thank you for that, most people don't realize how hard it is to just go in."

He gave her peck on the cheek. She lifted her lips toward him expecting a more passionate kiss, but it didn't come. Instead he pulled away from her.

That night her sleep proved to be restless as she relived the evening with Daniel and recalled his demeanor toward her. She needed to show him her changing heart. She wasn't the self-centered Barbara any more, she was truly seeking God's plan for her life; not Satan's.

The next day, Barbara saw Daniel at the hospital as he hurried down the opposite hall. They locked eyes for a minute. He smiled and waved and then turned toward the patient rooms. At the end of her shift she heard footfalls in the distance behind her. Her heart raced when she saw Daniel running toward her.

"Mind if we walk together," He asked as he came in step with her.

She smiled and a butterfly feeling flew across her stomach. "That would be nice," she demurred.

Once they arrived at Barbara's apartment, she offered Daniel an invitation to come stay for dinner. "I have a couple of steaks I can throw on the grill."

"Sounds wonderful."

Barbara's heart lightened when he accepted the invitation.

"Let me go home and change clothes. I'll be over there in thirty minutes." Daniel yelled as he headed for his own apartment.

The steaks hit the spot for two hungry people after a ten-hour shift.

"Are you ready for graduation?" Daniel prodded.

"I can't believe it's here already. My baby brothers will be coming next year."

"I enrolled for the residency program today," he said.

"That's great when do you start?"

"I don't know yet; I have a choice between two programs."

Barbara froze, she knew this meant he may not stay at Burlington Heights University Hospital, where she had obtained employment after graduation.

"Where are you going?" She asked as she tried to approach him again. He walked away from her and sat down on the couch.

"Not sure, there are options I have to consider." Daniel said.

"Can you share them with me?"

"I didn't think you'd be interested," Daniel responded.

"What makes you think that?"

"You told me."

"What? When? I don't know what you're talking about." Barbara wrinkled her brow in confusion.

"The day of Teresa's funeral."

"Daniel, that was years ago." Barbara attested. "What about it?"

"Remember the car that ran into us?"

"Yeah!"

"Right before it hit, you said you had a secret to tell me."

Barbara studied Daniel's face for some sign of emotion. It wasn't there. Before Barbara could start explaining, Daniel interrupted.

"After the car hit us, you screamed out, "Leave me alone. Remember?"

"Daniel I wasn't talking to you."

"I was the only one there."

"No, Jerk Fat appeared and he caused the accident. You were wounded and he laughed. I screamed at him. Is that the reason you've been pulling away from me?"

He nodded his head.

"Daniel, that was two years ago, but you only recently started pulling away," She contended.

"Barbara, you remember the car wreck victims I told you about in the ER?" Daniel asked.

"Yes." Barbara answered still feeling angry that Daniel wouldn't understand her words. She didn't get the relevance between his drawing away from her and the ER victims.

"As I stared into that precious baby's face, and wept for the loss of his unlived life. I knew. . ."

"Knew what?" Barbara rubbed Daniel's back as he hunched over. He pushed her away.

"I want. . . no I need, a family. I want children, I want a wife that wants to be a wife and mother. I need it. It's God's plan. God made the family and your activities in that women's group are destroying your mind and your soul. I don't believe you can be a godly wife and mother. I love you but I want a helpmate, not an adversary."

Barbara withdrew from Daniel's space. She didn't want to hear those words. She would have to face the truth of her own deception. She wanted to build her own career and be in charge of her own life. Even though her recent experience in prison led her back to her Bible study; a change of desire came slowly. She could tell Daniel had grown tired of waiting for her to get her priorities straight. She sat down and listened and watched, suspecting this may be her last time with him.

"I saw us."

"How?"

"After Teresa's horrible death, you were still more concerned with your women's group than about us building a family. In fact, you made it clear you didn't want a family, or to be 'drug' down by the responsibilities of marriage, you want a career. You know what's funny?"

Barbara didn't see anything funny in this conversation. "What?"

"You want a career in God's work but you are so far from the heart of God, you wouldn't even know what that work is."

Barbara fought the tears.

Daniel stood up and started pacing in the room as he continued his tirade. "God wants us to marry and multiply and take care of His earth. But you want to. . . I don't know, you want to be god!"

Barbara stood and faced Daniel, her mouth open. She no longer shed tears; she grew angry. "I don't want to be god." She said as she stood up and faced Daniel.

"Don't you?"

Barbara sat down on the couch. "Daniel the more I try to understand the more confused I become. I really believe my work is to help women."

"How? Equal pay? you are so deceived by your own agenda you can't even see the truth."

"What are you talking about?"

Daniel turned and looked straight into Barbara's eyes and with measured sentences said, "It's not about women's rights, it's about abortion. They think if it's legal then it can't be morally wrong. Look what that did for Teresa."

"What do you mean, morally wrong?" Barbara whimpered.

"The worse offense is hiding Jesus from those who need Him most." Daniel miffed and turned his back on Barbara.

"How is women's lib hiding Jesus?" Barbara screamed.

"Marriage and the different but honorable roles of men and women. You want to destroy men and yourself in the process." Daniel pointed his finger in her face.

"You want to be a god just like Eve in the Garden. Satan's lies haven't changed because they don't have to change, you are still foolish and vain." Daniel lectured with raised voice and red face. He sat down and crossed his arms.

Barbara clinched her teeth. She wouldn't engage in a fight with this man over the women's group. He is her rock, her love, her life; she couldn't breathe without him.

"I don't understand why your angry at me."

"Because you don't want a family, but I do. You aren't listening to me, but I listen to you. I heard you tell me to leave you alone and now you are getting your wish."

"Daniel, that was the demon two years ago."

"It doesn't matter anymore. I think you trust this demon more than you trust your friends, me, or God. I think you want to be like him." Daniel walked over to the door and opened it. "I'm going home. I'm moving and this is the end of my pursuit of Barbara Troye."

Barbara cried out, "Daniel, you can't mean?"

"I mean every word of it, I have given four years of my life trying to make you my wife, now I'm glad I failed because I don't want you anymore."

With that final statement, Daniel walked out of her apartment and slammed the door in Barbara's face.

33

Kidnapped

> Who is the wise man that may understand this? And who is he to whom the mouth of the Lord has spoken, that he may declare it? Why is the land ruined, laid waste like a desert, so that no one passes through. . .? they have walked in the stubbornness of their hearts and after false gods.
>
> ---Jeremiah 9:12,14a (NASB)

BARBARA PACED AROUND her empty apartment. *What am I going to do without Daniel? Now I'm truly all alone.*

When Sunday arrived Barbara felt loneliness surround her like a shroud. Sharon's visit to her mother's added to the feeling of loneliness. Sunday afternoons usually provided rest and play time for the two girls, but today, those activities escaped her because of her broken heart. Michael had joined some of the other guys from the psyche group for a fishing trip. Daniel, now absent from her life, left a huge gaping hole in her heart. She would spend the afternoon alone with her thoughts about the stupid things she had done in the last few years. She fondly remembered the first time she met Daniel. Oh, how I wish I could go back to that day, I would do things differently.

A passage she had read in her Bible Study only a few days ago came to her mind, "I the Lord search the heart and test the mind."

"Lord are you searching my heart? If You are then you see my sincerity in repentance. Please test my mind. I don't want to believe lies anymore." She wept at the hopelessness of her situation.

The phone rang. It was Patti. Even though Barbara didn't have much in common with this strange girl, the opportunity to be with people felt better than being alone with her own company.

"Grandmamma would like you to join us for dinner tonight, around eight," Patti invited Barbara.

Barbara answered. "What's the occasion."

"She wants to thank you for helping in my release from prison." Patti said. "I will send a car for you if you like."

"That sounds nice, I don't much feel like driving today." Barbara answered.

"You sound blue." Patti noted.

"Sorry, I find myself alone, so your call came at the right time." Barbara tried to explain without sounding pitiful.

"Glad to hear it. I'll see you soon."

Patti hung up and turned to grandmamma. "You were right, she's all alone."

"I told you Jorkphat would not fail us."

"I wonder how he discouraged the boyfriend?" Patti asked. "He's pretty devoted to Barbara."

"Our Jorkphat knows how to plant lies into the mind of even the strongest Christians. I'm sure it was an elegant break-up," Grandmamma suggested. "He is a colorful fellow."

"I'll say." Patti rolled her eyes upward as she reaffirmed Madame Lilith's comment.

"That felt strange." Barbara said as she hung up the phone.

Drained from the cry before the phone call, Barbara didn't let another thought come into her head. She put herself on automatic and walked to the bathroom, pulled a pill bottle from the shelf and took a Valium. She drew herself a bath, eased her relaxing body into the hot water, leaned her head back and looking up at the ceiling said, "I'm sorry, but I'm not strong enough. I've lost Daniel, the most valuable thing in my life. My heart is broken and hurts too bad. Tonight, Valium is my god."

Soon Barbara felt the, don't-care attitude and a sense of well-being, invading the shattered soul of the break-up with Daniel. After an extended length of soaking time she pulled herself out of the cooling water in the tub, wrapped a robe around her body and fell onto her bed. I have time to nap before Patti comes. Just before drugged sleep overtook her body, she heard the familiar laugh of Jerk Fat.

The clanging alarm clock entered Barbara's dream as gunshots. She could feel panic overtaking her. She groaned and rolled over. The Valium had not completely worn off. She needed more sleep but not with the memory of Mr. McCord and the dragon hanging around in her mind.

"Lord, is this part of your test of the mind?" She said with sarcasm born out of the deception of pharmacology. Patti would be here to pick her up in less than an hour. She swung her legs over the edge of the bed and held her foggy head in her hands. Life's the pits. She ambled toward the kitchen and poured herself a hot cup of coffee. The brew that would make her world sparkle in about three minutes. At least she hoped it would.

She wondered why she accepted the invitation to Patti's house. Although she had been dazzled by the house and its occupants, she noticed Patti wasn't much of a friend. She was more like a tour guide. Conversation did not come easy with her. Nonetheless, it would be a meal with people and maybe. . . just maybe. . . she could forget her broken heart and messed up life for a while. She headed to the bathroom and proceeded to get ready.

When the man Patti called Uncle appeared at the front door, Barbara wasn't surprised. Why would Patti come if she could send her butler/uncle or whatever? He handed her a note from Patti. Bring the red dress and the jewelry, we'll do your hair and make-up when you get here.

Barbara shrugged her shoulders and looked at the pant suit she had donned. We must be going to play dress-up. She left the door open and retrieved the items. She sat her purse down on the bed when she picked up the box.

"Okay, I'm ready," She told Mr. Uncle as she pulled the door shut behind her.

Daniel picked up the dishes with a blank mind. His empty heart yearned for Barbara's company. Why had he been so harsh on her? He went through the motions of Sunday afternoon living, when suddenly he dropped a glass with a loud crash. What have I done?

He called Barbara, no answer. He went to her apartment and banged on the door. No answer, but the door was locked. He looked in the window. In the crack of the curtains he could see her on the bed. He released a sigh of relief and went back home. He would tell her later he had accepted the residency at Burlington Heights and plead with her to forgive him. Maybe then they could make some life-long plans.

"What's your name?" Barbara asked Uncle.

"I'm called Uncle, but my real name is Lapetos." He said with a slight curl of his lip.

"Strange name."

"It's Greek; it means to wound or pierce."

Barbara shuddered at the way he said the words.

They rode in silence. Barbara's thoughts drifted to Daniel and his words. They had pierced her heart through and through and even now she bled from the wound she felt would never heal.

They arrived at the big house. Barbara noticed Lapetos moved his rear view mirror to look at her. She turned away from his stern gaze. Then she heard Michael's voice in the back of her head, "Be careful, little one, be careful." Barbara gasped at the warning she heard.

"What's wrong?" Lapetos asked when she gasped.

"Take me home, right now."

"I'm sorry. I can't do that."

"Why not?"

He licked his lips in a slow deliberate manner. He didn't give her an answer. Barbara could almost swear he hissed at her. She tried to shrink away from his gaze and review her plight; I'm alone, and no one knows where I am.

Daniel couldn't release a feeling of dread in the pit of his stomach. As he walked home from checking on Barbara, he decided to visit Michael. He paced up and down as he related the events of his break-up with Barbara to Michael.

"I said I didn't want to see her again. That's a lie! I can't imagine being without her. Why did I say it?"

"I know Barbara, and I know what we are seeing now isn't her. The demon that whispers in her ear makes her obnoxious."

"I know, but I still love her. It's like God placed a love for her that will not let go; no matter what she does. Before, her ideas of feminism seemed like a passing fad. It wasn't the same this time."

"Different how?"

"I brought it up and the more I talked the angrier I became. I sensed someone directing my thoughts and putting words in my mouth." Daniel moaned and sat down. He buried his head in his hands.

"You just described what happened; to both of you," Michael consoled.

"What?"

"Remember how the demon revealed himself to you on the bodies of that family?"

"They were on my mind when Barbara and I started talking, in fact I brought that up in my speech against Barbara," Daniel related.

"What happened, that brought it on?" Michael asked.

"We went to a movie, had a nice dinner and we were enjoying each other's company, then I told her about my residency applications."

"Go on." Michael encouraged.

"I made it sound like I would leave."

"You didn't tell her they were both local?"

"No, another person started speaking through me, and I wanted to hurt her." Daniel plopped down on the couch and lowered his head. "How could I have been so cruel to someone I love?"

"I'm not sure you were," Michael pondered. "I saw this happen in Nam. The stress, exhaustion, unfamiliar surroundings and strange people took over and we became different people, cruel people. It appeared insanity claimed us."

"That's exactly how it felt."

"Let's go see Barbara, she should be awake by now," Michael suggested.

Daniel agreed and jumped up, ready to make amends.

"She's not answering; is she still asleep?"

"Surely not." Michael answered him and turned the knob, the door was unlocked.

"We can't go in?"

"I can," Michael said without any hesitation. His manners had given way to concern. Daniel followed. Despite the late hour, the apartment had no lights. Michael flipped the switch to explore the kitchen, bedroom and bath. Daniel followed.

"Look!" Daniel exclaimed to Michael. "Here's her purse. She wouldn't leave without it and her car keys."

Daniel picked them up and paced across the room, muttering. Michael continued to search. He knew worry consumed Daniel and it would keep him busy while he looked for more clues. Something didn't feel right.

When Uncle pulled in front of the opulent house, Barbara attempted to open the door. Uncle came back and opened it for her. When she emerged, he took her arm in a firm grip and whispered. "Smile for your host."

She obeyed the ominous threat. "I forgot---"

"It's okay I'll bring the box in for you," he responded without letting her finish.

"Hello my friend," Patti greeted Barbara with a big smile. Her uncharacteristic greeting mimicked a lifelong friendship.

"Hi," Barbara managed to murmur in the midst of her host's enthusiasm. Her rapid heartbeat slowed down with Patti's exuberant recognition.

"I hope you brought the dress. We are having many guests tonight. It's a formal banquet."

Barbara looked down at her pants and slip-on flats. "I'm not dressed for a banquet." Barbara noted with apology.

"It's okay, Uncle is bringing that exquisite dress you modeled for me." Patti chimed in with a lilt to her voice. "You did bring that luscious red gown, didn't you?"

"I did. In fact, I brought the whole box," Barbara volunteered.

"Good, let's get you to the beauty salon where they can work their magic on you."

"Beauty salon?" Barbara raised her eyebrows at the suggestion.

"Yes, we have one here. We have three beauticians."

Before Barbara could ask any questions, she found herself standing in the doorway of the most elaborate beauty center ever. A middle-aged woman of statuesque build came over to her and took her elbow as Patti let go of her arm. It felt as if Patti passed her to the other woman, like a package.

"Wee, my dear, you have most beautiful cheekbones," She said in some kind of European accent. She ran her fingers through Barbara's hair. "Lush hair, good style; I have much fun to make you beautiful." She turned and winked at Patti. With that motion Patti left and shut the door. Barbara heard the click of a lock.

Quickly, the woman took her by the arm and lead her to the interior of the lush salon, "Come, we make you beauty shine." Barbara didn't argue or fight, why should she? It appeared the group prepared some first class pampering for her. Maybe the locked door kept others from taking sneak peeks?

Two hours later Barbara stood in front of a mirror. If it weren't for recognizing her obnoxious navy blue pant suit, she would not know the reflection she gazed upon, as herself.

"Wow, I'm beautiful." She gasped.

"Wee Mademoiselle, we show you natural beauty. Now, for wardrobe."

"I brought my own clothing," Barbara interjected.

"Yesss, I know." She hissed. "It's outstanding. Go, put it on. Michelle will help you." The young girl serving as her guide led her to an anteroom where the crimson velvet dress lay out perfectly pressed along with the sparkling heels and accompanying jewelry. How could I have been afraid? I'm queen for a day.

The dress formed to her body perfectly, the shoes enhanced the upturned circular flower petal hem with the flowing train. The sparkle of the diamonds gleamed against the crimson flow. Barbara smiled at the reflection. "I look like a princess," She said. The three women smiled and nodded.

The matron of the group spoke up, "Now is time to meet Grandmamma and her guests in the grand ballroom.

Barbara felt like Cinderella at the prince's ball. The dress moved in rhythm with her hips. She held her head up high and followed Patti to the ballroom. As they walked the length of the hallway, Barbara noticed that Patti dressed in formal wear yet not near so elegant as herself. She smiled at the thought of being the most beautiful woman at the ball. All eyes would turn to drink in her beauty and grace. A silly thought popped into her head as she wondered if her shoes were made of glass.

"Come my dear," Grandmamma motioned as she and Patti passed through the doorway of the huge room. There a grand appointed dining table with at least fifty people seated around it stretched from one end of the room to the other. Uncle held out his hand with palm down. He guided her into the room. They stopped at the end of the table and the grand baritone voice of Uncle announced, "Ms. Barbara Troye of Church Creek Falls."

The people around the table clapped as if she had finished a concert. Barbara continued to follow Uncle's lead as he seated her in the first chair next to Grandmamma. Patti sat at the opposite end. Uncle helped push her chair under the table as she sat down. She thought of her mother and grateful for her insistence upon learning Gloria Vanderbilt's rules of etiquette.

Grandmamma leaned over and whispered, "Follow my lead." Then she smiled and patted Barbara on the hand. Barbara looked around the table and studied her fellow diners. They were all beautiful. Suddenly, Barbara felt foolish for being so prideful of her own beauty. The women at this table appeared to be the loveliest of all women. The men were a miss-mass of older men sporting paunches and bald heads as well as handsome middle aged men with streaks of gray. They all looked distinguished. The women appeared to all be under thirty. The juxtaposition of the couples puzzled her. Sitting across from her was the only young man in the group. He looked handsome and distinguished but not near as handsome as Daniel.

"Oh, Daniel," she sighed quietly. Her heart ripped open with sorrow at the thought of losing him. She would have to endure this play-acting for the remainder of a meal, then maybe Uncle would take her home. She determined she would confront Daniel and find out why. . . why he didn't want her anymore. She hoped her hair and makeup would endure so that when he saw her, he would beg her to return to him. Of course he would.

"Any more clues?" Daniel asked.

"She left in a hurry," Michael pursed his lips as he continued to scan the apartment for clues. "There are no signs of any crime, but even for Barbara this is out of character." Michael mused.

"Do you think she's been kidnapped?" Daniel pleaded.

"Maybe, look at this."

"What is it?"

"A note from Patti."

"Isn't that Pap's daughter?"

Michael looked long at Daniel before he spoke. "Yeah, sort of."

"But?" Daniel encouraged Michael to complete his thought.

"She's not really his daughter, and she's not what you would call a good person."

"How do you mean? Would she hurt Barbara?"

"Possibly, she's a witch."

"How could she be Pap's daughter and be a witch?" Daniel contended the idea.

Michael gave him a glance with one eyebrow raised. "Never underestimate the enemy."

Daniel shrunk away from Michael's glare.

"Paps fell hard in love with Patti's mother; Karen Macklin was her name. He wanted to give her everything."

Daniel nodded wanting to hear this story if it had some clue about Barbara's whereabouts. "Yes," he said urging Michael to continue.

"She worked as a prostitute. Paps wanted to get her out of the life. He saved his money and bought her from the madam of the brothel where she worked. After they were married, they both flourished. Paps had finished his service to the Navy and found a good job as a welder. They were thriving. They were both thrilled with Patti's intended arrival even though they both knew biologically Paps could not be her father since Karen became pregnant before she and Paps met. They wanted to name her Patti Jane."

"What happened?" Daniel encouraged him to keep talking while he kept looking through Barbara's apartment.

"The madam realized her mistake at selling Karen, her big money-maker and a new baby too. The madam threatened their marriage with violence if Paps didn't pay another ten thousand. He didn't have that kind of money. A couple of her hired thugs kidnapped Karen. They beat Paps pretty bad as he fought hard for her."

"Why didn't Paps challenge her legally?"

"He discovered their marriage certificate was never filed. His claim could not be validated." Michael sighed with the painful detail.

"One day Karen showed up on his doorstep. Her bruised and broken body suffered from a beating she could not conquer. As a result, none of the Johns wanted her, so she wasn't making any money. Besides, Madam had the baby girl. She would groom her for the life of a prostitute and witch. Paps cared for Karen until she died. He said, 'I could never give her what she really wanted; her baby girl to be free of that woman.' After he lost the love of his life, he joined the Army and went to Vietnam. He spent his last nickel trying to get custody of that little girl."

"What does all this have to do with our situation now?"

"Pan is Patti, and she's the one that has Barbara."

Daniel whispered. "Do you think?"

"Do I think the madam would enslave Barbara? Absolutely."

As the word came out of Michael's mouth, his eyes widened. "The brothel," Michael shouted and headed out the door. Daniel followed.

The seven course dinner had been amazing. Barbara couldn't believe such food existed. Some of it delicious and some disgusting making her gag. Especially the sight of octopus still wriggling and other such "delicacies" She felt relief at the end of the meal. The young girls serving the final course of lime sherbet kept their heads down and exited the dining room. Young men serving as waiters brought coffee. They moved with robotic motions. Barbara looked at her waiter to tell him thank you and noticed a skeletal like face and body. He appeared to be starving. She gasped. The much needed coffee washed the awful tastes out of her mouth. . . and mind.

She could feel the stare of the man across the table from her. She didn't engage in conversation with him. The boring conversation with the woman next to her, gave her sympathy for the young girl. Her banter revealed a sullen unhappy person. In fact, smiles and humor didn't grace this place at all; only heaviness. She couldn't believe a house so beautifully decorated and filled with beautiful people produced such stale air. It stank of rot and decay.

Once the waiters completed the task of pouring coffee for the guests, Grandmamma spoke up.

"Let's go to the atrium and enjoy the beautiful night and full-moon. I believe the orchestra is tuned up."

The crowd politely worked its way to the outer courtyard, a display as beautiful as the inside and as stale. Barbara turned to the young man who had taken it upon himself to escort her out.

"Where are the lights?" Barbara asked him.

"Oh we don't need lights," he pointed up at the full moon. "When your eyes adjust you'll see all you need to see."

The orchestra struck up a waltz and the dinner party guests danced. The man next to Barbara put his arm around her waist and pulled her close to his body. She immediately backed away. "Hold it buddy, we aren't that close."

"Oh, but soon we will be," he said with a crooked smile and a wink. Barbara ignored him. With his sharp features projecting a handsome face and deep turquoise eyes that could melt stone, she wondered why she felt repulsed by him. Maybe the orange tie he wore.

"What's wrong, my love?" he asked as he twirled her around the dance floor. She stumbled over her feet and stepped on his.

"I'm not your love; I can't dance and why did you wear an orange tie?"

"Thanks for being honest," he smiled as he reached up and removed the tie. "It does clash with that gorgeous dress. Where did you get it?"

"A friend of mine gave it to me."

The dance came to an end. Barbara pushed away from him. Another dance started. "Please let's sit this one out," she said.

"Sure," he pointed to an area with two white garden chairs. Another couple sat in the grouping of chairs at a lone table. "We can join my good friend, Samuel."

After they sat down, Barbara introduced herself to the couple, an older gray-haired man and a beautiful young girl. He held her close to him. Barbara conversed with the girl. The man listened to every word Barbara spoke, the young girl nodded and tried to smile. Finally, she spoke with a weak voice, "Are you new here?"

Barbara took a second look; she couldn't be more than fifteen. She put her hand over her mouth to keep from showing her surprise. She whispered a prayer, "Oh God help her."

She felt her own escort put his arm around her and squeeze her, "Don't meddle." He said with a gruff growl. She pushed at him, but his arm didn't budge. She shuddered. The reality of this dinner party slowly dawned on Barbara. She felt the heaviness. She looked around the sky as she recognized. . . the presence of a dragon.

"Where are we going?" Daniel asked Michael as they climbed into his car.

"To find Barbara."

"At a brothel?"

"It's our only clue."

The two men drove up in front of an older apartment complex. "She's here?"

"No, this is Pap's place. I've been cleaning it, and I came across some pictures and notes he made. I think they're important to us right now. We've got to scour the apartment and find an address."

Daniel followed as Michael opened the door. When they entered, Daniel saw mountains of papers and newspapers. "What did he do with all this?"

"He kept track of any possibility of finding Patti, that's how he found her."

"So why didn't he throw all this stuff away?"

"Not sure, but we better be glad he didn't, because somewhere in all this is how we'll find Barbara."

Michael picked up the phone. He heard a dial tone. Thank goodness, now if she will only answer. He dialed.

"Hello."

"Sharon, this is Michael. Remember we said prayer is Barbara's only salvation?"

"Yes. What's going on?"

"Now's the time, call her parents, call anyone and start praying and don't quit until I call you.

Michael hung up and saw Daniel on his knees "Good idea, but right now I need you to help me find a picture, an address, something that will help us find that brothel where Patti grew up."

Barbara turned her attention to the people on the dance floor. Everything looked different. The vision of a beautiful atrium withdrew as if a veil lifted from her eyes. For the first time she observed a different environment of rot and decay. It no longer felt like an elegant dinner party but rather a Hell's Angels gathering, or hell itself.

The cool night air made the thin girls shiver in their sheer dresses. The boys wore lose slacks with suspenders and no shirts. The older men and women were holding them close. Many of them obviously in pain and discomfort from the cool temperatures and the hot-headed men.

"What's going on?" She exclaimed as she turned toward her escort. To her horror she saw---a man dressed in orange and turquoise - Jerk Fat!

"I found it!" Daniel exclaimed as he pulled a picture out. "Is this it?"

"It has to be. Let's go."

"Should we pray?" Daniel asked.

"Yes, continuously while we are moving. In war you don't have time to go to a prayer room. You pray in the midst of battle. Right now we're in hand to hand combat."

Everyone heard, the scream coming from Barbara's mouth. The men laughed, as the girls and boys wept. The old men abused their girls in horrific ways that Barbara could never imagine. "Stop!" she screamed. One of the young boys being tortured looked at her and said, "You can't stop it, you'll soon be one of us." She noticed a tear running down the young boys face, most likely in horrific pain.

Barbara turned away and saw a young girl being held by another old man. He held her tiny fragile body next to his with her arms clasped at her side. She didn't fight him; she endured. She looked at Barbara, "I'm so sorry they trapped you," she said.

Barbara responded, "Trapped?" The girl twisted her mouth in a semi-smile. Barbara asked her, "How did you get here? How old are you?"

"I'm sixteen. My parents wouldn't buy me a car so I told them they were cruel, and I would rather live with the devil than with them. Then I stomped out of the house and the devil brought me home with him." She nodded at the old man pawing her body. Barbara shuddered. Another young girl looked at Barbara with no expression and offered her own dilemma, "I played with an Ouija board; and the devil dragged me to hell." Another one spoke up, "I went to have my future read, I wanted to know where to go to college." Still another young lady spoke up, "I was hypnotized as part of the entertainment at a party." The saddest child groaned, "I was a reader, I liked to read about dragons and witchcraft and now I live among the dragons." A girl older than the others, spoke up, "I used chakras to heal. Funny thing how that old snake at the base of my spine rose up. You know what, there was no lotus blossom, only this hell." They all spoke up and told their entrance into this place of perversion and torture. A new wave of voices hit Barbara in the gut, "I aborted my baby; I left my husband and joined the women's liberation movement."

Barbara's mouth fell open at the last confession. Jerk Fat smirked, "And now you know how you got here."

At the same time one of the young girls asked Barbara, "How did you get here?"

"I'm not sure, I met a girl---" Barbara would not admit her involvement in the women's lib group. The group that took her away from her study of God's Word. She remembered the events her mother taught her during their Bible study. After Adam and the woman consumed the fruit of the forbidden tree, the ground and the serpent were cursed. God told Adam he would have to work by the sweat of his brow and the woman learned she would have pain in childbearing and... Barbara choked as she realized the rest of God's word to woman, "and you will want to be like a man, you will not be willing to be loved by him but desire to be like him. As a result, you will be blinded to My love."

"I've been. ---"

Jerk Fat interrupted her thought and returned her to the conversation. "You've been a friend to Pan."

"Pan? Yes, she invited me---"

One of the young girls interrupted with a harshness in her voice, "She's the devil's invitation, she brought us all here." The girl sighed and the old man repositioned her upon his knee. "If you have a chance, run, or you may be sitting here tomorrow."

Barbara took the girls advice and wiggled out of Jerk Fat's grasp. She turned toward the house to leave and gasped, the opulent house no longer existed, instead she saw a run-down moss covered shack crawling with bugs, spiders and snakes. She heard a guttural laugh behind her. She turned and saw Pan watching her. Barbara gasped at the horrible change she saw in Pan. The dark-eyed beauty Barbara knew turned into a ghastly shell. The dark circles around her eyes painted an empty orb. Her mouth turned in an awkward way. Her pale skin looked blueish like a corpse.

A young boy near Barbara saw the change in her expression. He spoke the truth she felt. "Creepy isn't it? It's all a lie."

"Everything in this place is a lie," Another girl said.

Barbara heard a smarmy voice beckoning. She didn't want to turn around to face Jerk Fat.

"Turn around my sweet," He hissed.

"No!"

"Look at the beautiful trees."

She looked up. She didn't see trees. She saw yellow eyes and flicking tongues with occasional bursts of flames; they all watched her.

"Come my dear, it's time."

"Time for what?" Barbara saw Pan beside her smiling. She appeared once again as the girl Barbara knew, wearing a silver gossamer gown with flowers in her hair and ribbons flowing down her back.

"Patti, what's going on?"

"It's your wedding day," She stated with a smile, "and my name is Pan."

Jerk Fat smiled and concluded the statement, "To me."

"You're a joke; you can't have me," Barbara responded in disgust.

"You've been mine for years now, darling."

"What are you talking about?" Barbara wrinkled up her nose at him.

"Remember the mask your mother hung on the wall?"

"Yeah, so what?"

"Remember when you saw the light flickering one night?"

Barbara paused and wiped her clammy heads on her dress.

"The next day you sat on the couch and the mask pricked you. remember?"

"Yeah, so."

"That was me, and you became mine when I pricked your skin. I poured the seeds of anger and rebellion in your heart."

Barbara protested, "You can't hurt me! I'm a Christian."

Jorkphat and the dragons all laughed. The largest dragon in the front of the gathering bent down closer to Barbara. She stared in the familiar face of Nisroch, the same dragon she confronted on the family farm and at the witches' coven.

"My dear, remember the church which trained you as you grew?" He cooed as much as a fire-breathing dragon could coo.

Barbara stepped back from the heat and stench of his breath and body. She didn't take her eyes away from him.

"Those people, the pastor, your Sunday School teachers and all the fellowship of that church...were some of my most faithful servants."

"What? . . . No!"

"I taught them to be good 'Christians.' It's easy to keep their hearts away from the Holy one once they became so busy with their goodness and service activities."

Barbara moaned. She knew he spoke a partial truth. The church always had something going on, and it seldom involved any teaching about Jesus.

"What about Mrs. Waithe? She was a faithful Christian?" Barbara gasped, searching for a defense for her home church.

"I told her to leave, and she did. Funny, she was the only one with the knowledge to stop me and she gave up." Nisroch raised his head and roared with the final statement.

Jorkphat bent over and licked Barbara's neck with his rough tongue. She resisted, or rather tried to resist. Her muscles refused to move.

A foul-smelling man picked her up. Her eyes grew big at the sight of her own personal horror story. Her body failed her. They carried her toward an altar similar to the one Teresa had voluntarily laid upon. Behind it stood Grandmamma, but she morphed into the same person Teresa had introduced as Madame Lilith, the high priestess.

Michael and Daniel pulled up in front of a badly-neglected house with tall weeds and all kinds of wild creatures roaming about.

"This is it." Michael said, but he sat staring and didn't move.

"Are we going in?" Daniel asked while opening the car door.

"No! Shut that door." Michael screamed. "We can't go in yet, there is much . . ."

"Much what?" Daniel's voice raised with anger.

Michael drove off and headed to a well-lit service station.

"You need gas?" Daniel smirked.

"No, we need prayer covering." Michael got out of the car and went to the payphone where he dialed Barbara and Sharon's apartment, hoping Sharon reached Barbara's parents and gathered prayer warriors. "How's the prayer group going?" Michael asked when she answered.

"I called the Troye',, they said Zay and Rance had left to come help us. I enlisted Dr. Greenstein and Mr. Young."

"I'm surprised Uncle Buster and Aunt Merilee didn't come."

"I asked them, but they said, the Holy Spirit told them to remain at the farm, not next to Barbara. Buster said, 'I can't fight this battle for her.'"

"I trust him. Right now, I need prayer for me and Daniel. We're facing the devil and frankly, I'm scared." Michael admitted.

"Remember what Barbara said to you in Vietnam?" Sharon prodded.

"The battle is not mine but the Lord's. For even a coward finds bravery with hope and hope came in the Christ child." Michael quoted Barbara's words from the vision.

"Michael, Christ is our hope. He's the child that brought hope to the world. Don't give up."

"Our only weapon is the Lord's words," Michael affirmed.

"Is your sword sharp?" Sharon entreated.

"I pray it is," Michael faltered.

"Like the father of the possessed young boy in Luke 9?" Sharon reminded him.

"Yes, "Lord I believe, help my unbelief." Michael relaxed at the mention of the event.

"Jesus told His disciples this kind of demon only comes out with much prayer and fasting," Sharon reminded him. "We are your prayer support. Remember what else Jesus said," Sharon prodded.

"Nothing is impossible for God!" Michael thanked Sharon and reminded her, "Pray hard, pray diligently and pray continuously. . . it's Barbara's only hope of escape."

"Michael, now are you armed with a sharp sword?" She asked him again.

He smiled at the question and calmly said, "Yes, Yes I am."

"Then go!"

Sharon hung up the phone and called the Troyes

When Buster answered the phone he held it out so Merilee could hear. She began to pray. "We need strength. We are few in number against an enemy that owns the world. We come in humility to approach the creator of the universe and the one and only true God."

All the listening party-line members shouted "Amen." Sharon and the small group gathered together, fell on their knees and added, "God's plan will not be stopped. Not one that God gives to the Son will be lost."

A band of warriors, fully armed and suited in the full armor of God, plowed their way into the throne room of

Grace. As the Holy One saw and heard the pleas of His servants in that sacred setting, He armed His angel with a message and a mission. The angel dressed in military fatigues prepared to join a small band of warriors for hand to hand combat against a formidable gathering of dragons.

Barbara couldn't move or speak, although her senses of sight, sound and touch still functioned. Her heart pounded in her ears as she imagined the tortures the devil planned to inflict upon her. She thought of the vile exploits these dragons committed to Teresa. All of the young girls and boys gave her a final look of pity before they turned their heads away. They couldn't bear more than their own torture and hopelessness. Even a coward is brave with hope. Where is my hope?

Barbara saw the beautiful crimson dress turn to heavy chains holding dying babies next to her dripping with their innocent blood. It bound her in a hold she could not break. Jerk Fat picked up her hand and fondled the diamond bracelet in the image of a dragon.

"Thank you for the welcome sign as I enter my new home."

Barbara tightened her muscles hoping to move, to run, to escape before. . .

Pan took a ribbon and wrapped it round Barbara's forearm and then placed Jerk Fat's hand on top of

Barbara's arm wrapping the rest of the ribbon around Jerk Fat's hand.

"As this ribbon binds you together so shall Jorkphat be joined with your body," Pan said as she lit incense and raised her wand between the couple. Jorkphat said, "And now my beloved, let us be joined together."

"No!"

The shout heard across the room by all occupants. Michael stood calmly as the audience parted allowing Jorkphat to see the one who dared to stop the possession ceremony. "Move away from her."

Jorkphat laughed. "You can't stop me now, army boy."

Michael shuddered at the voice that had tormented him during the years of battle in Vietnam.

Buster and Merilee held hands and fervently prayed for their daughter. They knew their daughter's rebellion brought on this trouble. They didn't understand why they couldn't be near her, but they knew to be obedient to the direction of the Holy Spirit, even when it didn't make sense.

They prayed for Rance and Zay as two young teenage boys traveled alone to Burlington Heights to help their sister. Merilee didn't want the boys to go without them. How would they know what to do or say?

Her faith taught her to trust her Lord. She prayed for her children, both for their safety and their wisdom. The phone call from Sharon revealed the boys hadn't arrived. Merilee wept in deep painful sobs as she pleaded for her sons to arrive at their destination and with her whole heart, she beseeched the Holy One for the life and soul of her daughter. She prayed to the only one who could save Barbara - Jesus, the Holy One of God, who came to earth in the human body of a child.

34

Lost And Found

"Then you will call upon Me and come and pray to Me, and I will listen to you. You will seek Me and find Me when you search for Me with all your heart."

---Jeremiah 29: 12-13 (NASB)

"DO YOU SEE the street?" Zay asked Rance.

"I can't see anything. The rain puddles reflect all the street light."

"This farm boy don't like no city driving anytime, but night time in the rain is the worst. What do you think we should do?" Zay mocked himself.

"I don't know, nothing looks familiar," Rance moaned. "We haven't even seen the university. Do you know where we are?"

"No." Zay snapped at his brother. He had slowed down as much as he dared. Nonetheless, they were still moving, hoping to find their sister's apartment.

"Let's call Barbara, can you see a street sign to tell her where we are?"

Zay nodded. He pulled into a service station and waited while Rance went to the phone booth. He returned in a few minutes, "I need change." He stated. The two boys looked in every slot of the car for change, they came up with fifteen cents.

"It takes a quarter to make a local call." Rance said. Zay didn't answer, instead he studied the city map.

"Mom and dad will have to send a search party for us now," Rance joked.

"Naw, I think I can get us there. Here, navigate," Zay handed Rance the map with markings on it.

"Is this the way to Barbara's?"

"Yes, this is our starting point, here." Zay pointed to the end of the line.

"In that case, we are only three inches from her." They both gave a nervous snicker.

Thirty minutes later Rance asked, "Are we on Hempstead Road?"

"Look!" Zay pointed to the highway sign over the traffic signal.

"That's strange, I thought this Hempstead was a major street, not a side gravel road," Rance directed.

"Either way, it is the right name and fits the map. We're taking it, unless you have a better suggestion," Zay exclaimed.

A yellow pickup with flashing red lights pulled in front of them.

"Oh no," Zay cleared his throat.

"What? Oh no?" Rance repeated and turned around, "Police?"

Zay answered, "it doesn't look like police."

"I know."

Four yellow vehicles with flashing lights surrounded them.

"What the heck are they?" Rance wiggled around looking at the vehicles.

"What's going on, Zay, what do they want?"

Zay shook his head. "I only know we go where they want us to go."

The vehicles took the two boys about half a mile before they pulled them into a small parking lot in front of a small wooden barracks. The gentleman in the front car, dressed in military fatigues, and heavily armed with a pistol strapped to his side and a military M13 clutched in his hand, came to the window. Each car held two soldiers. The one in the passenger seat pointed weapons at their heads and surrounded the boys.

"Zay are we going to die?"

"Looks like we might."

Zay rolled the window down as the commanding gentleman approached.

"What are you boys doing?"

"We're looking for our sister's apartment. We're lost."

"Why are you lost, if she's your sister?"

"We're country boys and don't do much city driving. It's dark and raining, we got lost. I think we missed an exit." Zay explained.

The soldiers lowered their rifles. "Where does your sister live?"

"On University Drive," Rance squeaked out. He cleared his throat and continued, "She's a student at the university."

The military man looked over Zay's driver's license, "You registered boy? He asked with no inflection or emotion.

"We're seventeen." Zay answered politely.

"Let's see your ID." The military man demanded of Rance.

"I don't understand how you boys got here," he said.

Zay showed him the map, "This is the route I plotted at the gas station back there a few miles."

The man studied the map for a while, took it over to one of the other men. He walked around the car making notes. He went into the barracks building. Rance and Zay watched him through the window as he made a phone call.

"It's a wicked night for anyone to be out, much less a couple of plow boys still wet behind the ears." The gruff military man guarding them scolded.

Zay and Rance both nodded. The man handed them their ID's.

"It seems you have wondered onto private property. We will escort you to a city street and Sgt. Davis over there is going to escort you to your sister's apartment. He will confirm your story."

Rance took a deep breath to slow his beating heart, "Thank you Sir," he proclaimed and gave a salute. The man let his lip curl into a slight smile. "Your welcome son."

Once Sgt. Davis pulled up in front of Barbara's apartment, he and his partner walked the boys to the door and rang the bell. Each one held a boy with a grip made of iron. Both boys prayed Barbara would answer.

They gasped when a woman came to the door they didn't know. "Is Barbara home?" Rance managed to whimper.

"Are you her brothers?" The woman said and they both smiled and nodded. She looked at the two military men. "Who are these gentlemen?"

"We are helping the boys find their sister, is there anyone here who can identify them?"

Dr. Greenstein thought for a while, "Yes, come in."

Sharon saw the boys and jumped up and ran to them, hugging them before she noticed the extra visitors.

"Ma'am these boys say their sister lives her, can you confirm?"

"Yes. Their sister lives here with me, she's my roommate."

Sgt. Davis looked around. His partner did the same. "Is she here?"

"No, she's in trouble. That's why we're all here."

Davis noticed the group on their knees around the coffee table with an open Bible. "What kind of trouble?" Davis asked.

Sharon sighed and said, "spiritual trouble."

At her statement the two military men let go of the boys' arms.

"Where is she?"

"Her cousin and boyfriend are looking for her," Sharon said. "They're. . ." Sharon hesitated and gulped. "on their way to confront the —-"

"Demon?" Sgt. Davis completed her sentence.

Sharon looked up at him and smiled, "Yes! Yes!" Her shoulders relaxed and Davis took up her thought.

"Then you better start praying." Davis said.

He signaled for Zay and Rance to join the prayer group. A warmth permeated the room with a soft glow as the warriors of heaven joined them. The two listened to the pleas of the prayer warriors assembled. They opened a path to the eyes and ears of heaven. With a twinkling of an eye the two warriors joined the battle at an abandoned run-down hotel near the heart of the city.

"Thank you." Sharon whispered as she glimpsed a bright light passing through the room.

After the soldiers disappeared, Rance asked a question he had been pondering for a while, "Why is the military so protective of that empty dirt lot?"

35

Fighting A Dragon

> The effectual fervent prayer of a
> righteous man availath much.
>
> ---James 5:17 (KJV)

MICHAEL FELT HIS resolve fading as his stomach churned and his legs felt like wax melting beneath him. He bowed his head.

"Thought you were strong, huh? Jorkphat mocked.

Michael froze, unable to think or act. Daniel stood beside him,

"What are you doing?" Daniel shouted at the demon.

"Calm down," Jorkphat chuckled.

"I will not calm down! I want my fiancée."

"But remember you rejected her? She remembers," Jorkphat mocked.

Daniel knew the accuracy of the accusation. Jorkphat passed his hand over Barbara's mouth releasing her tongue to speak.

"I love you," she sobbed to Daniel. Her small form remained rigid preventing her from turning her head toward Daniel.

"Leave her now," Michael shouted. He knew the plans of Jorkphat, they lived in his memory. "You will not get any of us tonight."

With that statement, Daniel comprehended the meaning of Michael's words. He felt his knees go weak as he realized the action that Jorkphat must be plotting for Barbara. Daniel stood up and joined Michael. He whispered in his ear, "Is he possessing Barbara?"

"Yes."

"What do I do?"

"Remember, you belong to Christ. Shout His words at him." Michael instructed.

Daniel shouted, "The Lord weeps because His people have been taken into captivity."

Jorkphat backed off. He stared at Daniel with fixed eyes and stern jaw. Daniel brandished his sword of the spirit.

"How do you know?" Jorkphat demanded of Daniel.

"Don't answer, he will try to draw you into an argument, you can't win against him." Michael admonished. "Just quote any scripture. It's like a spear piercing him."

Daniel nodded. "Give glory to God before He brings darkness." Daniel shouted.

Jorkphat jerked and the dragons above roared.

"See, it hurts them." Michael smiled as he pointed out their pain. "The Lord will not abandon His people because of His great name." Daniel and Michael released a volley of scripture.

Jorkphat again jerked as if he had been hit in the back. He took Barbara's voice again. At that moment, Michael felt a surge of electricity go through him. He recognized the jolt as their prayer support delivering angelic help. With renewed strength he shouted toward Jorkphat, "We are overcomers through the shed blood of Christ who overcame the power of the evil one, the power of death!"

Once outside, Sgt. Davis said to Paul, his fellow soldier, "I think this is our mission."

Paul answered, "I agree. I can feel the power of darkness creeping over me."

"We're in the right place. Let's go spread some Light." Davis held up a golden flashing sword and disappeared into the air. Paul followed.

"Look," Paul said as they found themselves standing behind Michael and Daniel. "Listen, they are using their swords, they know God's word," Davis chuckled.

"Look at that wimpy orange demon. He can't stand against these two." Paul observed.

"I love seeing earthly soldiers fighting the dragons." Davis responded.

"And this one, called Michael displays a strength born of experience against that dragon," Paul announced.

Davis implored, "That's right, you ready to do some hand to hand combat?"

A roaring sound came rushing from the trees. It built into an ear-piercing scream. Flashes of light came with it and one deep strong voice said, "Jorkphat, get on with it."

Jorkphat looked at his wrist tied to Barbara's. "Now!" He shouted.

Jorkphat's visible body melted into orange smoke surrounding Barbara's body.

At the same time two soldiers stepped up beside Michael. They both held flaming swords. They approached the altar shouting, "By His redemptive work on the cross. He delivered us from the domain of darkness, and transferred us to the kingdom of His Beloved Son."

As the four men shouted in unison the words the Holy Spirit gave them, Pan stepped in front of Barbara. She pointed her wand toward the men and the dragons roared as lions. Fire came from the tops of the trees and lapped at Michael, Daniel, Davis and Paul. The four men surged forward through the fire and toward the dragon's altar where Barbara sat bound by chains. Again they shouted in unison, "When you walk through the fire, you will not be scorched, nor will the flame burn you."

The dragons' flames didn't touch the group. Michael called out to Barbara, "Put your eyes on us, look at the cross of Jesus. Come on, look only at Him!" He shouted with fervency. When she managed to move her eyes toward the small band of warriors, they again shouted, "For I am the Lord your God, the Holy One of Israel, your Savior. You are precious in My sight, and I love you."

With those words Barbara raised her hands and shouted. The dragons turned their flames on her, but once again they did not touch her body. She shouted back at Michael and the little band of soldiers coming to rescue her. They moved slow. She could feel Jorkphat's spirit pushing on her mind and soul. "Don't stop, he's taking me over," she screamed. Then she started singing, "At the cross, at the cross, where I first saw the light and the burden of my heart rolled away."

This time Daniel shouted "I love you with a love that will not cease. It will endure all things; Christ loves His bride. Barbara, you are my bride."

With those words a tear crept down Barbara's face. Her hope appeared in Daniel's love for her. She saw the Christ child as man's only hope. Now she felt brave. Even with bravery, her body jerked in convulsions.

"You will not get her back so easily you fool." The dragon known as Nisroch growled. "This woman belongs to me. We are deeply ingrained in her. Go away and leave us to our celebration."

Davis stopped running and stood up straight, he held his arm in the air and his body changed from that of a man dressed in military fatigues to a man dressed in fine white linen with a belt of pure gold around his waist. His body bronzed like a topaz gem. With the appearance of lighting and his eyes like a flaming torch. His voice carried the volume of a great waterfall.

"Let the Spirit lift you up, Barbara Troye, and take you away, the hand of the Lord is strong. It will lift you from the darkness."

The small band of soldiers stood meekly by the angel of the Lord and whispered words given them by the Holy Spirit, "The Son of Man will send forth His angels to gather out of His kingdom all stumbling blocks and those who commit evil. They are thrown into the furnace of fire; a place where there is only pain and violence."

With Davis' words, Barbara felt the invisible bonds around her body relax. She jumped off the altar and ran as fast as her numb feet could carry her to Daniel, Michael, Paul and the beautiful angel who had freed her. A noise like a massive landslide came from behind her. She turned and watched the earth swallow the dragons, Jorkphat, and Madame Lilith.

The bronzed man spoke again, but in softer tones, although still powerful, "Then the righteous will shine forth as the sun in the kingdom of their Father."

Barbara fell down at his feet and declared, "I'm not righteous." Davis picked her up, and said "only one deserves your worship and I'm not Him. He only can make you righteous." Barbara stared at a normal man dressed in army fatigues with her mouth agape.

Then Davis said, "Those who seek the Holy One, who entered the world of man as a human child, will hear and see truth."

With that Davis and Paul left as quickly as they had come. Paul looked at Daniel and winked, "Best duty ever!" He said as he pointed to the man in front of him.

Daniel held a shaking Barbara. She shivered as if her body were freezing. She leaned into him, "He. . . he . . . was. . ." She stammered and clung to Daniel with a fierce grip.

"I know sweetheart," Daniel rubbed her face as she rested it on his shoulder. She shuttered.

"Daniel, he. . ." She couldn't complete the sentence before she burst into tears. The release of terror flowed from her eyes.

"Are the dragons . . . you. . . know. . . still there?" Barbara pointed toward the trees.

"I don't see them," Daniel answered, but he had never seen them. Barbara buried her face in Daniel's chest, but she turned her head and looked up.

"Are they there?"

"No."

Daniel looked at Michael waiting for instructions. "What do we do now?"

Michael joined Daniel and Barbara, "We need to get out of here and get all these kids out." It seemed all the captors are gone. I'm calling Dr. Greenstein."

"Good idea, they're going to need her," Daniel said.

Michael herded the fifteen or so young boys and girls out onto the street. He didn't want to leave them in this dank, dark prison of the soul any longer. Once they were all on the street, Michael found a phone booth and called the police. Daniel stayed with the huddle of scared shivering young ones while he continued to comfort Barbara.

A groan came from the gate they exited. Michael turned and saw Patti Pan. "Patti, are you okay?"

"No, you idiot," Patti stumbled toward the group spitting and cursing. "You just destroyed my home!"

She turned back and looked into the darkness where the marriage of Barbara and Jorkphat had been interrupted. She sighed. "What do I do now?"

"You can come with us and be free." Daniel offered.

"No! she snarled and called out, "Nisroch, please come back." Her appearance changed before their eyes. A beautiful young woman transferred into the colorless black hole of emptiness when she called for the dragon. Barbara saw smoke surrounding Pan and it entered her body. A smirk appeared on Pan's face.

She sneered at her and licked her lips sending Barbara a kiss through the air.

One of the frightened young women rescued from the brothel turned her gaze from Pan to Michael and with a trembling voice said, "They'll beat us, you know. Not all of us will survive it. Those who do will be starved into submission." She made the horrific announcement stating facts which she knew.

"Not this time, honey," Michael reassured her. "We're taking you to a safe place until your families come."

"There's no safe place," Another young one spoke up, and Michael noticed tears tracking down her cheeks. He put his arm around her. "I understand," He said with great tenderness.

She turned, looked at him and asked, "How can you understand?"

"Dragons captured me too."

"How did you escape?"

"With my life and my faith. They can be overcome. Look to the One who has power over them."

"Who's that?"

"Jesus Christ."

"I've heard that line before," she answered as she pulled away from Michael's embrace.

"Not all who speak the truth, know how to get it," he replied to her objection. She stopped.

"What do you mean?"

"Many people hold a truth that has never been tested. You have been tested and now you are given truth."

"You mean---"

"You witnessed God's angel release you."

"I believe what you say, especially if you will get me some food and warm clothes. It will make the beating easier to endure."

"In faith, accept your rescue. It's a complete rescue, which means there will be no more beatings or starvations." Michael hugged the young girl. "Just believe, that's all."

"Believe what?"

"What you have seen tonight and let the truth be seen with the eyes of your heart. Believe in the One who came to set us all free from the demons, Jesus Christ."

Michael saw the police coming with a bus. "You go with them; they'll take you to a safe place. There you'll see kind people," Michael told her and the other young people as they blindly obeyed him. They were too weak, too cold, too hungry and too defeated to care.

Daniel, Barbara, and Michael stood alone in the dark. "Let's get out of here," Michael urged them toward his car. He turned and looked at Pan, "Last call for redemption." Pan returned to the decrepit house apparently with her dragon in tow. She lifted her hand and made an obscene gesture at Michael.

Sharon and the assembly of prayer warriors poured their hearts cry before the throne of Grace. Sharon stopped in mid-sentence, rose from the floor, and sat. The rest of the group looked at her.

She announced, "they have her. It's over."

The group stood from their kneeling positions and collapsed on the chairs. "I'm exhausted," Rance declared.

"You've been to war," Sharon reminded him.

The phone rang.

Dr. Greenstein took the call, "It's Michael, he said I needed to get to the mental ward, they are bringing in a group of young captives they've released. Mr. Young I'm going to need your help."

"So, it's really over?" Zay asked for confirmation.

"It's not over, but the immediate danger is past," Dr. Greenstein restated.

Zay called his parents.

Buster answered, "Yes, thank you, son." Buster turned to Merilee, "She's okay. Michael found her. She's safe."

Rance answered the door and paid the pizza delivery guy. The smell brought the group together once again.

"What do you think we should do now?" Rance asked anyone listening.

"We wait," Sharon responded. "And eat," she smiled and took a bite of her pizza.

36

Facing Truth

> All day long my dishonor is before
> me and my confusion has overwhelmed
> me, Because of the voice of him who
> reproaches and reviles, because of the
> presence of the enemy and the avenger.
>
> ---Psalm 44:15-16 (NASB)

WHEN MICHAEL, DANIEL and Barbara arrived at Barbara's apartment, Zay and Rance jumped up and embraced their sister. "Sis your shaking."

"I was. . . I saw. . . the dragons. . . they were gathered around me. . . and," she stammered.

"The event has left her shaken," Daniel explained.

Sharon took her by the arm, "Let's get you into some clean, warm clothes."

Barbara nodded. "Burn this dress and---" She took off the dragon diamond bracelet. "Get rid of this."

Rance took the bracelet and slipped it into his pocket, "No problem, Sis."

Sharon disappeared into the kitchen and Daniel followed. "I think some hot cocoa will help. It's her family tradition, you know."

"I've noticed that. Probably 'cause she's a farm girl." Daniel concluded.

Sharon laughed. "Can't think of a better sedative. Can you?"

"Right now, a natural, God-given sedative is the best medicine for us all," Michael informed them as he entered the kitchen in the middle of their conversation.

The weary group of spiritual soldiers sat and sipped the hot cocoa. Michael broke the silence, "Now I know how Elijah felt after his great victory."

"How?" Zay asked.

"Depressed," Michael related. He sighed.

"The battle with Jezebel? Zay asked again.

"Yes, and 400 pagan priests."

"I don't understand."

"Neither do I, but I feel it. We just saw an angel defeat the devil and we're depressed and hiding." Michael said with another deep sigh.

Everyone in the room nodded. They were all drained.

Barbara sat her cup down on the coffee table, shivered, and pulled her blanket tighter around her. "I'm still cold, you guys can't imagine the frigid temperature. I thought hell would be hot, but. . ."

"Extreme cold burns, ya know," Zay answered the comment.

"Did you guys see them . . . what. . . the one who . . ." Barbara mumbled.

"The angel warrior?" Michael finished her thought.

"Yes! He was beautiful," Barbara exclaimed.

Rance looked at Michael with knitted brow. "What?"

"He must have come because of your prayer. He and another man walked in dressed in army fatigues."

"Wow! That must've been Sgt. Davis," Rance grinned.

"Who?"

"Zay and I got lost. We ended up in an empty pasture, and all these army guys led us to their little guard station. Davis and another soldier named Paul escorted us to Barb's apartment. They said they did it to confirm our story."

"So how did they get to us?"

Sharon picked up the story and explained their prayer time. "Our prayers sent you an angel." She concluded the story with a smile.

"A powerful one," Daniel whispered into Barbara's ear. "For which I am thankful." Daniel put his arm around her and planted a kiss on the side of her head. "He gave me back my girl."

Barbara smiled at him and then leaned her head on his shoulder.

"I wonder why they had that empty lot guarded?" Zay asked.

"What are you talking about?" Michael inquired.

"We were looking for Hempstead street. We took the exit marked Hempstead and drove onto a gravel road in a deserted block." Zay related their harrowing experience. Rance picked it up. "And then all these armed guards surrounded us. One of them was Sgt. Davis."

"Michael pondered a minute, "Did you see trains?"

"Yeah, and that's all, beside that little guard station at the gate," Rance explained.

Michael shook his head with a big grin. "God watched out for us."

"Whad'dya mean?" Rance asked.

"That place. . ." Michael stopped and chuckled. "Those trains you saw were loaded with armed warheads and other weaponry. That place is locked down tighter than lions in the zoo. There is no way you could have just wandered onto it. . . unless---"

"God was leading!" Zay exclaimed.

Michael nodded, leaned back in his chair and smiled, "God armed us at a military arms depot."

"So what about Sgt. Davis? Zay asked.

"I don't know, but I bet if you could ask, there is no Sgt. Davis there."

"So why get us lost and take us there. Still doesn't make sense," Zay contended.

"We can't understand the ways of God, but we know we can trust Him," Michael sighed. "God's ways always have a purpose, even when we can't see it."

"What happens now? You know, to me and Patti?" Barbara ask in a weak voice.

"By the way, where is Patti?" Daniel asked.

"She stayed at the house," Michael divulged.

Barbara listened to the conversation of the people she loved most. She watched them interact and realized how much she loved them all.

The only man missing from the group was her father. She really missed him and his wise guidance. She felt a sharp pain in her chest, then she heard a quiet voice in the back of her mind say, "Your missing both your Fathers."

37

The Worse Is Yet To Come

Yet they did not listen to Me or
incline their ear, but stiffened their neck;
they did more evil than their fathers.

---Jeremiah 7:26 (NASB)

BARBARA WOKE UP early. Zay, Rance and Sharon were still sleeping. Slipping out of the apartment she went to the coffee shop for breakfast.

The plans for today included Zay and Rance visiting the campus, having lunch with her and then head home to Church Creek Falls. Until the activities began she basked in the stillness of the early morning. It had been wonderful having her brothers here. The experience with dragons, demons and warrior angels brought them together in a manner that could not be explained, or understood.

During the quiet respite of peace gained from that experience, she seriously thought about going home with them. Peace had been a stranger to her for so long. She reflected on the events of the past years she spent as a college student. With that chapter of life coming to an end she focused on her future life with Daniel and her friends. She now knew her place in life would be serving her Lord with Daniel at her side. They made a great and formidable team. A little giggle escaped her lips at the idea of a new life and family with Daniel. She held up her left hand admiring the engagement ring he slipped on her finger a few days ago.

When Barbara entered the campus cafeteria, it felt like the lights shone brighter and the crowd buzzed with laughter and conversation.

"Tell me what's on your mind?" Sharon prodded. "You look worried."

Barbara sat down at the table with Sharon and Michael.

"Since McCord is dead, where's the demon?" She absentmindedly stirred her coffee in rhythm to Sharon's movement as the three of them pondered the question.

Before Sharon could answer, Zay joined them. Barbara greeted him with a kiss on the cheek.

"Hey, you remember my baby brother?"

"Yes, we spent a long evening together."

"You guys are too good for me. If I were you, I wouldn't have spent my evening praying for me. But, I'm so glad you did."

"We wanted you to stop those women's lib meetings." Sharon grinned.

"It's still hard to turn away from them. I agreed with several of their key points," Barbara replied.

"We know. Sharon said as she placed a book entitled, *The Power of the Positive Woman* on the table.

"Another women's lib book?" Barbara snickered. "thought you wanted me to drop this."

"It is, but from a Christian's point of view," Sharon added.

"Who's Phyllis Schafley?" Barbara thumbed through the book and asked about the author.

"She's a lawyer, mother, wife, politician, publisher and Christian. She truly does it all without violating God's role for women."

"Does being a Christian make her reasonable?" Barbara squirmed in her seat as she tried to make her snarky comment sound better.

Sharon ignored Barbara's sarcasm and addressed the statement with seriousness. "She shows the trashy side of the feminist movement and how it conflicts with God's plan for women."

"I saw that side of feminism." Barbara whined.

"Schafley asked the question you avoided," Sharon pronounced.

"What question was that?"

"The cost?" Sharon took a sip of her warm coffee brew and watched Barbara over the rim of her cup.

"Not sure I understand, my dear friend." Barbara responded to Sharon.

"What is the cost to women if the ERA passes?"

"No cost, only benefits," Barbara exclaimed with a firm voice.

"Really? You want to fight on the front lines in a war?"

"Well, no but that's not what this is all about?"

"Isn't it? Equal rights mean that women will be treated the same as men."

"Yea, that's right." Barbara agreed but with less confidence.

"So what do men do now that women don't?"

"Go to war?" Barbara let the truth meander around her brain even though she questioned Sharon with mockery.

"Among other things, there will no longer be male and female dressing rooms or rest rooms."

"Aww, you just went too far, there are differences in men and women that can't be changed."

"Uh hu." Sharon moaned and let Barbara continue to reason her own arguments.

"Can you imagine women playing professional football. The tight pants would scare me off." Sharon snickered at her own little joke.

Barbara laughed too as she imagined herself in a football uniform.

"Women's sports should be as valuable as men's." She responded in defense of women.

"Should be, but if there is no division between men and women's sport, then men will slowly take over women's sports and push women out completely. At least with a division of the sexes women can enjoy sports." Michael chimed in with his evaluation. Barbara sneered at him.

"Women's sports are beginning to gain some notoriety, that would all be lost." Sharon rescued the thought.

"Why?" Barbara pondered.

"A woman's team that 'cannot' exclude men will soon become another men's team, pushing women out of the sports arena all together. That extends to Boy Scouts and Girl Scouts. The equal rights amendment is a two-way street. It has the potential to push women out of many activities they enjoy. Where's the benefit?" Michael schooled Barbara on the meaning of equal rights.

"Still, I think you're taking it a bit too far."

"Maybe, but she's telling ways the law can be interpreted. Remember she's a lawyer."

"She has something to gain from its failure, I bet."

Sharon shook her head and took another sip of coffee. She needed to keep a calm demeanor and not have a shouting match with Barbara. She changed the topic but remained in the context of the discussion.

"I want to be a wife and mother, what does that rule do to me? Will I be required to get a job?" Sharon posed her own thought. "I want to raise my own children."

"To me the worse part of the ERA is their method of destroying fathers. Men want to be a part of their children's lives too." Michael interjected into the conversation. He dropped his head a bit. "Men want a helpmate, not an enemy."

Barbara sat back in her chair and snickered. "Those things you've mentioned do seem unreasonable."

"And that is why she is the voice of reason; she reveals the unreasonable problems with women's lib.

"I don't see any of those things happening," Barbara retorted.

"Really? You didn't hear those women shaming their husbands and sons just for being men? Didn't you notice the pro-choice signs they held up or the homosexuals with their nasty little slogans? Your saying you didn't see that the day you were trampled by a mob of angry women?"

"Okay, maybe but women in combat, never," Barbara mocked.

"You never knows who's going to challenge the status quo and force their opinion with a law that can go either way. Did you know the abortion debate was won with the fourteenth amendment?" Sharon cautioned

"I don't even know what the fourteenth amendment says," Barbara groaned.

"It's the right to due process and privacy. Abortion is legal because someone presented a viable case for abortion being a right of privacy."

"I guess you have a point. But why would those things happen if the ERA became an amendment?" Barbara contradicted Sharon.

"Because, my dear idiot friend, God made women different and He gave us super-human abilities in the family unit. Destroy that and like the London Bridge everything else comes tumbling down."

"I need to think on this."

"Remember Schafley's credentials as opposed to an angry, bored housewife."

"Yeah, yeah. I will." Barbara mocks.

Barbara stuffed the book in her oversized purse. "Right now, Zay and I have an appointment with Dr. Winegren."

Barbara bid her friends goodbye and took her handsome brother by the crook of his arm. He stood more than a head taller than she. He had beautiful wavy blond hair. He would be the talk of every girl on campus. Barbara felt the need to protect him from girls who would use him for their own needs; but then hurt him because he had a tender heart. She sighed, *Chaos never allows for peace.*

"What's the matter Sis?" Zay asked.

"Thinking how I can protect you from overzealous women," She answered with a smile and a hug,

"You mean women like you."

"What do you mean?" She saw the knitted brow in her brother and realized he was concerned,

"I heard you back there, you're a hypocrite and a floozy,"

Barbara felt her heart sink to her knees. Her brother had called her a floozy. That was the word their mother used for women who exposed too much of their bodies and flirted too much.

"I'm not a floozy." She retorted.

"Not the way Mama uses the word, but you are mean to Daniel. He loves you more than you deserve."

"I can't argue that point. But I'm different now." Barbara argued,

"You're not as mean, but you still try to be something you're not, Paul said it best when he said, 'don't think too highly of yourself.'"

Barbara groaned at his analysis. She dropped her head for a moment and then looked up at Zay and countered his thought, "Zay, how do I accept the submission of womanhood as a Christian and still be true to myself?"

"You don't."

"What?"

"That's an oxymoron, if you're true to Christ then you will be true to yourself because of Him."

Barbara pondered Zay's wise words. He was a spiritual man with a close relationship to his Lord. Finally, she spoke up with a tone of humility. "Your words make that old agitation and anger rise up."

"Sis, I love you with my whole heart, but you need to discover who you're really mad at and why?"

"I guess the conversation about the reasonable voice raised questions. I guess I am self-centered."

"And self-worshipping." Zay patted her on the hand.

"How? What does that mean?" Barbara retorted.

"It means you are trying to make things work the way you want them too and you think you have the power to do so."

"I am confused. I hate this. It feels like the orange cloud is still talking to me," Barbara growled.

"Maybe he is, after all it was the demon that convinced you that you didn't need God."

"You go on. I need to reason the events and conversations from the last week."

"What are you going to do?" Zay asked cautiously, not truly trusting his sister to be alone.

"I'm going to find a quiet place. Pray and ask my God to give me direction in His will." She answered in a firm confident voice and a tender smile.

"Good idea," Zay patted her hand, and proceeded to his appointment in the science building.

She headed toward the grove of trees behind the science building which had the beauty of a city park but few students knew about it. She and a few other students had adopted the area as her own personal quiet place.

She sat down on the one lone bench under the only full grown tree. "Looking for quiet?" A strange small voice asked.

"I guess not since you are here, she groaned.

"You know who I am?" the voice said.

"You didn't disguise your voice. What do you want?"

A dark figure stepped out from behind the tree.

"Haven't you done enough damage?" Barbara screamed at the figure.

The black clothed person raised her head, removing the hood from her coat and looked directly into Barbara's eyes.

"We have plans."

"Who is we?" Barbara asked the dark clothed figure of Patti Pan. Turning her gaze at Patti Pan Barbara saw the yellow eyes of Jorkphat

"You!"

"You didn't think I would give up so easily, did you?"

"But, you were swallowed by the earth with the other dragons."

Patti laughed out loud and answered, "Yes, but I'm spirit and cannot be contained by the earth's bowels. The only thing that happened that night was your rescue by delay."

"I don't believe you." Barbara stood firm although her heart raced within her. "Peter said, 'God didn't spare angels when they sinned but cast them into hell'."

"Aww, you're right." Jorkphat snickered. Do you know what else Peter said?"

Barbara's mouth came open but no sound came forth. Jorkphat laughed. "I didn't think so."

"You know just enough to make it easy for me. If you ever really read your Bible, you would be shocked at what it says, especially about your shallow man-made religion."

"I don't understand." Barbara stammered.

"Peter said, 'God knows how to rescue the godly. You all think you are in that camp, so you don't read the rest.'"

"OK, smarty pants," Barbara said, sounding a lot more assured than she felt. "Why do you think I am not among the godly. I know Jesus and I belong to Him."

Jorkphat laughed and then quoted Peter, "The Lord knows how to keep those who indulge their lust with the perverted desires they feel. They are daring in their arrogance against authority figures. They seek their own will above the law and above others. They have no trouble cursing angelic majesties. Because of this they suffer the consequences of doing wrong. They have a heart trained in greed, and they never cease from sin and find delight when enticing gullible naïve and unstable souls into a life of indulging the wants of the flesh."

Barbara put her hands over her ears and groaned. "I'm a fool."

Jorkphat raised his voice in his condemnation of Barbara still using the words of Peter, "You entice others and promise them freedom when you yourself are a slave to corruption."

Barbara put her hands down and looked at the body of Patti with the spirit of Jorkphat and exclaimed, "Your right, but now I know that there is an escape."

"I don't care, I have plans for you and I will not give up until they are complete." The voice of Jorkphat announced.

"I will not follow you. You distort the scriptures in my mind but it will return to you as your destruction not mine." Barbara exclaimed.

"You're right." Jorkphat said in a small voice. "So I have nothing to lose."

Patti's head turned upward. Barbara followed her eyes and saw Zay standing on the third floor of the science building. He was scared, really scared.

"But you have much to lose."

"You can't hurt him?"

"I can and I will, don't ever forget it." Jorkphat laughed at Barbara. She turned back toward him.

Barbara regretted her delay in praying. She felt naked against this entity of evil.

"Are you ready now?" Patti asked with a hypnotic threat that transformed Barbara into a willing subject.

"Yes," She droned.

The two girls got into the car. Lapetos sat behind the wheel. "You know where to go Uncle."

He nodded.

She looked at Barbara and smiled, "You ready?"

"Do I have a choice?" Barbara asked with sarcasm

"Always." Patti snickered.

In the quiet, Barbara wiped the tear off her cheek as she watched the neighborhood scenery change from bright to dark.

"At least this time there will be no one to rescue you." Jorkphat screeched.

Barbara recognized the neighborhood. They were taking her to one of her former women's lib meetings.

"Why?" Barbara asked about their destination.

"Because we have a task for you to do. There is a tender young girl there who needs someone to encourage her to carry out her thoughts. You will be that voice of encouragement."

Barbara sat still and gazed out the window. She silently prayed, *Lord, give me wisdom to help not injure.*

With the realization that she had to prevent her arrival at that meeting, she screamed, "No, no, no."

"No what?"

"You're not going to take me there again." The car neared an intersection. Lapetos slowed the vehicle. Barbara opened the car door and fell onto the pavement. She rolled as far away as possible. It would be better to be dead than to be trapped in that witches' hell.

The car squealed as it turned back toward her. Barbara stumbled and tried to raise herself. Pain ripped her body where the pavement met tender skin. She ignored it and pressed toward her goal. The urgency of getting away and reaching Daniel, Michael, Sharon, anyone flooded her brain. "Oh Jesus, please help me." She cried scurrying into an alley way. An indention appeared in the wall. With feet pumping and pain coursing through her body it provided protection. Suddenly, a door opened, she entered and the door closed behind her. Out from behind the door stepped a soldier.

"Ms. Troye," He said in a kind voice.

"Who are you?"

"I'm Sgt. Davis."

"You were there at---"

"Yes. The Father will not let go of those who call upon Him with a sincere heart."

Barbara collapsed on the floor. Sgt. Davis came over and bandaged her bleeding arms and legs. "You took quite a fall."

"I had too, I couldn't go back to a place of lies," Barbara moaned. "Today, I heard the truth. And that demon quoted scripture to me."

"Yes, demons will use God's words to confuse and entangle you in the corrupt ways and thoughts of the world in order to overcome you."

"But how, if I am a Christian?"

"Knowing Christ and having knowledge of Him are not the same thing."

"Explain, please."

"Everyone knows Christ, even the demons know. There is historical evidence for His existence and records of His miracles, but only those who have knowledge of Him as their Lord and Savior belong to Him."

"I can't go back there, ever. Help me understand." Barbara pleaded through trembling.

"Some things are hard to understand, it is those things that the demon will distort in order to capture. You have been searching for truth and finding deception."

"Why?"

"Because you did not trust the knowledge you had, but you let your guard down and the demon took you down a path of unstable ideas. Peter tells you to be found spotless and without blame through the strength of first-hand knowledge."

"I don't understand." Barbara asked Sgt. Davis with a sincere desire to know the answer.

"As you seek now, you seek with clarity, you truly want to know."

"Yes, I want to know."

"Then understand this; it is the patience of our Lord that is your salvation."

"He isn't giving up on me?" She smiled at the revelation.

"He's working to reveal Himself to you in such a way, that you will see Him."

Barbara smiled. "I see! I really see. He's showing me, not punishing me."

Sgt. Davis smiled and nodded. Then he looked her in the eyes. "It's not over yet. You have work to do and it may be the hardest work you've ever done. It's the Master's plan for your life and it's a plan for your good not for evil. Remember that!"

Barbara recognized the quote from Jeremiah 29:17 delivered to her in person by an angel. She nodded and smiled as she wiped the tears from her face and blew her nose into the tissue Sgt. Davis gave her.

"What is it?"

"I can't tell you, but your first instruction is to trust your God and don't fight your captors."

With that statement, banging assaulted her ears as the door broke from its hinges. Davis was gone. The angry face of Lapetos stared down at her. "Stupid girl, you can't get away from us. You belong to us."

With renewed strength and trust, Barbara thought of Davis. She kept her tongue quiet. The big man pulled her up from the floor and without any regards for the wounds he pushed her toward the door. "Get in the car and don't give me any more trouble."

The women's lib meeting presented the same content. Today, this routine put Barbara on mission. She listened for her cue from the Lord while cautiously watching for any lying cue from Jorkphat.

The speaker droned on and for the first time she heard the idiocy of the babbling. She was speaking without knowledge of the only true lawgiver-the Lord. Their concepts urged the destruction of men as husbands and fathers; men like her daddy.

Barbara shook her head and whispered, "Wow! This is all an attempt to destroy God as a Father. Their words sounded good, but were filled with lies. Yet the very words they spoke destroyed their value as God's beloved. While pushing their goal of government as provider instead of husbands, they denied themselves the God-given companionship and protection of a committed, loving, marriage.

A tear crept down her cheek as she realized God gave femininity to women as a gift. A verse from first Peter walked across her mind, "Husbands, dwell with your wives according to knowledge, giving honor to the wife and be together as heirs of the grace of life."

God made women to be honored by their husbands. This was the true definition of femininity. Suddenly, Jorkphat jumped in front of Barbara's face.

"Doesn't it feel good to be back in the old school." He snickered.

Barbara nodded but said nothing. She had seen that Jorkphat was nothing compared to the power of Christ. Like an angry feminist is nothing to the beauty and grace of marriage.

"Daniel and I are heirs together of the grace of life," she muttered out loud. "That's true beauty." With contentment in her heart she looked up at the speaker on the podium. For the first time listening to the message rather than the emotions of the speaker. Barbara felt her stomach lurch when the speakers urged the attendees to abort their burdensome babies. Barbara knew this was her cue, but was it from God or Jorkphat?

She ducked her head and once again heard that still small voice. *I wouldn't ask such a horrible thing; I wouldn't have even thought of it.* She knew this kind voice." The Lord God Almighty, *her* Lord.

A chant started in the room, "My body, my choice." Barbara looked around at the women raising their hands in the air and shouting. The mob mentality scared her. She heard a small whimper next to her. She looked and saw a petite young woman with her arms wrapped tightly around her middle. A mist covered her eyes.

"Barbara sighed, "If this is my mission, give me wisdom, if it isn't then stop my intervention into this young woman's sorrow." Barbara prayed.

"May I sit with you?"

The young woman nodded and wiped her tears. She looked at Barbara and grimaced.

With trembling voice, she spoke to Barbara. "I had an abortion and I would give my right arm to undo it. They don't know what they're asking for, it's awful. I get drunk every year on the date of my baby's death. How I wish I could hold him. I haven't been totally sober since that awful day."

"Why did you abort?" Barbara asked before she weighed her words and realized it wasn't any of her business. She feared Jorkphat may be the one directing her thoughts.

"I'm sorry, I shouldn't have asked that." She tried to cover her mistake.

"It's okay, I'd like to tell you. I need to tell someone."

Barbara took her hand. "I understand." With confidence she recognized the cue came from God. With that thought her spirit relaxed and Jorkphat faded into forgotteness. She trusted her God completely.

"I loved the baby's father. We were young and planning our wedding." She stopped and looked at Barbara.

"Go on, I understand." Barbara assured her.

"When we discovered I was pregnant, his parents presented a reasonable argument. They said, if we aborted this baby we could have more children later, after we married and became financially stable." The girl began to wail and couldn't speak for a while. Once she gained some of her composure, she continued her explanation.

"We agreed to the abortion. I didn't want it."

She stopped and sucked in air. "The people were rude. They rushed me through. But the worse part came afterwards. My boyfriend was nowhere in sight."

"Were you alone?" Barbara gasped.

"No, his parents met me and took me home. They were stone cold silent and wouldn't even look at me. When we arrived at my house, his dad looked at me with a hard scowl he said, 'we never want to see or from you again, understand.'"

Barbara patted her hand. The young woman continued, "My baby and my love are both gone." She covered her face with her hands. Her stomach lurched with the silent cries she held under her breath. "I know he loved me and our baby, but they wouldn't let him see me again."

"Do you know where he is now?" Barbara asked. They girl nodded her head and wiped her tears from her face. After she blew her nose, she said with great effort, "he's dead, they killed him."

Barbara wrinkled her brow at the horrible announcement.

"They said it was an accident but I don't think so. I think he drove his car into that lake on purpose."

"Why do you think that?"

The girl reached into her jacket pocket and pulled out a letter. She waved it in front of Barbara. "He told me what he was going to do."

The girl couldn't hold it together anymore, she leaned on Barbara and through language broken with sorrow and tears she moaned, "If only I hadn't killed my baby, I would have a family now."

Barbara took her hand again and stroked it, while thinking about Teresa. The girl looked at her and said, "There's no good reason to murder a baby, not a single one."

Barbara noticed Pan stood at the front of the room leading the chant. She also noticed a cloud of orange around her. "Let's get out of here." Barbara urged.

With the girl as cover, Barbara bent low as they walked through the crowd out the door. Barbara crept past Lapetos. She felt like he may have seen her, but he didn't make a move toward them. She wondered if this young woman was the task Jorkphat mentioned. Nonetheless, the comfort of Jesus leading them caused her to push forward. With Lapetos behind her, she whispered, "Jesus I need you to give me wisdom and a ride home."

"Do you know where we are?" She asked her new friend.

She nodded. "By the way my name is Donnetta."

After a few blocks, Donnetta stopped, "Here's my pad." She pointed to a small but neat house.

Barbara gave Donnetta a hug. "If you need to talk some more, call me." Barbara jotted her phone number down and handed it to her and bid her goodbye. Before leaving she turned toward Donnetta.

"Why were you at that meeting?" Barbara requested.

"I don't know, today would be my baby's first birthday if I hadn't murdered him."

She dropped her head. "My baby needed justice, I was his murderer so tonight I was executing his murderer. I went to the meeting to get the courage."

"I don't understand how the meeting would give you courage to commit suicide." Barbara said while searching for some words of comfort and encouragement.

"By listening to those idiots talk about killing their baby, I would realize how big a fool I was for falling for the lies and how much I deserved to die. I met you instead. You encouraged me to struggle through."

Barbara then realized she was supposed to encourage Donnetta to follow through on her suicidal plan, instead God stepped in and she became an encouragement to Donnetta. What Jorkphat meant for evil, God turned to good. She started walking away with a lightness of spirit.

Barbara stopped and turned back toward Donnetta operating the key in her door, "Do I need to stay with you?"

"No, I don't feel the need to die to honor my baby, I think I need to help others avoid the same mistake."

"What do you have in mind?" Barbara asked.

"I don't know, but the urge is strong. There is nothing to make me forget."

With that last thought Donnetta walked inside leaving Barbara on the doorstep to ponder her last statement

"Wait," Barbara called to her before she shut her door. "Can we meet again?"

The girl smiled and nodded. "I would like that." She scribbled her phone number and name on a piece of paper and handed it to Barbara.

"I need a friend. My boyfriend's parents blame me for the loss of their son and their grandson. Can you believe it?" She shook her head. Then she gave Barbara a slight hug.

With the conversation ended, Barbara noticed her surroundings were dark. Barbara had no idea how to get home. "Sgt. Davis, I could use some help right now." She said as she walked.

Davis didn't appear. Instead a car pulled up beside her. She started to run until the sound of a familiar voice called her name. She made a small turn of her head and saw Daniel getting out of the car and running toward her. She leaped into his arms. "How did you find me?"

"He smiled at her and helped her into the car. Once they were in he explained. "I'm not sure, I asked Jesus to help me find you and I started driving and there you were."

"Wow! Barbara wrinkled up her nose with a big grin. "I'm grateful."

"It's funny, but I would swear I heard Sgt. Davis, telling me where to turn."

Barbara smiled and said, "Thank you, Sgt. Davis" She turned her attention to Daniel and in a quivering voice urged him. "get outta here fast."

"What's wrong?" Daniel could see the anxiety in her face.

"I didn't come here of my own free will and my captors are going to miss me real soon."

Daniel sped up and headed for the main highway. "I think they may have found us. Hold on."

Barbara looked behind them. The car followed close enough she could see Lapetos angry face. They would both be items in the morning obituary if he caught them. "Oh, Lord, we are in Your hands." She said out loud.

"Amen!" Daniel confirmed.

38

New Beginning

> Now therefore amend your ways and your deeds and obey the voice of the LORD your God and the LORD will change His mind about the misfortune which He has pronounced against you.
>
> ---Jeremiah 26:13 (NASB)

SHARON OPENED THE door to greet Michael, "Come in, I'll be ready in a minute"

Michael slid into the chair across the room. "You alone?"

"Yes, Barbara took Zay and Rance to visit the campus. They're pretty excited."

"Me too! It's nice to have family close by."

Sharon came out of her bedroom. "I don't have that luxury."

"I thought you were going to move back to your mother's before. . . you know . . .all the excitement."

"So did I, but when I visited her and my dad, I realized real fast they needed to be alone to work out their problems. I have enough trying to keep Barbara corralled," She snickered.

"I've been trying to do that most of her life and haven't succeeded yet."

"Why do we love her, Michael?"

"I love her because she's my family, and you love her because she will be your family too after we're married," He put his arm around her and kissed her on the forehead. Sharon giggled and turned her head up to catch the next kiss on the lips.

Interrupting the intimate moment Barbara and Daniel came through the door with a loud rush.

"It's Pan, he's in Pan." Barbara blurted out when she came in.

"And he's still after me."

"What?" Michael said.

"Jerk Fat. He took over Pan's body when. . . you rescued me."

Daniel added, "Her bodyguard chased us, but we lost him."

"He knows where I live." Barbara shouted."

Michael came over and with a calming voice reminded Barbara, "He's not coming here for you. That's why he lured you away."

"Why, I don't understand?" Barbara moaned.

"He has to get you away from God and convince you to turn away from Him."

"Then why did he threaten injury to Zay?" Barbara pondered.

"A deception to pull you away from God's protection. It didn't work did it?" Michael grinned.

"No, it didn't. In fact, in worked against him." Barbara whispered remembering her meeting with Sgt. Davis. She rubbed her sore arm. She smiled when she remembered his gentleness. The smile turned to a frown with the memory of her encounter with the other young woman.

"Davis . . . He---"

"He, what?" Sharon prodded.

"He brought a young woman to that meeting where Pan took me. I think she's part of God's task for me," Barbara looked at Michael.

"God's task?" Michael interposed.

Barbara sat down and took a deep breath, "Yes several years ago, my mother told me God had a task for me to do. I think tonight's encounter with Donnetta may have been the introduction to that task." Barbara mused.

Zay and Rance stood in their sister's living room telling everyone goodbye. Zay noticed Barbara's face. He gave her a hug, kissed her on the cheek and whispered in her ear, "We'll be back soon."

Rance waved to the group and with his usual exuberance shouted, "See you all next year!" Then the two senior high school boys headed back to Church Creek Falls to finish their obligation to the state education system before they joined their second family at the university.

Barbara fell into a chair and despite all her efforts she started crying. "I feel so alone."

Her friends looked at each other and shrugged their shoulders. "We're still here."

Barbara laughed, "I'm sorry guys, I said that wrong. I meant, I miss my brothers."

Michael chuckled, "We know how you are. We're going out for breakfast, you want to join us?" Michael asked as he took Sharon's hand in his.

"No, you two go. I have an appointment later."

When the door closed, Barbara pulled her legs up under her and buried her face in the palms of her hands. *I'm scared, not sure I can do this.*

She got up, put on makeup, combed her hair and put on a nice dress. Grabbing her keys and her purse she headed out. She needed to have some alone time with her Lord before her appointment.

She considered going to the church where Sharon attended. When she approached the church she realized she didn't want anyone else's opinion. She wanted communication from the Holy Spirit on a personal level. She wanted first-hand knowledge of her Lord and Savior.

She drove to the park, found a secluded bench to sit. She stared up at the sky.

"Lord, you know all about Jorkphat. Can he still get to me? Is he still with me?" She addressed her questions to the one sending her on the task.

Taking a deep breath, she uttered her first sincere prayer in more than three years, "Jesus, if you're real give me answers."

She yawned and shook her head. Without thinking about it, she took her jacket and made herself a pillow. She lay down on the bench and went to sleep. Upon awakening she felt rested and strong.

She pulled her knees up to her chest and chuckled, "Mom, God gave me a task and I've just had my nap. Now I'm ready to see what He has done. I wish you were here to go with me to this appointment."

She looked at her watch. She had time to make her appointment. The feeling of fear no longer consumed her, instead there was excitement.

39

Answers

It is He who made the earth by His power, who established the world by His wisdom and by His understanding, He has stretched out the heavens.

--- Jeremiah 10:12 (NASB)

DANIEL CAME TO see Barbara. She wasn't home. Instead Michael and Sharon answered the door. He joined them, or tried to, he kept walking to the window and looking out.

"She's okay Daniel," Sharon said.

"How can you be sure?"

"After what you guys went through for her, I should think no harm can come to her."

"I wish I had your confidence. Oh, Oh, here she comes, everyone act normal," Daniel almost shouted. Michael and Sharon chuckled since he was the restless one.

"Hi guys," Barbara said with a genuine smile as she entered the apartment. "It's a beautiful day."

Daniel scolded. "Where have you been?" He said working to contain his anger mixed with relief.

"Seeking answers," she said calmly.

"Did you find any?" Sharon asked.

"Not all of them, but it's still early. However, I did discover another question."

"What's that?" Michael asked

"How did a demon get on me and try to possess me if I'm a Christian?"

Sharon spoke up, "Sin!"

"That's a simple churchy answer. Tell me what's sin?" Barbara said with raised voice.

"You missed it." Michael responded.

"No, I didn't. I heard Sharon say sin," Barbara retorted.

"No, what is sin? Sin is missing the mark, the goal, the object."

"So what did I miss?"

In unison the group said, "Christ!"

"That's right. We sin only against God, so anything we do that misses Christ is a sin," Barbara retorted with a crooked grin.

"You set us up?" Sharon countered.

"I guess I did, but I needed your confirmation that I had found the right answer. I tell you one thing for sure, I ain't missin it anymore," she smirked. "Sin hides in our very relationship to Christ, I've been trying to 'serve' Him, when I needed to 'seek' Him." Barbara intoned.

"Then all the other things come to you," Daniel finished the thought.

"The question becomes how can we see sin if it's hiding in our good works?" Michael asked Barbara.

"Bingo!" Barbara chimed in. "Some of us are more hard headed than others. We judge ourselves by others accomplishments."

"When you should be judging yourself by what Christ did for you." Sharon remarked.

"Right on, sister." Barbara intoned.

"Evil imitates good. It cannot create, so it imitates. It hides in the goodness of the good," Sharon added.

"You sound like a philosopher." Barbara laughed at her friend.

"When you quit studying your Bible and started studying the women's lib literature, you lost your vision of good and evil. That's why the demon could reveal himself to you, you didn't know the difference," Michael lectured.

He sighed and continued with a further explanation. "It happened to us in Vietnam, we saw the evil of the Vietcong, we saw them go into villages and massacre the people. We saw the people give allegiance to them out of fear. We saw war without rules. After a while, it became normal. People called us liars when we tried tell what we saw. So we quit talking." Michael said.

"When others won't see and won't believe, we quit talking about the goodness of God and His wrath toward sin. That's when sin grows among people," Sharon added.

"When did I fall for deception?" Barbara asked her friends.

"When you were denied your own plan, you didn't seek the plan God had for you, you attempted to make your own plan work." Sharon answered.

"So my sin was women's lib," Barbara repeated.

"No, you sinned when you turned from truth and started creating your own truth. The women's lib served the demon as a tool to capture you."

"I felt angry," Barbara said under her breath.

"That's when Jorkphat stepped in and started fueling the anger with his deception. He wanted to get your eyes off Christ," Daniel said.

Barbara ducked her head and changed the topic. "I've got something to tell you."

Daniel was standing near the window. He thought he heard something and looked out.

"Does it have anything to do with the people standing at your door?"

"I'm going with them."

"Where?"

"To look at a building,"

"What?" Daniel jumped in.

"I spent my morning with the Lord. I quit trying to make my own plans and I asked Him about His plans."

"What happened?"

"He brought Donnetta into my life. She survived an abortion but lost everything. I met her the night you picked me up off the street. I went back to see her."

"What did you do?" Daniel groaned.

"I invited her to join me in building a ministry." Barbara smiled as she vocalized aloud the plans God had given her.

"What kind?" Michael prodded.

"I'm going to start a center to help women know the truth about abortion. We will have Bible studies and offer pre-natal classes, as well as give physical help with the needs of raising a child. I'm calling it, *Hope of the Child.* My new friend consented to be my partner."

"You know abortion is legal now?" Sharon reported.

"The greater reason to build a place of hope for those who suffer from the lies. We will educate those considering an abortion and restore those suffering from an abortion."

Michael smiled and wiped the mist forming in his eyes with his hand.

After the group inspected the building with the realtor, they made plans for repairs of the building as well as furnishing it for a grand opening. The group buzzed with the excitement of the project. The group decided to celebrate by going to a nearby coffee shop.

"I know a place where we can have some privacy." Michael told the group and they all piled into the car.

Michael took them to the busiest place on the city block across from the court house. A little bistro with fancy pastries and wonderful coffee.

"This is private?" Barbara inquired as they stood staring at a limited menu.

"Yep, there are few ears here who care about our conversation." Michael ordered them muffins and coffee. "Besides the best stories are enjoyed over a cup of coffee and pastry delights with good company." Barbara laughed at him. He made her feel better, alive, next to Daniel she loved being with Michael, he was like a younger version of her daddy.

They found a table in the corner of the room with a radio playing softly in the background. "See what I mean?" Michael waved his arm around the room. He adjusted his seat and spoke. "I have a story to tell you."

"Goody, I love stories." Sharon leaned in closer to him.

"Let me start with the night before I shipped out for Vietnam," Michael began his oration.

Barbara held her coffee cup in both hands blowing on the hot liquid. She gave Michael her full attention.

"That was a horrible night, I never felt so alone and frightened. I held on to the prayer of my Uncle Buster," Michael said and Barbara smiled at the reference to her daddy.

"I repeated his prayer over and over. I would pray and then cry a little. I would pray that if I was killed, my family would be comforted, then I cried for my family. I prayed that if I was wounded, I would die before I would be captured, and then I cried at the thought of torture. It went on like that most of the night, until about 3 a.m. The man in the bunk below me, reached up and patted me. He said, 'It's okay to be scared son. Your prayers put you on the right track though.'"

Barbara leaned over the table and Michael continued, "That was Paps, the old man in our squadron. He signed up for WW II as a sixteen-year-old kid. He said he cried all night long and wanted to go home to his momma."

"Why didn't he? If he was only sixteen?" Barbara asked. Michael ignored the question and continued.

"He said another soldier, one a bit older, maybe twenty-five or so encouraged him and prayed for him." Michael stopped, took a drink of his brew and stared at the ceiling.

"Humm," Barbara said to keep Michael talking.

"The name of the soldier that helped him was Buster Troye."

"Daddy?"

"Yea. When I told him he's my uncle, he told me how Buster brought him through one of the bloodiest battles during WWII --- when Corregidor fell to the Japanese in May 1942. Eleven thousand men pushed into that doomed mission in the early stages of the war. Among those seven thousand Americans was Paps and Buster." Michael stopped his story and worked to gain his composure.

"Paps promised to watch over me in the same way Buster watched over him."

"How did he do that?" Daniel prodded.

"He kept a watch over me and prayed for me every night."

At that moment, the radio music stopped and the beeps and whistles of a special announcement came on. "Shhh." Michael said as he tuned into the announcement.

"April 30, 1975 the ten-year war is over for American soldiers," The radio announcer said.

Michael shook his head. "It's hard to believe. The old codger did it."

"Did what?" Daniel asked not understanding Michael's thoughts.

"Nixon, ended the war, I had heard rumors that the North Vietnamese were scared of Nixon. I guess it's true." Michael pondered to himself aloud. "Praise the Lord, the North Vietnamese communists signed the treaty."

"Why is that important?" Barbara asked not understanding Michael's statement.

Michael chuckled, "I forget you at home thought we only fought the Vietnamese but we were fighting communism which devastates a people while making power hungry millionaires of its leaders. We lived and fought beside the South Vietnamese, they were our brothers. A peace treaty will allow them to grow their crops, raise their families without fear of invasion by a vicious enemy, killing and taking their food and children."

Barbara sat staring at Michael in both wonderment and admiration, "Wow, you invested yourself over there."

"Sure did, that's why the war America knew was not the war American soldiers fought. At home the Vietnam war created a culture of rebellion and protests at home. Over there the war created hardened and broken men and women who saw first-hand the work of evil dictators; both American and Vietnamese. When evil reigns, people are destroyed."

Barbara ducked her head and confessed, "I'm one of those rebellious people, or I was."

"I remember how you developed into an activist. How many protests marches did you attend?" Sharon mused.

"Not as many as I could have but more than I should have." Barbara grinned. "The war protests gave me a way to be angry and act it out without consequences; or so I thought."

"Is that what led you to the women's lib meetings?" Michael asked her.

"Yeah, I was invited to my first women's lib meeting at one of those protests. It was a natural movement from protesting the war to protesting the men of government, to protesting the abuses of men, period."

Michael took a long draw on his cooled coffee. The music started back on the radio. "It was the times."

"How do you mean?" Barbara asked him.

"We're like Solomon; we enjoyed the fruits of our fathers' battles. Like David fought the battles and collected the goods and the labor to build God's temple, our fathers collected freedom for us to honor God, instead we honored ourselves."

"I guess we had it easy, we were the first teens to have our own cars."

"The first to live in relative peace," Michael said.

"So what happened that we ended up in the worst war ever?" Barbara asked.

"I think it's like Paps said to me that night in the bunker; we weren't the first generation to fight the dragons of evil but we were the first to be deceived so easily."

"Why do you think that?"

"Because we had it so easy, we thought we had all the answers to create world peace, until we saw---" Michael stopped.

"Saw what?"

"The absolute hatred of the dragon and his ownership of this world."

The two sat in silence for a moment each thinking in terms of their own life.

Barbara broke the silence, "Michael, did Paps know Patti thought he was her dad?"

"Yes, he knew. He saw the dragon devour that baby girl."

"Still he never gave up hope." Barbara reasoned.

"He clung to the vision of you. Because of his relationship to Buster, you belonged to him as much, if not more than Patti," Michael explained.

"Once Patti's mother died, the madam at the brothel claimed to be Patti's grandmother. Paps fought the claim but since he had no means of support, the old woman claimed Paps unfit to raise a child, unfortunately, the judge agreed."

"Paps must have gone crazy," Barbara moaned.

"He did, that's why he signed up for a tour of duty in Vietnam even though he was really too old. He waited for his first day to be shipped out. Difference between me and him was that he wanted to stop a bullet. He had lived his life. He was ready to die. So he dedicated himself to keeping me safe and alive. I really think he saw that booby-trap that took his legs. He stepped in front of me."

"Wow!" Barbara said. "How do you repay something like that?"

Michael winked at her. "Good question."

"You know, that's a picture of what Christ did for us on the cross," Michael continued. "He took the pain and penalty of death from us."

Barbara looked up at the ceiling. "Like He pulled me from the open throat of death." She mused. Daniel took her hand and kissed it. "That started me on the path of seeking knowledge. You know what this means?"

"No. What?" Michael responded.

Barbara smiled with a glow of confidence, "I trust Him."

Epilogue

> For I know the plans I have for you declares the LORD, plans for welfare and not for calamity to give you a future and a hope. Then you will call upon Me and come and pray to Me, and I will listen to you. You will seek Me and find Me when you search for Me with all of your heart.
>
> ---Jeremiah 29:11-13 (NASB)

GRADUATION DAY ARRIVED for the group in May, 1976. Daniel completed his residency and Michael received his law degree. Barbara and Sharon received their Bachelors of Science in Nursing. A great time for a little band of warriors to celebrate. They faced the next step of life with anticipation and excitement to see God's plan for their lives unfold.

Their new life started with the marriage of Michael and Sharon a few weeks before Daniel and Barbara took their vows of marriage. The two couples stayed close as they pursued different life careers.

Michael and Sharon moved to a suburb area of Burlington Heights where Michael took a position with a law firm as a tax attorney. Sharon worked at a small private hospital, until their twins were born in 1980 and she happily became a stay-at-home mom.

Daniel and Barbara stayed in an urban area of Burlington Heights where Daniel set up a family practice. Barbara's crisis pregnancy center grew to a staff of ten, offering pregnancy tests, ultra-sounds and counseling to anyone at no cost. Barbara held regular Bible studies at the center with an average attendance of six to ten people. The center found financing through donations and volunteers.

Barbara served the region as a high demand speaker. She shared the gospel to a diverse group of people across the nation. She completed her master's degree and took a teaching position in the school of nursing at the university. Often taking little Joseph Troye Holloway with her or leaving him to play with Sharon's twins.

The next morning after Lapetos chased Barbara and Daniel, his obituary appeared in the Burlington Heights newspaper. He died in a fiery car crash. There was no acknowledgment of Patti in the crash.

Daniel and Barbara watched Zay and Rance graduate in 1981. Zay received a degree in microbiology. Rance received a Bachelor of Science in investment banking.

Zay joined Dr. Winegren in the university laboratory and began working on his graduate studies in biomedical engineering. On his first day on the job, Dr. Winegren took him to a basement four stories underground where a titanium four-foot-thick cage held a giant creature that had the body of a goat and the head of a serpent, *a cursed dragon.*

><

An unknown spirit drags Zay Troye into hell and introduces him to a cursed dragon.

Zay Troye accepts a two-year fellowship working with DNA and a malformed cursed dragon. He didn't expect to be dragged into the sordid plots of evil before he found his answers. Will Dr. Troye and his assistant escape or become victums of hells plan?

Stones in Clay
PUBLISHING

Available wherever books and ebooks are sold.
Bible Study guide available only from StonesInClay.com

Acknowledgements

A special thanks to all who helped make this book a reality. First I want to thank those who encouraged me with their enthusiasm for the release of the novel.

I thank my cousin Michael Nelson who gave me insight into the life of a Vietnam Veteran. To all who have suffered through the decision of abortion or the aftermath of abortion. I love each and every one of you. I hold a special place for you in my heart and pray for your healing.

Amy Mykytiuk, who included my works in her already packed schedule of editing, teaching, writing and serving her church community as an active pastor's wife and mother of five children. She served as editor and prayer partner as this book was born of a spiritual battle all its own.

For my first editor Jeanne Marie Leach, who pushed me over the first hurdles.

Mindi Stucks lent her exceptional talent to the visual appeal with the cover and graphics. Thanks to Judith Voss Photography for contributing her skill in capturing an expressive author photograph.

My husband Gary Cooner, the technology expert that keeps the engine running both with encouragement and his technical expertise.

To you; the readers, thank you for reading and recommending the book.

Warning: This story reaches into volatile subject matter, both politically and religiously. If you have been offended, I offer my apologies for that but I encourage you to seek God's word for yourself in making a decision regarding feminism, paganism, witchcraft and abortion. This story is written from the biblical viewpoint of the book of Jeremiah. Those who are opposed to the Christian worldview are encouraged to be open and learn. These topics are addressed throughout scripture and as such should be presented with the absolute of scripture.

The main character in this story searches for answers to her quest to fulfill her perceived purpose in life. If you find yourself in this spot and want more information about finding biblical answers, Well-trained biblical counselors can also be found at biblicalcounseling.com.

I thank you all for your contributions and encouragement to make *A Gathering of Dragons* a reality. This novel is a product of Along Side You Ministries; a counseling and teaching ministry dedicated to the spiritual needs of teens and young adults, their parents and leadership. All profits from the sale of novels and materials help support this ministry and future publications.

The characters of Gloria Steinham, Betty Friedan were some of the founders of the second-wave of feminism as described in this novel. Phyllis Schafley efforts to mobilize opposition to stop ratification of the Equal Rights Amendment gave birth to the Eagle Forum founded in 1972. It became one of the most influential Religious Right organizations in history. Schafley continued to take a hard line stand in political and cultural issues until her death in 2016 at age 92.

Notes About Lilith And The Satyr

The desert creatures will meet with the wolves, the satyr also will cry to its kind: Yes, the Lilith (night monster) will settle there and will find herself a resting place.

-----Isaiah 35:14

The Scripture information about the Lilith or the Satyr is limited. Since they are mentioned there is reasonable evidence that can be found about them in ancient historical records, Homer's Iliad, Mythology, Jewish literature, and The Book of Enoch.

Lilith is a Hebrew word used for night monster, it is referred to by some cultures as a banshee. The Lilith is said to devour new life and mothers were particularly afraid of the monster.

The satyr is defined as the hairy goat. It is also used in reference to the scapegoat. The name given the satyr in Leviticus is Azazel. The book of Enoch attributes' all sin to Azazel the angel who aligned with Satan. He taught man how to sin. Enoch is an apocryphal book mentioned by Paul and Jude in the New Testament.

The whole earth has been corrupted through the works that were taught by Azazel; to him ascribe all sin.

— 1 Enoch 2:8

Cross references giving more information about these creatures can be found in scripture, they are:

Genesis 6:2-4 - Also associated in the Book of Enoch which is available in English, The Complete Book of Enoch by Dr. A. Nyland is recommended.

2 Kings 23:8 can be interpreted as worship places for the demons. This same idea is expressed in:

Deuteronomy 32:17, Psalm 106:37, Matthew 12:43, Mark 5:13, Luke 11:24 and Revelation 18:2

Dragon Series

Buster Troye comes face to face with a horrid Dragon. Will he overcome the dreadful beast?

Barbara Troye is lured by her selfish needs into revolt? Can she be rescued from the Dragon's demon?

Dr. Zay Troye sees a Dragon carrying the secret of hell. Can science find the truth?

Rance Troye's wedding is cut short when the Dragon steals the bride. Will Rance's search save her or destroy him?

The pain of Buster Troye's Dragon bite grows from a family division. His final battle is fought by the Dragon warrior.

During World War II, military "Operation High Jump" explores Antarctica and finds the Dragon's lair.

www.StonesInClay.com   Stones in Clay PUBLISHING   www.AlongSideYou.org

Available wherever books are sold.